The Queen's Fencer

The Queen's Fencer

To the Maine State Library Readers! Caitlin Scott-Turner

Caitlin Scott-Turner

Five Star • Waterville, Maine

First Edition, Second Printing

Published in 2005 in conjunction with
Tekno Books and Ed Gorman.

Set in 11 pt. Plantin by Al Chase.

Printed in the United States on permanent paper.

Library of Congress Cataloging-in-Publication Data

Scott-Turner, Caitlin.
    The queen's fencer / by Caitlin Scott-Turner.—1st ed.
      p. cm.
    ISBN 1-59414-302-1 (hc : alk. paper)
    1. Great Britain—History—Elizabeth, 1558–1603—Fiction.
I. Title.
PS3619.C695Q44 2005
  813′.6—dc22   2004028110

Dedication

For
My beloved husband,
Steve
Always and always.
And
For the memory of my father,
Robert E. Scott, Jr.
Scholar, historian, theologian.

CHAPTER ONE

Hampton Court Palace: July, 1597

The afternoon sunlight glinted on the steel of the rapiers.

"Riposte!" Will Trevallon called from the side of the tiltyard as the two fencers clashed before him. "Recover! Do not give ground, anticipate every move!"

Ardys heard her father's hoarse shout, but did not answer. She concentrated only on her fencing. She held her weapon in a firm, flexible grip, and moved the blade with remarkable speed to parry her opponent's thrust.

The gentleman who sought to break through her defense was able, but no match for her. He was younger, being but eighteen when she was almost twenty, and though he outweighed her, that gave him no advantage. The skill was hers.

Colorfully dressed in the current fashion, he wore pumpkin hose of red satin slashed with dark green flaring out from his hips like two cannon balls. His trunk hose was orange; covering thigh to toe as tightly as a second skin, and the velvet doublet-cape flung loosely across his shoulders and secured with a gold brooch was teal blue. Despite the splendor of his rainbow hues, he still seemed clumsy and inept when he faced the young woman.

The weapons in their hands were not blunted, but sharp and deadly. The girl's father, William Trevallon, Fencing Master to the court of Queen Elizabeth, did not allow that. Ardys had learned early of the blade's sting, and was not afraid.

Ardys cared not for the man's dress, nor did she waste a

thought on his rank. Henry, Earl of Southampton, was merely another opponent to out-guess and out-maneuver. It did not matter that he was an intimate friend of Robert Devereux, the Earl of Essex.

She knew that Robert Dudley, Earl of Leicester, the Queen's greatest love, had died soon after the defeat of the Spanish Armada in 1588. His twenty-eight-year-old stepson, Essex, was now Elizabeth's favorite and her Master of Horse. Henry of Southampton was a loyal follower of Essex, but he had slow reflexes, and Ardys did not hesitate to take the offensive.

"Come, then, Henry! She'll have your head! Faster, ye gommerel!" one of the spectators yelled encouragingly to his friend. "Can ye not see she's fast?"

The hilts of the two rapiers scraped together as she lunged forward expertly, her weight on her right leg. Henry awkwardly deflected her blow by falling back, angling his sword across his chest, nearly losing his balance altogether.

"No, no—cease fencing!" Will commanded and stepped forward into the arena. The spectators, men always present in varying numbers at the public lessons of the Fencing Master, quieted, awaiting Will's instruction.

Drawing his own rapier, Will impatiently motioned Southampton aside. The master's weapon was long-bladed, boasting an intricately carved steel swept hilt in a triple braid design, the initials WT in script on the grip. Trevallon touched the tip of his daughter's blade with the point in formal salute.

"Keep your weight forward, gentlemen. How many times must I say it? Do not allow yourselves to be pushed off balance by your opponent's lunge. Back if you must, but maintain the stance. You cannot move freely otherwise. Observe."

Will and Ardys began to circle, intent on each other's

faces. At the same instant they lunged. The blades rang together, but the sound was fleeting; they parted and clashed again. In the silence of the tiltyard the clang of steel was like a song, with its own melody and rhythm.

"Well, my girl, you've defeated yet another potential suitor," said Will under his breath as he parried her stabbing thrust.

"Suitor! Henry of Southampton?" She hissed in reply. "I need no suitor—and never one that prefers the beds of boys!"

"You need suitors, Ardys! You're all of twenty already—would ye be an old maid?"

"Ha! An old maid—like the Queen! Pay heed to your sword, Father, and leave my unmarried state be!" She bore down on him harder, forcing him to step back.

Ardys had fenced with her father for years. Will brought Ardys to the Queen's court in London when she was fifteen, to help him with his teaching.

While his was the greater experience now, her youth gave her the faster reactions. They were very nearly equals. He had taught her everything he knew, and had not spared her, treating her as roughly as he did his male students.

"Bear in mind," Will said, "the Spaniards do not arm themselves with blunted swords. No more do the French or the Scots. Nor will any enemy. For us, fencing is a sport, but the true objective in any form of combat is the death of the opponent. This is not a game to be taken lightly."

The Trevallons matched thrust for parry and never broke stride. Their finesse and agility were inspiring, but they were unaware that the majority of their masculine audience admired the graceful curve of Ardys's body more than her fencing technique.

Ardys invariably wore men's clothing to the tiltyard. She preferred simply-cut apparel of unembroidered black velvet:

a doublet with tight, slashed sleeves, straight gray hose, and a close-fitting white shirt with a high collar. This was her uniform, the mark of her position as assistant to the Fencing Master. The title was unofficial, and she received no pay for her work as Will's other assistants did; but she knew she had earned the right to consider herself a step above them all.

The severe masculine clothes did nothing to disguise Ardys's figure.

Watching her, Henry's friend Hal Clipton remarked, "Still lusting after her, Henry? She's a fine one, she is."

"No more! I went after her once, in one of the gardens here as it was drawing to dusk. I gave her sweet words and smiles, but when I pulled her into my arms she gave me the knee! 'Tis not a surprise I'd care to repeat. And that was five years ago, when her father first brought her to court . . ."

Her admirers kept their distance. Ardys had only two passions: fencing and learning. A better scholar than Will had ever been, she was proficient in history and languages, and had a rudimentary knowledge of mathematics and astronomy.

Will teased her, telling her she should marry and bear children, as befit a woman. Ridiculous, she laughed, reminding him that the Queen they served was a brilliant and powerful monarch who had lived long and ruled well without a husband. It was an argument they both enjoyed, and neither of them acknowledged the flaw in comparing any woman with Elizabeth Tudor. The Queen was above them all, set apart. She was not a normal woman.

If an unlucky opponent lost his concentration when the sun glinted red on Ardys's shining hair, or found himself contemplating the black depths of her eyes, so much the better. Ardys always pressed home an advantage, regardless of how it was gained.

Henry of Southampton remained standing with his fellow students and watched as Ardys parried Will's flawless thrust, feinting to her left.

"Jesu! Still, I would do battle with that wench in bed," Southampton said thickly.

"Aye," smirked one of his friends. "But you'd best keep your weapon sheathed in your codpiece or ye'll come to some hurt again."

Laughter rippled through the crowd, and when Will heard it he put up his sword abruptly.

"We've lost them, Father," Ardys smiled as she and Will bowed formally, signaling the end of the match.

"And do you know," she continued, a bit breathlessly, as they turned to walk across the yard, "I believe I could best you."

"Someday we must remember to fight for the instruction of my students, not for our own pleasure!" Will said with a smile. He put his arm around her shoulders companionably.

She wiped her shiny face with a soft towel handed to her by a servant boy.

Ardys noticed that her father's arm seemed somehow heavier, but she did not mention it. He was tired, that was all.

He was winded, too. "But do not forget that I am master here, not you, even if you do have a certain skill at fencing."

"A certain skill?" Ardys echoed and raised an eyebrow. "Well, fear not. None shall see that a mere woman can beat the grand master fencer."

At the edge of the ring Ardys handed her practice rapier to the weapons-keeper, a boy who received it with reverence. Will did not surrender his sword. He kept it always by his side. Trevallon had been given his rapier by the Queen, as a token of her favor, and he would use no other.

"Tomorrow afternoon, once again," he told the students.

"There is much to be done before the celebrations. And for God's sake, do not spend all your energies in dancing and drink! That will affect your speed. Now go."

Southampton cast one last lascivious glance at Ardys as the men dispersed. She did not notice, and after she linked her arm through her father's, the Trevallons walked in comfortable silence toward the palace.

CHAPTER TWO

The sun rose a fiery orange over Hampton Court on the twenty-ninth of July. No one paused to admire the dawn, however, for even at this early hour the palace was bustling with preparations for the coming day. The weeks of planning and rehearsal were at an end, and anxious participants counted the hours they had left.

The Master of the Revels, Sir Thomas Benger, raced down the long galleries knocking on door after door, rousing his troops like a general before battle. He was a nervous, thin man with a talent for organization unparalleled at court, and he was in charge of the day's events.

Richard Edwards, Master of the Children, a select choir of small boys, ran among his charges in the long hallway where they all slept together, clapping his hands. Richard saw his friend Thomas going to each door, but did not disturb him and instead roused the children.

"Up, rascals! Up! We must rehearse at least once before the Triumph, at least once!" Edwards hurried his charges out into the courtyard to warm up as soon as they were dressed. Singing without accompaniment, their high sweet voices blended in harmony while they rubbed the sleep from their eyes.

On July 29, 1588, nine years before, the Spanish Armada sent by Philip of Spain to invade England was defeated in a long, running battle in the English Channel near Gravelines. It was a triumph for the kingdom, and for its beloved Queen. In her honor, the Earl of Essex had planned a reenactment of the fight, to take place on the

13

River Thames in front of Hampton Court Palace.

Carpenters had worked for weeks fitting out large pinnaces to duplicate, in small scale, the principal vessels used by both countries. The miniatures measured roughly one-third the size of the originals. Floating there were smaller versions of the *Ark Royal*, the flagship commanded by Lord Admiral Howard of Effingham; the *Revenge*, under the able hand of the one-time pirate Sir Francis Drake; the *Victory*, captained by John Hawkins, and the *Triumph*, commanded by Martin Frobisher.

The English Fleet met the mighty Armada with only thirty-four large ships, and the ambitious Essex had planned to reproduce them all. But each of the models was forty feet long, and ten feet across at the beam, with three or four high-rigged masts, and Devereux had finally been persuaded that his first scheme would be prohibitively costly. Besides, the Thames at Hampton would never accommodate so many ships, even small ones. As it was, any spectator that stood too near the shore would be in danger from the pointed bowsprits.

The model Spanish galleons, proud three-masters topped by tall castles, were the *San Martin*, flagship of the hapless Commander Don Alonso Perez de Guzman, seventh Duke of Medina-Sidonia (who despite his distinguished title had never been to sea prior to Spain's Great Enterprise); the *San Juan*, captained by Vice-Admiral Juan Martinez de Recalde; and the *Gran Grifon*, under the command of Pedro Alvarado.

Numbers of lesser ships, flyboats, and launches were also constructed, some specially prepared to burn brightly, like the small English fireships that had in the dark of that July night confused, panicked, and scattered the Spanish Fleet out of its impressive crescent formation. This flotilla was kept company by the many birds and small boats that always crowded the river.

The decks of the model ships were mobbed with men who would play the parts of the admirals, sailors, and soldiers; so there was no room left for the ships to carry artillery. Demiculverin were set along the banks of the river instead, pointed at the sky, and musket-men were stationed at strategic intervals to create the noise of the battle.

A quarter-mile down the Thames dense trees lined the waterside, and here a clever fabrication of boulders and logs was placed, the image of the rocky and inhospitable Irish coast.

Many of the Spanish ships, harried not only by the pursuing English but also by a fierce storm that lasted for days, went aground along the western coast of Ireland. Low on ammunition, victuals, and morale, the Spaniards found themselves at the mercy of the native Irish, and were slaughtered as they waded ashore. Now, local Sussex villagers were hired to play the Irish: dressed in furs and carrying axes and other crude weapons, they were to lie in wait behind those boulders. Benger's lackey, Sampson, had been rehearsing their war cries for a week, and today they would rush out at the defeated Spaniards.

In all, this year's extravaganza would last four hours, covering a distance of over a mile down the Thames. The audience, led by the Queen, would view it from graveled paths that ran the river's length. Elizabeth, for her comfort, and so that the crowd could better view her, would be mounted, the rest of the crowd on foot. The entire court, plus as many commoners as could crowd in, was expected to attend.

"Well, my friend Thomas," Edwards called at last to Master Benger. "Be all ready? God's teeth, but these fellows best sing well or they'll feel my boot!"

Benger stopped, perspiring, and turned to his old comrade. "Edwards! If we pass today without a mishap, I will become a poxy monk!" he cried, knocking on yet another door. "Will we ever forget the Accession Day celebration five years ago when that large fake whale, floating so proudly down this river with three musicians in its mouth, sank like a stone?"

"Oh, never!" Edwards laughed. "And the poor knaves kept playing until the water reached their eyes! You nearly fainted, Thomas! But mark you, there were so many things to see that the Queen didn't notice her swimming musicians. She had more interest in the banquet to come after, I vow."

"Would that we are at least able to attend the banquet this evening," Benger said, "a most pleasant feast will be had. And there will be a new play by Master Shakespeare, a new comedy. 'Tis called *The Merry Wives of Windsor*."

Inside the palace, numerous cooks, scullions, and pastry boys slaved at the intensely hot ovens. Twenty oxen, as many cows, sheep, and calves, were roasting for the main courses. For the more delicate tastes of the diners there were nightingales, herons, pheasants; peacocks and peafowl and chickens; onion soup, pea soup, oyster soup, artichoke pies stuffed with grapes, dates, and hard-boiled eggs. Before dessert was served one of the boys would have to run to the baker's kitchen to fetch the fresh "maids of honor," tiny almond cheesecakes much loved by the sovereign but too complicated for the baker to make in bulk.

An army worked in Hampton's eighteen palace kitchens, but the distinguished members of the court would not know of it. Only Thomas Benger knew and worried over the whole of the production, each and every detail, and he would not relax until the last drunken guest had been taken to his chamber much later that night.

"Well does Her Majesty know the value of a good spectacle, even one with a sinking whale," Benger said. "She's a Tudor all through—I heard that the old King her father was a spectacle in himself, just as she is! It's as well that my Lord of Essex is close to her heart—and therefore her purse . . ." He straightened, realizing he should not speak so of the Queen's favorite.

"Godspeed, Edwards, and may your boys sound more like angels than they look!" he said, and scurried off toward the kitchens.

Ardys was awakened shortly after dawn by the delicious smells drifting into her chamber from the nearby kitchens. Her maid touched her shoulder gently.

"Come, madam, 'tis time! Ye bade me wake ye early and so I've done!"

"Be still, Anna, I am awake. Jesu, what smells from the kitchens!"

Ardys swung her bare legs out of the bed and reached for her shift. Anna yanked open the curtains at the single, high window.

When the court was at Hampton, Ardys and her father slept in two separate rooms on the ground level, near the inner courtyard. Each chamber was plainly furnished with a velvet-hung bedstead of carved oak, a three-tiered open court cupboard, and an ornate wooden chest supported on stout, short legs to house personal belongings and clothing. The walls were paneled in rich dark cherry, polished, like the furniture, to a high gloss.

In each room a great stone fireplace, four feet high and three feet wide, took up one entire wall. In Ardys's chamber the stone was a deep green, and matched the emerald color of the bed drapes.

The window was many-paned but the thick glass allowed

little light into the room. In the winter Ardys would leave a tiny blaze in the fireplace all night, and snuggle into her bed, pulling the velvet covers to her chin and drawing the curtains closed around her, so that she slept in a warm cocoon.

The fire was not lit now, nor were the drapes pulled around the bed. The night had been unseasonably warm, even for July; and she slept under no cover at all. Ardys yawned and stretched, and as she did the velvet spread slid silently to the cool green and white-checked tile floor.

Rising, she folded the spread and placed it on the bed again. The air was heavy with humidity, and the sun blazed onto the stones of the cobbled courtyard. She glanced up out of her window to the elegant blue and gold astronomical clock, high in the gateway arch. That clock was once the pride of Henry the Eighth, and each day she spent at Hampton Court Ardys began with a check of the time, the zodiacal signs, and the tides on the Thames.

The thin white linen nightshift clung uncomfortably to her body while she washed at the basin. It was not a day for formal dress. She found herself glad that she could wear one of her lighter silk gowns instead of the new doublet of the finest blue-black Venetian velvet that had been made for her for this occasion.

"Anna, bring my blue gown," she said, anticipating the lightness of the fabric on her skin. "If I cannot fence today, at least I will not die of the heat in that thrice-damned new velvet doublet."

"Nay, madam, you mustn't say such things! That doublet be the latest style and all the gallant young men are wearing it."

Ardys laughed. "No wonder then that no care was given to my silhouette when it was designed," she said.

The new doublet reached upward almost to her chin, and

a stiff white lace ruff flared behind her head like a halo. It was constricting, heavy, and most unflattering to Ardys's womanly figure. She was happy to don the light blue gown with its darker blue undersleeves and bodice. The gown had a large ruff set with pearls, and one also dangled from her left ear. Anna pinned up her mistress's long, thick hair, damp-feeling in the heat, into a heap on the top of Ardys's head.

"Do not bother to frizz it," Ardys said. "The air will do that today, without help."

Soft heel-less black leather shoes completed her outfit. She tugged, irritated, at her collar, but it did not loosen, stiffened as it was by thin slats of wood. It was probably better this way: there were endless hoops and petticoats underneath the skirts, but at least the fabric did not cling to her skin. Ardys refused to wear farthingales unless absolutely necessary and at least this outfit spared her that. She should count herself lucky.

It would not matter what she wore this day, at any rate.

"I still canna believe ye will not fence today, Mistress," said Anna as she finished the fastenings.

"No more can I. And I was not told until last night! It must have been an arbitrary decision of Essex's, I vow, probably because of the stories his friends told him of the ruthless girl who will not allow a man to beat her at fencing. My father tried to have the decision reversed by the Master of the Revels, but he had his orders too. From Robert Devereux, Earl of Essex, of course. Damn him!"

"Hush, my lady. Remember that walls can hear! But ye do look right lovely in that, I trow."

A low wooden clothes chest stood at the end of Ardys's bed, and she opened it carefully. On the underside of the heavy, silk-lined lid five straps had been attached to hold her rapier and dagger. These two handsome weapons were a gift from her father on her eighteenth birthday, and she used them only in tournaments or other state occasions. The weapons-keeper looked after all her other equipment.

She drew the rapier from its supple leather sheath and ran an admiring finger down its sharp length. The steel gleamed quietly in the meager sunlight that struggled through her window. The blade reached three and a half feet from tip to tip; double-edged and lightweight, superbly balanced. The ornamented guard, designed to protect the fencer's hand, was carved with delicate scrollwork and had a swept-hilt that wound sinuously upward from the cup-like basket in three lacy S-curves.

"I love the open work of the swept-hilt, Anna! 'Tis better than cup- or basket-hilt rapiers. It suits my style of fencing, and 'tis lighter for a small hand. How glad I am that Father chose to introduce the new style here!"

At the top of the blade, flush with the leather wound grip, were engraved the initials "ST" in calligraphic lettering. This was the mark of the Italian sword maker, who signed each weapon he created as proudly as an artist signed a painting. In truth, this man was a close friend of Will's, but Ardys liked to think of "ST" as a rare man with an unfailing, steady eye, working hour upon hour in some dark Italian room, a rapt apprentice at his knee, as he fashioned each intricate part of the sword. She never told Will about that—such flights of imagination were unworthy of the Fencing Master's daughter.

Each nick on the blade told a story, too, of the battles she had fought, the blows she had parried, the opponents she had faced. The blade bore the scars of wounds she had never felt.

Held in her white-gloved right hand, the rapier was a part of her, a natural extension of her arm. It belonged in that hand and no other: Ardys allowed no one to touch her sword, including her father. Fellow fencers and students could admire it if they chose, but any request to test the balance of it met with a glare that silenced more effectively than any word.

Slicing the air a few times, she listened with delight to the song of the blade before she resheathed. She strapped the leather girdle round her waist and slid the rapier through it till the hilt rested against her left hip. Slim-fitting, the gown did not bunch overmuch under the girdle. She might not be fencing, but she would still wear her sword, by God! The dagger, a short, wicked length of steel with a gold hilt, leather-sheathed like the sword, fit into the belt at the small of her back. One final glance in the mirror, and she was ready. The weapons were quite incongruous with her gown, but Ardys shook her head and went out.

Will grunted, "Come," when Ardys knocked on the door that connected their rooms. He stood beside his bed, bits of clothing on the floor about his feet. He was struggling into a heavy breastplate, and had almost tipped over trying to fasten it behind his waist without assistance.

"Father, are ye all right?" Ardys asked, pulling at the buckles of the breastplate.

"My page is elsewhere this morning—curse the rascal! And I am not so thin as once I was. This breastplate was made for me ten years ago." He winced as Ardys tugged at the buckles. "It's that thrice-damned pain in my side again, today of all days! No matter, I'm well enough. Here, this buckle goes there . . ."

"You'll need reshaping, Father, before this old armor will fit you properly," Ardys said, trying not to smile as she buckled the back of the peascod breastplate.

"I've worn this old armor for many years without trouble, well you know. And it still shines like it was new made."

"It does that."

"I have never been beaten when I've worn this. In any

contest—broadsword, mace-and-chain, ax, or—"

"You have never fought with the rapier in armor, Father. 'Tis foolishness. Any soldier knows a rapier will not pierce armor."

She held the puffed velvet sleeves out as he pushed his arms into them. "Stand still, and stop wheezing, won't you! How you expect to move about, much less fence, while carrying such weight is—well, such folly is like the Earl of Essex, but it hardly seems well to fence in a breastplate on such a hot day."

"Aye, it was Devereux's idea, right enough. Steel shining all about the arena will be a stirring sight, ye must concede . . . Not so tight, my girl! D'ye think to smother me?"

"I could understand if the contest was to be with battle-ax, or two-handed sword, or mace-and-chain. With those weapons you simply stand in one place and hack at your opponent. But a breastplate! In this heat?"

"It is Devereux's wish," said Will patiently, trying in vain to stand straight. His right side caught at him, and he winced again. "Be glad you do not own armor, else you would have to wear it, as well as I."

"That I doubt. You well know Essex is determined to keep me out of the tourneys, for some reason. Jesu! That pompous, preening, thrice-cursed . . ."

"Hush, child!" Trevallon glanced about. "Never speak thus! Essex is a great warrior. He proved himself in the Netherlands, did he not? He has killed more than his share of the Queen's enemies. One day he shall be a great leader of armies. Be content!"

Will patted Ardys's shoulder to silence her. "It is he who sponsors this event, and on this day at least, from him we take our orders. It is for the honor of our Queen. We would fight unclothed if he required it of us. At least that would be cooler!

But I am sorry he has banned you from the fighting, my daughter. Do not fret. Mark you, there is always another tourney."

Ardys said savagely, "He is no fencer." It was the worst insult she could think of. "I have bested all his lackeys, and by God I'd best him if he had the stomach to meet me! I'll wager he's afraid I'll challenge him, and in front of the Queen he could not refuse me—a mere woman against a grand knight. He cannot bear to be beaten in any contest. He is not like his late stepfather Dudley, who had much dignity . . ."

"Hold your tongue, Ardys!" Will said sharply. "Your temper causes my head to ache—Jesu, it reminds me of your mother! How can you have lived at court all these years and still not have learned discretion? Essex holds the Queen's heart in his hand: if Her Grace loves him, he must be worthy. Or do you question the wisdom of the Queen? No, I thought ye would not!"

Ardys knew she should learn to control her quick temper. Her mother, Alice, was sharp-tongued, it was true, but Alice's storms passed quickly; and Ardys's younger sisters were all gentle, quiet girls. Well, Will had taken Ardys from her home and brought her here to court as though she was his son. What did he expect, that he should make her strong in combat and yet keep her meek like other women? The two of them visited Cornwall but once a year, and they invariably became bored by Alice and the other girls: the embroidery, the sewing, the endless playing upon the virginals. The Fencing Master had not taught his eldest daughter to love womanish things, and her mother, God knew, had given up trying.

What had prompted him to put a rapier into Ardys's hand when she was young? Sometimes Ardys wondered. The wish to pass on something of himself, she supposed; he had no son.

If Ardys had not proved so able at fencing, perhaps her life would have been more akin to the lives of most women. She had thrived and her progress as a fencer thrilled her father.

The majority of women were ignorant souls, particularly in the counties far from the capital.

Their Queen was an obvious exception to this norm, as she was to all the others. Disgraced as a child, abandoned as the daughter of an executed traitor, declared bastard at the age of three, Elizabeth's father had nonetheless seen that she had the best of tutors, beginning with Roger Ascham in the old days of her secluded childhood at Hatfield. When her royal siblings, Edward, and after him, Mary, came to the throne, they had denied the Princess Elizabeth much, but not the training of her mind. Learning was Elizabeth's solace, and her joy. She surrounded herself with educated people when she took the throne, and would not tolerate ignorance.

Will had presented Ardys to the Queen at the age of fifteen, and Elizabeth had been appalled that the girl not did understand Latin. It was a tale Will repeated so often that Ardys knew it by rote.

"God's death!" the Queen had sworn, "is fencing all this girl knows? She must learn other things if she is to be a member of our court! She shall have our private secretary for a Latin tutor. He shall have to find the time for her when he is not fulfilling his other duties. Her mind must be trained to be as quick as her blade."

According to the royal command, the Fencing Master's daughter had been drilled in Latin, French, Greek, German, literature, history, and mathematics. The English court was like a university, attracting philosophers, writers, and scientists from all over the world; there was always an interesting discussion going on, always something new to be learned.

That, combined with the glorious fencing, filled Ardys's life as no embroidery ever could. Life at Elizabeth's court was exciting and colorful. Ardys did not miss her home in Cornwall, and the infrequent letters she wrote to her mother at first had ceased within a year.

Will shook himself, clanking a bit, and brought her attention back.

"Time draws on, my daughter. No more prattle. Look how the plumes on my helmet droop in this heat! A pity—they bounce most becomingly when there is a breeze. I dare say there will be a crowd gathered by the river already; we had better go."

CHAPTER THREE

Elizabeth Tudor, by the Grace of God Queen of England, Wales, Scotland, Ireland, and France, stood with her long pale hands upon her hips, surveying the scene as the players took up their positions along the banks of the Thames. At sixty-three, she yet had her moments of great vitality, though she was feeling the inevitable drag of time more and more. She still never sat when she could stand, danced for hours, delighted in playing cards into the small hours of the morning, and could out-curse the roughest seaman. Few of her younger courtiers could match her level of nervous energy, and the older and wiser among them had long since ceased to try.

A peacock feather fan, iridescent in the sharp sunlight by the river, shielded her fair skin. Her face was white from the powders she applied with a heavy hand, but from a distance she was a picture of smooth, glowing youth.

Around her the gaudy crowd of her ladies-in-waiting swirled, and beyond them were the strutting gentlemen of the court: a kaleidoscope of bright, shifting hues reflecting on the water of the Thames. The Queen was the magnificent center of it all, more spectacular in her own right than any of the entertainments planned for her amusement.

The sovereign was resplendent in a low-bodiced gown of shimmering black silk, with a drum-like farthingale billowing the untold yards of skirt out more than a foot to each side of her tiny waist. The proportion of the sleeves was as grand: stiff and rucked, they tapered from padded shoulders that matched the farthingale's width into tight, ruffled white cuffs. The large cream-colored collar extended up into a wide

26

ruff that framed her face. She looked regal, and it was no wonder that her subjects stood in such awe of her. She was the embodiment of power, the epitome of maidenly virtue.

The jewels that winked and glittered whenever the Queen moved, like thousands of tiny stars, captivated the crowd. The entire surface of the black gown was embroidered with gold and silver threads, and it was also set with pearls, rubies, and garnets. From Elizabeth's waist hung a mirror encrusted with diamonds, held by a silken cord, and at her breast lay a gold brooch two inches long in the shape of a woman gathering stalks of wheat. This was the symbol of Virgo, the Queen's birth sign, and a motif she wore often.

The scarlet red of the Queen's hair shone an unnatural livid color in the sunlight.

The crowd pressed Will and Ardys closer to the bank of the river as it followed the Queen to the graveled paths. With a hand up from a groom, Elizabeth mounted a handsome white horse, acknowledging the cheers of her people with a graceful wave.

"Well, my lord Essex!" Elizabeth cried when she spied the handsome earl coming toward her. "Think ye the Spaniards shall win the battle this day—as they could not the first time?"

"Ha! Philip's pride never let him believe we could best his mighty Armada with our small navy and our fireships!" Essex called back. "He knows better now, my Queen, does he not?"

Essex came to her side and bowed formally, extending an elegant slender leg before his sovereign.

The English victors would not let the Spanish defeat slip into the comfortable oblivion of history. If there were those who rebuked Elizabeth for dismissing her able seamen without pay, if her own fleet had been dangerously short of ammunition because of her parsimony, it did not matter now.

Providence had intervened, and Providence clearly favored Elizabeth of England. The English fireships had scattered the mighty Armada, and the storm had finished the Spaniards. Only a few of the twenty-seven thousand Spanish troops had made it back to Spain.

Ardys, making her way to the river, felt her throat tighten as the throng bore in upon her. She was sometimes frightened by crowds, an unease she tried to conceal and which years of life at a densely populated court had not eradicated. Will laid his heavy arm across her shoulders as they walked slowly with the crowd, swept along behind the Queen.

Glancing up at her father, Ardys could see beads of sweat on his forehead and upper lip. She was hot even in her light gown; it molded itself to her back, and under her arms. How Will must be suffering in his breastplate of steel! Mercifully, none of the men as yet wore their helmets and Will carried his under one arm.

Trevallon's helm was of shiny polished steel, with thin horizontal slits for his eyes and mouth and tall plum and yellow feathers curling forward from the top point. Will continued to wear the Helford colors, although he had ceased to serve Sir Richard Helford when he became Fencing Master to the Queen. Trevallon wore those colors out of respect and gratitude to the Lord who had established him at court. Ardys, when she wore colors at all, wore those of the Queen.

"Father, how is it with you? I worry for you," Ardys said.

"My sword arm is already weary with the weight of the headpiece I carry," he said, "my shoulders are fair cracking— and the day is hardly yet begun!"

Ardys gritted her teeth as another rivulet of perspiration rolled down her back into the pool that had formed at her waist. Inwardly she cursed the stifling heat and was ashamed of the effect it was having on her. None of the others appeared to be suffering, although some people did look flushed. That could be excitement, of course. Her own breath caught a little when she heard her father's sharp intake of breath; it must be that damned pain in his side again. He was only forty-six, but was moving like a much older man.

Ardys looked up, hoping to see some sign of rain. She saw none, only the cloudless, merciless blue of the summer sky.

Elizabeth's horse pranced sideways as she called, "Excellently spoken, Sir Captain!" to the master of the *Ark Royal* when he concluded the first oration. Ardys and her father could see the Queen well, but were far enough away that they missed most of the words of the speeches.

Some of the cannons were touched off before the second speaker finished and he had to shout to be barely heard above their throaty roar. Thomas Benger must wish he were safe in his grave, Ardys thought wryly, where he could not be made to answer for such mishaps. The Queen took no notice, however.

The day went on with man after man discoursing on the myriad virtues of the monarch. Ardys smiled proudly and watched Her Gracious Majesty beam through every speech, compliment and thank each speaker, and clap delightedly when the *Gran Grifon* sank, its crew foundering in helpless realism in the muddy water of the Thames.

The fireships did not function properly. When the torches were put to them, they merely smoldered and gave off an evil smell. Ardys spied Benger wringing his hands as he watched from the shore, but the actors outdid themselves, recreating the confusion the real fireships had caused. They shouted curses and prayers to the Almighty in Spanish, to the great amusement of the spectators.

The drama continued and the crowd moved in its wake down river. When the sorry remains of the Spanish fleet finally reached the mock Irish shores to begin its last flight, the assembly applauded as much with relief at the coming end of the spectacle as with pride in the relived victory.

Elizabeth's white hand rested on Essex's arm as he helped her dismount. Ardys narrowed her eyes with dislike when she saw the Queen look at him with affection. The young Lord, just twenty, rivaled the Queen in magnificence of dress and bearing. Ardys had a good view of the man from where she stood, and she tried to understand why the Queen seemed so fond of him. Extremely tall, he was broad-shouldered and had long, muscular limbs. His thick square brown beard reached the front of his breastplate, which was decorated richly with scrollwork and incised geometric designs. The Queen raised her hand to shield her pale blue eyes when she spoke to him, for he was one of the few men at court taller than she was.

"Ah, Robin, what delights you have shown us this day! How wondrous to see the battle of Gravelines as it must indeed have been. And how true the sound of the guns! Were ye not at our side, and our loyal subjects all about us, we would quake with fear that the Dons had come up the Thames to our very doorstep!"

"If they dared, sweet lady, I would prove my love for you in battle," Essex declared eloquently, and bowed.

From the corner of her eye, Ardys saw Benger rushing to the water's edge to try and put out one of the fireships. Now that the spectacle was over, it was burning furiously. She pointed it out to Will, but he seemed not to notice.

Devereux spoke again. "Your Grace, the sun begins to lower. Still to come are the fencing matches and the jousting, the banquet, Master Shakespeare's play, and the dancing—and then we shall play at cards till morning! Shall we to the tiltyard?"

Elizabeth took his proffered arm. The two of them led the assembly away from the river, through the palace, and out into the tiltyard where the outdoor galas would conclude.

Ardys felt her father's fatigue as he leaned surreptitiously on her. She was becoming more concerned for him by the moment but hoped that the fencing would bring him back to himself. And if she could not fence, at least she would then be able to watch her father. She was confident that once he took the rapier in his hand, his discomfort would vanish. A true fencer, Will had taught her, was transported into a realm beyond pain, where mind and spirit ruled.

The crowd arranged itself around the edges of the tiltyard. Servants ran to fetch cool drinks for the noble guests.

She watched her father and his nineteen fencers, dressed alike and handpicked by the master for their high skill in the art, range themselves in a line across the center of the ring. They stirred up little dust in the humid air, the red glow of the setting sun reflecting blood-like on their breastplates. Ardys's heart swelled with pride at the sight.

After a sign from Will, each man raised his helmet, set it in place on his head, saluted the Queen, and unsheathed his rapier.

The list of challengers had been drawn up weeks before; Ardys had assisted her father in assigning the pairings. Though a general challenge was read to the crowd, there would be no spontaneous duels this day.

The exclusion of the Fencing Master's daughter at so late an hour caused some logistical problems: no one was skilled enough to fight her matches but the master himself. He would have to face twice as many opponents. Anger replaced pride as Ardys watched and saw how pale Will looked.

The breeze was not even sufficient to ruffle the gay feathers adorning the helmets.

Will lifted the light rapier to salute the Queen once more, and only Ardys saw him wince with pain. Ardys now stood near Elizabeth, at the front of the throng.

The Queen spoke to her familiarly, "Well, Mistress Trevallon, why are you not costumed for the fencing today?"

"Lord Essex—" Ardys began.

Essex interrupted her reply ungraciously. "My Queen, it begins!"

Everyone fell silent as the first pairs of fencers, Will among them, turned to face one another. The contest began, rapiers whistling harmlessly against steel breastplates in carefully orchestrated parries and thrusts. The fencers circled together, shifting position. Ardys thought her father lagged out of step, but he recovered himself. Elizabeth imperiously shushed Essex when he tried to speak to her.

Night began to fall as the fencers fought on. Servants brought torches from the palace to light the arena. There was some confusion among the combatants as the lamps were lit in a wide circle around the tiltyard, and the crowd murmured restively. There had been no plan to fence in the dark: it was difficult enough to move in the confined space of the tiltyard without the added worry of poor visibility. The sun had gone, but Ardys was grateful, for it had taken some of the heat with it: she hoped her father's pain would lessen.

The torches were lit; a ring of fire illuminated the fencers.

At the start of the third heat, Trevallon collapsed quietly in the dirt at the feet of his opponent. He lay on his back, staring up, and did not move.

Ardys saw him fall, and for a helpless moment, blind fear held her still. Then she was at his side, desperately yanking the helmet from his head. His face was ashen and red-blotched, his breathing uneven. He tried to speak but could not.

The Queen stopped the tourney with a gesture, and sent a page to enquire what was amiss. The boy ran, and returned to inform her that the Fencing Master had taken suddenly ill, but was not injured. At her order, the boy scampered into the palace to fetch her physician.

"Take this off him!" Ardys frantically clawed at her father's steel breastplate. Her fingers bled where she scraped at the metal. If she could just free him of the steel, he would be all right. His armor was too tight, and he was tired and overheated, that was all.

"No!" she screamed as someone behind her pulled her to her feet.

It took four strong men to lift Will, and she followed, gripping his hand, talking to him, trying to ease the fear in his wide staring eyes, as they carried him through the crowd across the courtyard and into his own chamber. She clutched at him, trying to give him some of her strength, and they had to disentangle her so that he could be gently laid on the bed and undressed.

One of the students who had come with them wordlessly handed Ardys Will's rapier, rescued from the dirt of the arena. She held it helplessly.

For three days Ardys sat, pale and stiff-backed, on a stool by her father's bed. Silently she hovered by him, watching for some flicker of consciousness, listening to the harsh rasp of his breathing. He had collapsed into a heavy, dull sleep as soon as he was laid on his bed, and he would not awaken.

Dr. Ruy Lopez, the Queen's personal physician, attended the sick man, but clysters, bleedings, and purges brought no improvement and may indeed have done more harm than good.

The old court astrologer, Dr. Dee, came as well, but could offer no help: he saw the future plainly enough in the face of the Fencing Master and would only shake his head as he left the chamber.

Ardys watched her father sink a little deeper into his last sleep with each passing day. His skin took on a grayish cast, and his mouth became cracked and dry. He could no longer swallow, and water poured between his lips flowed freely out again, soaking the pillows. From time to time Ardys touched a damp cloth to his lips and forehead. There was no response but the constant harsh sound of his breathing, noisy and unnerving.

Ardys thought little, and felt less. It was not happening. It could not be; it was not possible. This man who lay so still under the blankets was not the smiling, athletic father she loved. It had to be some other man, or this was a dream from which she would awaken. She viewed the entire scene with detachment: Will's body, shrunken somehow, drawing in upon itself. The whispering servants, the darkened room, curtains drawn to keep out evil vapors. It was as though she stood and watched from a distance.

The candles sputtered in the airless chamber. She touched Will's face softly. Cold and moist, he lay with his eyes half open and rolled back, unseeing, behind his eyelids.

"A growth," Dr. Lopez said. "It must have been there a long time, for it is very large, filling most of the lower part of his body. The heat of the day, combined with the strain of the heavy breastplate, must have simply overwhelmed him. 'Tis hard to believe that he did not collapse weeks before, for his pain must have been much."

"I never knew. He gave no sign, no complaint. He said it was nothing," Ardys said softly.

Ardys needed to apologize to her father because she had not known. She loved him and she had not known.

The door to the courtyard swung back abruptly and the

Queen swept quickly into the room. With her came Archbishop Whitgift, the head of her household church, in his black robes.

All those present, including Ardys, went to their knees. Whitgift, his black vestment flowing about him like wings of a crow, stepped to the bed, knelt, and began to pray quietly over Will. Elizabeth waved the attendants about their duties. Dr. Lopez, unable to face the Queen's accusing glance, left the chamber in despair.

She pulled Ardys back onto her stool, and with one slender white hand on the girl's shoulder she leaned forward with a hush of silk and velvet to speak to the Fencing Master.

"Master Trevallon," said the Queen gently, "we are most sorely vexed by your illness. We have need of you, of your sword . . . Ye have been faithful in our service for many years, and we cannot lose you now."

The only answer was the rattle of his tortured breathing.

Ardys said: "He is dying." Her voice sounded foreign to her, for she had not spoken above a whisper for three days.

"Aye, we see." Elizabeth had seen death before and knew when she looked upon it; she had smelled the sour-sweet, cloying odor of sweat and fever and ended time.

"There is a cancer, Majesty. There is no room left for him to live; it fills his body and nothing can be done," Ardys said quietly. "Why must it be Will Trevallon instead of some other man? What have I done, what sin have I committed, that my father should be taken from me?"

She must not look away, she must concentrate on his dear face. She must remember every detail of his features, for when it was over she would not see him again.

"His brow is smooth," said Elizabeth, touching his face softly. "He sleeps, we think, without pain. Be glad for that, Mistress Trevallon."

★ ★ ★ ★ ★

The Queen turned away. Henry the Eighth's daughter had never truly known or loved her own father, and she could find no comfort for this sad young woman who kept vigil for the coming of death.

Elizabeth went to the door, motioning the servants to follow. When the Archbishop rose, she stopped him: "Stay, Whitgift. The rest of you, come away. Allow the man some dignity in his dying."

"Ardys," the Queen whispered. "Death awaits us all; there can be no escape. Be content, if you can, that your father has served us well, and has earned the respect and love of all who knew him. He will not be forgotten."

Ardys did not look up as she murmured, "Thank you, Your Majesty."

Whitgift continued to pray, holding one of Will's hands while Ardys held the other.

Elizabeth walked out into the blinding sunshine of the courtyard, thinking back to the young, gifted swordsman who had spoken boldly to his Queen at her birthday celebration an age ago. Her mouth compressed bitterly and she brushed a stray tear from her cheek.

She commanded everything, except Death. Death had robbed her of her dear Robert Dudley, years before. He had lived to see the Armada defeated and then he had gone off and died, and Elizabeth had not been with him. In his last letter he had written of his love for her, and had thanked her for the diet she had prescribed for him. Poor Dudley, he had become so stout and his hair had thinned and Elizabeth had loved him still, not perhaps with passion as of old, but because the ties between them were so strong. The friendship, the understanding, and the loyalty: all lost. Only the letter remained, in a small locked box by her bed. Nothing else to hold.

She was Queen, but she did not rule all.

Ardys did not hear the sigh as the door closed behind the last retreating page. Whitgift prayed, and Will's breaths came further apart, shallower, and weaker. Ardys kissed her father's cold cheek and held his blue-nailed right hand, that strong hand that once had wielded a sword with such power.

It was some time before she realized the end had come.

CHAPTER FOUR

The palace of Greenwich lay some distance up the Thames from Hampton Court. Closer to the Channel, the river was deeper at Greenwich, and full-rigged ships could stand at anchor at the palace stairs. William Trevallon had landed here in 1579, when he first came to the court in the entourage of Lord Helford.

Almost twenty years had passed; now Will's daughter Ardys would take her leave of the English court from the same dock.

Ardys stood on the stone steps that led down to the river, awaiting the small ketch that would ferry her out to the ship. The morning was bright, though the sun could not penetrate the thick cloud cover. Behind her, beyond the sloping green lawns, was the palace. The turrets and chimneys and the massive gatehouse were a pleasing sight, but today Ardys did not spare them a glance. Her eyes felt sore and dry, and she found that light made her squint.

The long dark cape she wore billowed around her, stirred by the gentle breezes that blew from the river. Her thick hair, dampened by the mist, hung limply about her waxen face. She stared straight ahead at the wide expanse of the water, her mind a murky haze that held but one coherent thought: today was August the seventh, and her father had been dead one week.

She was not alone. The Queen had seen to that. After a brief memorial, presided over by Whitgift in the gilt and blue chapel at Hampton, Elizabeth had kindly invited Ardys to remain at court indefinitely. Shakily Ardys had thanked her but refused, unable to face court life without her father.

They had never spoken of it, but she felt that he would have wished to be buried in Cornwall, near the sea, at Helford House. That was his birthplace, and his wife and other children were there. The Queen agreed that Trevallon would probably have wanted that, and her servants made the necessary arrangements for transport of the body and the journey of the daughter.

Two ladies-in-waiting had appeared in her rooms to assist Ardys with the packing and various preparations for the journey. These women were both widows. They left Ardys alone most of the time, did not chatter, and worked efficiently and quietly. Ardys supervised as they closed her father's garments and personal things into the trunk that had stood in his room. She was glad of their assistance. She could not bear the thought of touching any of Will's things, nor could she bear to stay long in his chamber. She believed it smelled still of death.

Trevallon's rapier, his gift from the Queen, lay with him in his coffin. It rested, as it had in his lifetime, on his left hip. There it would remain, forever.

Ardys dispatched a messenger to Helford House on horseback the day Trevallon died, directed to make all possible speed to inform her mother of his death. But no one would gamble that the lad, even with a pocketful of gold sovereigns to spur him on, would reach Cornwall before the ship that carried his daughter.

The corpse that had been William Trevallon was not being transported to Cornwall by the sea route, but was instead to be carried over land, with his belongings, southwest to his home. This was not Ardys's wish, for she would have preferred to stay with him, but the Queen said that would be too much for her and would not change her mind.

Like a sleepwalker, Ardys left Hampton on one of the

barges that regularly traversed the river highway between the palaces. Two elderly gentlemen helped her with her trunk and stayed with her on the short jaunt from Hampton upriver to Greenwich. These men stood on the dock now, their responsibility almost discharged.

Ardys disagreed with the Queen's decision about her travel arrangements, but of course she said nothing. Elizabeth was not to be questioned.

The roads south were in terrible condition due to the rainy spring and humid summer and were not much more than mud-choked mires. Ardys would therefore reach Falmouth days before the body, and she would be with her family when it arrived, able to take part in arrangements for the interment. It was better this way.

Ardys's passage would be swifter than her father's and smoother as well: the Fencing Master, suitably enclosed in his massive oak coffin, would no doubt be bounced and battered on the roads. Barring a storm, Ardys would travel in comparative peace.

That coffin, large as it was, did not seem big enough to hold Trevallon's body. Ardys stood next to its cart for some time before the mules pulled it away. That such vitality could be shut in a box was absurd. Tearless, Ardys lingered at the main gates of Hampton and watched the mule-drawn cart roll down the long drive. When it had passed from her sight, she turned and patted the cold stone base of one of the King's Beasts. These gargoyles sat majestically to the right and left of the arches that led into Hampton, and Ardys was in the habit of rubbing them for luck each time she entered the palace by that gate. She caught herself and felt foolish: as good luck talismans, the beasts were miserable failures.

A wave frothed against the dock as the ketch drew alongside. One of her gentlemen touched her arm and she jerked her head up and blinked him into focus. He was a benevolent-looking man, solemn in his black robes. He and the other lifted her chest and heaved it into the boat, where some unkempt sailors steadied it.

Through the fog in her mind Ardys tried desperately to remember her helpers' names so she might thank them properly. Surely she must have been introduced to them, and they had been so kind. But she could not recall, and could not think of the correct words to express her gratitude. She said nothing as they handed her into the dinghy.

"Come then, Mistress, gently now. Step to the center, 'tween the seats, that's right, now sit slowly. All right, are ye?" The leader of the seamen lent his hand as she balanced clumsily and the boat rocked. "Then we'll be pushin' off. Thank 'ee, sirs."

A purse filled with gold exchanged hands over Ardys's head. This was money for her passage, and would directly be paid to the captain of the ship.

The black-robed men turned and walked slowly up the incline to the palace as the ketch skimmed across the surface of the river toward the vessel. Absently Ardys trailed her fingers in the cool water, but there was no pleasure in anything that touched her now, and she withdrew her hand.

How odd that men lived still, she thought, when her father, a better man than any of them, did not. They were not to blame for their living, she supposed, any more than birds should be blamed for singing, or the sun for rising and setting.

The world would not change for the passing of one man, and the change in her could not be seen either. She was not what she had been: a dark void had opened in her breast; her heart plucked from her at the moment her father ceased to breathe. If she did not weep, it was not because she was brave, but because she could not.

When she closed her eyes, she saw his face as it was in his last days. It was a mask of death, thin and pale, not at all like him. She suddenly realized she could not remember what he had looked like when he was healthy, however hard she tried to conjure up his image, and this fearsome thought made her shiver. She could smell the chamber still, as though she had never left it. As though she had not bathed and perfumed herself to wash the odor away.

She burned her black velvet doublet and the blue silk gown in the fireplace in her room after he died. The steel breastplate he had worn she gave to one of the smiths to be melted down and remade for some other man. It could still be of use to someone else. She supposed there should be some solace in that.

The ketch reached the ship, nudging at its side by the rope ladder. The jarring motion caught her attention. Ardys climbed nimbly to the main deck fifteen feet above, scorning the hands extended to help her aboard. Like all Cornish-born, she was used to the sea and its vessels. Her years at court had not erased her memories of salt water and creaking decks. Will had taken her fishing for pilchards when she was a child, and they had gone sailing together for pleasure after their long voyages home from Elizabeth's court.

Now Ardys sailed alone and was glad of it. She begged not to bring even Anna, and the Queen had relented on that point. Ardys wished only for solitude.

The *Plymouth Rose* was a three-masted carrack of some four hundred tons, clumsy-looking and riding low in the water, fully cargoed. Visible above the water line were the forecastle with its painted bowsprit, the main deck on which Ardys stood, and in the aft was the balcony, higher than the rest and ornamented with carvings colored red and gold. On the deck above this was the great wheel.

Here in the balcony, the captain and his first mate had their cabins, and here also was accommodation for any wealthy travelers who chose to sail on the merchant ship. The *Rose* was no pleasure craft, nor was she equipped for war, but a sturdy cargo carrier, owned jointly by several traders in the port of Plymouth.

The captain was a rotund man, well paid by those traders.

He swept off his cap and made a knee before her, and when she extended her hand to him, he kissed it gallantly. The incongruity of that elegant gesture in a man as wide as he was tall was not lost on Ardys, and she fought down a laugh.

"Welcome, Mistress Trevallon. The *Rose* is honored by the presence of a lady from Her Majesty's court. Ye have brought no maid? Then I shall escort you to your quarters, if you'll permit me. You there, bring this lady's trunk."

The anchor chain whined rustily as it was drawn up into the capstan. The crew hurried about the decks as the ship began its slow ride down the river. Ardys jumped back, heart pounding, as a curl of rope, stout and wet, snaked around her feet like a live thing. Above her the three mainsails unfurled with a rush of thick canvas.

"Keep a good watch, Mistress. The footing can be chancy, especially when we are coming about to catch the wind. We'll not reach open sea for a time, so it would be best if you would confine yourself to your cabin."

They traversed the fifty feet to the rear 'castle, and the captain opened a door in its center with a flourish. Beyond him Ardys could see the dark interior of the cabin that would be her home for the journey through the Straits of Dover and down the English Channel. Cramped and airless, no doubt, but she was not bothered by the thought of that. It seemed womb-like and therefore welcoming. A place to be alone.

"Thank you, Captain," she said, her voice sounding hollow. "I promise I shall not interfere with the running of your ship; if I feel a need for exercise I will stay on the main deck, out of the way. Pray do not concern yourself for my welfare . . . Perhaps my meals could be brought to me here also?"

"Aye, one of the lads can bring 'em to you. If there is nothing more—? Then I'll bid ye good day."

He was quite kind. She endeavored to smile and was not really successful. She stepped into the room and closed the door, blocking out the light.

The gloomy darkness enveloped her immediately; she stood still a moment while her eyes adjusted. Daylight burrowed in through the porthole in the far wall, and gradually she picked out the scant furnishings.

A bed was built into the wall on her right, straw-mattressed and probably hard. A rugged table was fixed to the floorboards directly in front of her. Above it, an unlit lantern swung on a short length of rope. The ceiling was not high. She would have to be careful not to bump her head against the lantern. Her chest stood next to the table, taking the rest of the limited space. She shoved it under the porthole where it would serve as a bench. It weighed a great deal and would not slide too much when the ship rocked.

She sat on the chest and looked back over the Thames, wishing the carrack could move faster. If she had to leave, she wanted to go as far as she could as quickly as possible; but the *Rose* cruised sluggishly along and Ardys's view of Greenwich receded slowly around a bend in the river.

Her father in his coffin rolled along slowly too: she could picture it.

Ardys removed her floor-length cape, draping it across the table. She tested the bed: hard as a stone. With a sigh she lay down on her back, arranging her skirts around her.

44

Her closed door did not block the noise of the ship. She listened to the shouts of the men, the creak of the masts as the sails filled, the flutter of the wind they caught, and the constant lapping of the water. Pleasant sounds.

It was the first time she had been alone since her father fell in the tiltyard. No one could see her now, no one to whom she must speak, nothing she must do. She pushed the farthingale she had worn for propriety's sake under her dress and behind her, and curled onto her left side, facing the rough wooden planking of the cabin wall. Like a child she touched the wood with a hesitant hand, running her fingers along the rough cracks as though this was a texture new to her.

The wall was solid and real. She felt something inside of her letting go. Her face grew warm and her eyes stung with the tears that had been dammed up so many days.

Once released, the tears flooded from her. She buried her face in her hands and wept great, wrenching, gasping sobs. She rocked gently with the rhythm of the ship, abandoning herself at last to her grief.

CHAPTER FIVE

The first two days of the voyage passed uneventfully. The weather held clear and the wind was steady, though not strong. Each evening Ardys emerged from her cabin to stroll about the deck and ease her cramped muscles. She spoke only to the cabin boy who at regular intervals brought her trenchers of plain food and ale. She had no appetite, but she ate to keep up her strength.

The rest of the hours she spent weeping, for now the tears had come there could be no stopping them, and they did bring a kind of release: she slept often and heavily; drugged by exhaustion.

The third morning found the ship through the Straits of Dover and in the Channel proper. The breeze appeared to be lessening, and the sails flapped loosely. The lack of wind brought an odd quiet to the ship.

There was no land in sight, although the coast of England, possibly the Isle of Wight, could sometimes be seen hovering on the horizon.

Ardys arose at dawn, as did most of the crew. Her long weeping spell and the deep sleep of the previous night had cleansed her somehow; she felt more alive and aware of her surroundings than she had for days.

The formal black gown with its farthingale and starched white ruff was suddenly uncomfortable. She took it off and donned instead a worn green velvet dress that she found in the depths of her trunk. The gown was out of style, as it flowed in a straight line from the low square bodice to her slippered feet. The sleeves were of the type Anne Boleyn had favored, as they hid her extra finger—a tight white under-sleeve to the wrist beneath a longer green satin over-sleeve that was slit from the elbow. A lighter green underskirt accented the center of the gown from waist to floor.

Ardys lovingly touched her rapier in its place in the lid of the chest and looked with longing at her doublets, packed so neatly away. To be able to move freely, without all these petticoats and skirts, would be a true luxury. But sight of a woman in man's attire would probably attract too much attention from the crew, and that would bring the fat captain puffing to her side. Sickening thought. The gown would have to do.

She did not know if the captain had been told anything but her name, and she preferred if possible to keep him uninformed. She and her father were both relatively well-known. If the ship's crew found out who she was, she would be besieged with questions about fencing technique, and with expressions of sympathy for her father's death.

She was tired of thinking of death, and irritated at the ship's obvious loss of speed. The gown annoyed her; it was too stiff. She was used to daily hard exercise, and had had none for over a week. She felt full of unspent energy.

Before she opened her cabin door, she stood and listened to the sounds of the ship. It was too quiet. Something was wrong, and it must be more than the loss of forward motion. She stepped out onto the main deck and realized that the crew, normally noisy, shouting to be heard above the creak and flap of the sails, had fallen silent.

At first she thought the sailors were staring at her, but their gazes went beyond her. She felt a prickling at the back of her neck, as though the air would soon be charged with a storm, but the sky was a deep clear blue, marred only occasionally by feathers of high clouds.

She crossed to the starboard rail, looked out over the vast

expanse of the sea, and then she saw what it was the crew stared at so intently.

A vast ship, four-masted with spars tall as trees, towered like a castle on the western horizon. She caught her breath, understanding why the seamen around her were so silent. As the ship advanced on the *Rose* its high fore- and stern-castles became clearly visible, with the two decks above the water line. It had to be a hundred and fifty feet long, and thirty-five feet wide at the beam. The English did not build great fortress ships like this. Such vessels were designed for the carrying of troops, horses, and cannon.

The Spanish, who still viewed their navy as a land force deployed by sea, built such ships. Involuntarily Ardys took a step backward. A tiny breeze lifted her dark hair.

Spaniards giving chase to an English ship, a merchant whose peaceful intent could not be doubted, in the middle of the English Channel! It was unthinkable. Ardys had seen the mock Spanish ships at the Armada Day, but she was not prepared for this overwhelming sight. This ship was huge, and with its higher ratio of sail it was gaining on the *Rose* even with the scant breeze.

Soon it would loom above the *Plymouth Rose* like an owl swooping down on a mouse frozen with fear.

Her elbow bumped something soft, and she saw that the captain was at her side. She had no idea how long he had been there, and when he spoke, his voice was a hoarse whisper.

"Go back to your cabin, Mistress. We can do nothing—we can't maneuver, not with full cargo; we can't outrun her—there's enough wind for her, but not for us! And we surely cannot fight her. If those damned Dons want my ship, they'll take it. I was hoping we were too small for them to trouble with. Jesu, a ship that size must carry forty guns!"

"But ye must fight!" Ardys whirled to face him and saw his

48

look of despair. "If you allow a Spaniard to take you here in the Channel—almost within sight of the mainland—no English ship will be safe! They will feel they can sail our waters as they please! Do ye not realize what shall befall you and your men if the Spanish capture the *Rose*? The slave galleys— or the Inquisition! At court I heard the stories—the Dons carry their instruments of torture and their priests with them wherever they go. Do ye believe they will show you mercy? They have none!"

The Spaniard was now so close that the rows of eighteen-pound culverin that gaped from its sides were mere yards away.

A cold rage washed through Ardys. This fat idiot would stand by and let Spain have his ship without striking one blow in its defense. He thought to save his unworthy skin by surrendering, the coward! If the Spanish did not destroy the *Rose* outright, one battery of their guns would doubtless be enough to disable her and they would certainly imprison the crew. Or worse.

"Fight, damn you!"

The Spaniard hove into position for boarding. She could see the enemy clearly, swarming about the middle deck, readying the grappling hooks, climbing the rigging to make the swing across open sea onto the *Rose*. They did not even wear any steel protection.

She spit at the feet of the fat captain and ran back to her cabin, throwing wide the door. In her haste she fumbled with the clasp of her chest and had to wrench it open.

The *Rose* convulsed as the Spanish ship rammed into her port side; Ardys could hear the shouts of the enemy as they swung aboard the main deck.

"God's Blood, I will fight, if I have to fight alone! Trevallon's daughter will not die a coward's death!"

She pulled her rapier from its hooks, flicked the scabbard away, and turned to dash out to the deck. She stopped in mid-stride and stood very still.

A man blocked the doorway of her cabin. The light was behind him so she could not see him well, but she could sense the tautness of his body, the wariness of his stance: here was the enemy.

Tall and lean and all in black in the fashion of the Spanish, with a delicate white ruff and lace at his wrists, he also stood very still, waiting. His doublet was open to the waist, and so was the white silk shirt beneath it; she could see the gleam of some Papist medal on a gold chain round his neck. In the halo of light she could not make out his face.

She listened as the Spanish crew scrambled onto the *Rose*, laughing and cursing, their weapons clanking. There were no sounds of battle, however, no clang of sword or bark of musket and no screams of wounded men. The ship now belonged to Spain.

Ardys was silent for a few seconds, shaking with anger.

"I find myself on a ship manned by craven half-wits," she said quite distinctly in Spanish, "but, by God, I will not cry mercy."

Her rapier nestled securely in her grip.

"I wonder," the man remarked gently in English, "what an armed lass would be doing on an English merchant ship."

Insolently, his gaze swept slowly over her. Then he leaned against the doorjamb and crossed his long legs at the ankles.

He casually brought the tip of his sword down to rest lightly on the floorboard by his right foot. She saw it was a basket hilt, longer-bladed than her own.

He spoke without a trace of Spanish accent. It had taken her a moment to realize it, and she started with surprise.

"You are English—or once you must have been! Your

accent betrays you," she hissed. "I tell you then, as a courtesy to a countryman, that you have made a grave mistake attacking and boarding this peaceful trading vessel. The Queen will soon hear of this treachery, and I have no doubt that she will tell all the world!"

"Perhaps," he said agreeably. "But we did not attack. There was no need. And your Queen's opinion means nothing to me. Your Queen means nothing to me. I answer to no one."

Ardys raised her chin. "Inform your captain that I wish to speak with him."

"You are speaking to the captain. And I warn ye, I have little time for conversation."

A shout from behind him made her start.

"Cap'n 'Connell! She carries wool—high quality by the look, and lots of it! Come an' see!"

Another man appeared in the narrow doorway, much smaller than the captain.

"Not now, Bled," said 'Connell, never taking his eyes from Ardys's face. "You see to the loading. I shall join ye shortly."

The tall man nodded in Ardys's direction and she glimpsed his face: high forehead, long nose, neat mustache, and beard on a strong jaw. Angular, hard features.

The other sailor looked in at her, startled, his eyes wide.

"So be it, Cap'n," he said. "I'll tell 'ee when 'tis done." He turned and sprinted out of sight.

The captain swept her with another mocking glance and stepped over the threshold into the cabin. He tucked his blade under his elbow and deliberately began to peel off his long leather gloves.

"Cease waving that sword about, girl, before ye prick yourself with it."

His voice was deep and resonant, with a touch of Irish lilt. She could see his face clearly now. It was a hard face—but for the wide, sensual mouth. His eyes were a very deep blue-gray. Ardys stopped breathing for an instant before she shook her head angrily.

"I am in no danger, Captain. It is you who are. Challenge me, damn you!"

He said offhandedly: "Can you use that weapon as it was meant to be used? D'ye plan to defend your honor to the death? That may be amusing."

In the dim light from the porthole she saw the flash of his white, even teeth as he grinned.

He advanced a pace to the table but she stood her ground. Two sailors passed by the open door, lugging bales of wool. Tossing away his gloves, the captain took up his sword again. When he raised it, Ardys's blade flew up in a blur. He touched its tip with his own. The hanging lantern was in the way.

He looked at her then, taking her measure with a practiced eye.

"Ye hold the sword well," he said. "As though ye are used to it. And the stance is good as well. By my troth, I never saw a comely wench wield a weapon before."

The tip of his blade began a graceful dance in the air with hers. He moved so that the table was no longer between them. Only the length of the blades separated him from where she stood in front of the porthole.

"I like the idea of fencing with you. If you wish to do battle, I might oblige you. And then what will you do?"

"I will teach you better manners," Ardys said, her eyes narrowing as she took his measure in turn.

The steel shifted subtly as Ardys began to circle him slowly, gathering her long skirts in one hand. 'Connell matched her moves. He smiled again.

"You have me at a disadvantage, Mistress. I do not believe I wish to harm you."

The two blades shivered, steel against steel.

"That is indeed your disadvantage, sir."

"Wait." He held his sword still a moment; she followed suit. "I'll strike a bargain with ye."

"Are you then a coward, that ye must bargain with your enemies? Why should I listen to you?"

He let the insult pass and went on: "If ye draw first blood, you are free. I will leave you on this carrack with its overfed captain and those of the crew that do not join mine. You may take your chance with them."

"You are setting them free?" It was said before she realized it. "When have Spaniards ever freed their captives?"

"Never that I know of. But then why should I know? I have nothing to do with Spain."

"Not with Spain? But you captain a Spanish ship! To whom is your allegiance then?"

"It is of no moment. We are talking of a bargain. D'ye take it?"

She paused to consider. "If you draw first blood, what then?"

He cocked an eyebrow. "Why, then you shall yield."

"I will never yield!" she cried and lunged at him, slicing at his left arm.

He parried but she had caught him by surprise and he shifted a bit off balance. Instantly she took advantage of this, and pressed him back to the doorway with a series of quick thrusts. The captain's head brushed the ceiling of the cabin and he could not maneuver freely; he gave ground, backing out of the door onto the deck.

His crew halted the tiresome process of transferring the

wool to his ship. Both crews watched in astonishment as the tall pirate came stumbling backward out of the balcony cabin pursued by a beautiful woman whose sword flashed quickly in the sunlight. The sailors broke ranks when the combatants approached, forming a ring about them, a living arena.

There had been no battle that day, the vanquished captain having done the intelligent thing and surrendered to superior force. The pirate crew watched the two fencers eagerly, and there was no attempt made to interfere.

Ardys was used to fencing like this, surrounded by gaping spectators. She was in her element, and her heart swelled with the joy of action, the exultation of battle.

"My father taught me well how to fence. I am not afraid of you!" she said.

"Ha, good! Then this shall be even more pleasant."

The sunshine was blinding after the darkness of the cabin, and she was unprepared for her first view of the captain she fought. They closed together and blades and wrists intertwined; for an instant she could feel his breath, warm upon her cheek. His blue-gray eyes were heavy-lidded and long-lashed, and his hair was the color of mahogany glinted with reddish gold, curling thickly to his collar. His mustache and beard were fairer, blonder, and he was tan from the sun.

He was no longer smiling, and was losing his air of condescension. His jaw was tight with concentration. He continued to give way, defending himself expertly but seemingly reluctant to strike. It looked therefore like she was winning—when luck turned against her.

In the midst of a running thrust she caught a heel in the hem of her gown and nearly fell, her blade sliding uselessly along the length of his. He bore down on her as she went to one knee. She parried as she struggled upright and furiously kicked her skirts to untangle them. She had lost her rhythm, and their graceful dance became clumsy. 'Connell's foot struck the edge of the second deck and his right arm shot out to counterbalance as he fell to his left. At that moment Ardys's sword ripped his doublet from shoulder to waist; he parried too late to stop the strike, but with a feint to the right and a twist from below he sent her weapon flying. It whistled through the air and came to rest, quivering with its point buried in the wood of the deck, fifteen feet away.

Panting with exertion, Ardys waited for his move. She was unarmed and helpless. It had never happened before, and she had to respect a man who could do it. He kept his blade within easy striking distance as he glanced down at his ruined doublet and pulled at the fabric with his free hand. His shirt was sliced through, but the brown skin beneath was unscathed.

"No blood," he said softly, his voice low and dangerous. "We have not finished yet."

Impatiently she shook her hair out of her face.

"You shall not be so fortunate next time. End it now," she said. She drew herself up to her full height and met his hard gaze without flinching.

His eyes narrowed.

"Do not court death so calmly, Mistress. Bleddyn! Fetch this lady's sword and return it to her."

Ardys watched him. She could not look away.

Bleddyn tugged her sword from the planking and tossed it over his comrades' heads. Ardys caught it neatly by its hilt, and raised the point in mock salute as she resumed the stance.

"So! Ye wish to continue, Captain?"

"Oh, aye. I think perhaps I have never faced a better swordsman and I would satisfy myself that this is so."

With deliberate step the captain advanced, his feints and thrusts so rapid they were all but invisible. Ardys had never encountered such speed, nor had she faced such fearsome skill. He forced her to retrace her route, back across the deck to her cabin door.

In a frenzy she parried, but he gave her no chance for riposte. Her heart began to pound in her ears as she backed away. She knew he had resolved to beat her, and was more than her match: for the first time Ardys felt she was fighting for her life.

Inch by inch he drove her back, his sword flashing. She fell back over the cabin threshold, her own momentum propelling her farther off balance. She bumped into the table and sprawled against her trunk, bruising her knees and thighs on the hard wood. He stepped into the cabin and slammed the door shut behind them.

His voice was quiet and menacing in the sudden stillness. "I grow weary of this. Put up your sword before I injure you. If you value your life, yield."

Anger gave her strength. She lunged at him wildly, her sword arcing with deadly speed. He parried and pushed her on her back onto the bed, his attack never faltering. She deflected the blows he rained about her but she could not sit up.

She felt the bunk sag with his weight as he swung his right leg across her body and knelt over her. She was beaten, and she knew it. She had no room to move and his knees on both sides of her skirts pinned her down. 'Connell wrenched the rapier painfully from Ardys's hand, sending it clattering against the opposite wall. Drawing his dagger from his belt, he touched its sharp point to her white throat and leaned down.

He whispered: "Yield. Or do ye wish me draw blood now?"

She thought wildly: Jesu! He is going to kiss me, and I can

do nothing to stop him. She watched his full lips curve once more into a smile.

He threw the dagger down and she felt the warmth of his hand on her neck.

"I fancy I can see myself reflected in your eyes," he said softly. He brushed the hair from her forehead and then eased his long frame onto the bed beside her. He reclined there, his fingertips delicately outlining the curve of her cheek before his mouth grazed hers. She could feel her heart beating; feel the warmth of his body on hers. His kiss became more urgent.

Warm and soft, his lips tasted of the sea, and his mustache tingled on her upper lip. Confused, she moved slightly under him, and a lock of his dark hair spilled onto his brow. She was aware of every inch of her body beneath his. She felt his hands under the small of her back as he molded her to him, pressing her closer still.

Then, with a strangled curse he pulled himself away and stood beside the bed so abruptly that she nearly rolled off onto the floor. He stared down at her, his eyes clouded by desire, and then he bent to retrieve his dagger and sword and turned away.

He paused at the cabin door.

"You may keep your rapier," he said, his voice still husky. "You fence well: indeed perhaps better than any I have met before. But you allow your emotions to overcome you, and in a true battle that would be your death. You must learn to feel nothing."

"Who are you to teach me what to feel?" she demanded, sitting up.

"One of my men will see to your things. You may consider yourself my guest, or my prisoner. As you please. We depart shortly; make ready. The *Espada* can always make use of a good fencer."

She cried, "No! You cannot!"

"It shall please me to cross swords with ye again."

The door creaked open and he was gone.

CHAPTER SIX

The little seaman touched his hand to his forelock in a gesture of subservience before Ardys. "My lady," he said hesitantly, "Cap'n 'Connell says I'm to escort you across to our ship. Prithee."

Her hand went to her sword.

"Prithee, my lady," he repeated.

"Nay, nay, I will not offer you combat," she said, shaking her head. "To continue to fight after one is defeated is undignified, though you must not believe that I come with you without protest."

Ardys took a bit of the velvet rag she always carried and wiped the blade of her rapier as she would after any match. A shred of black velvet from the captain's doublet clung still to the sharp tip; when she pulled it impatiently away she nicked her index finger, and swore.

"Damn your captain's eyes!" she said furiously to Kennwyn, who blanched before her sudden temper. "Does he think me some prize cargo he can simply take because it pleases him?"

Bleddyn stared at the floor as she angrily thrust her rapier back into its sheath and returned it to its place in the lid of her chest, slamming it shut.

"We bain't never taken no prisoners afore," said Bleddyn. "We be honest seamen, my lady."

"Honest?" Ardys looked at Kennwyn and saw his abashed expression. "Go to, I understand not how you can call yourselves 'honest' when you are all cutthroats and thieves. And how do you explain that a Spanish ship comes to be crewed by

Englishmen, and preys on English ships?"

"Well, my lady, ye see we bain't none of us English."

Bled took hold of the leather strap on the outside of the trunk, pulling it out of the cabin and onto the deck where the rest of the crew had finished transferring the bales of wool. The chest was heavy, and his face became red as he tugged.

"Then you are all in the employ of the Spanish," Ardys said with contempt.

"Nay," he stood and mopped his brow with his sleeve, resetting his feet wider apart to get a better purchase on the stubborn trunk. "I be Welsh, and the Cap'n, he be mostly Irish. Some o' the men is Scots, some Irish. There's even a Frenchie or two."

"Then tell me—whom do you serve?"

"Why, Cap'n Desmond Kirkconnell, my lady, and no other. I serve Cap'n 'Connell as first mate, Mistress, and have done these pretty many years," Bled said.

Ardys laid her hand on the mate's arm. "What will happen if I refuse to come with you now?"

The small man sighed. "Then I am told to hoist you over my shoulder like one o' them bales of wool."

She stayed a moment, her hand on his arm.

"That," she smiled a trifle thinly, "would be a feat for you, my honest fellow. I am as tall, and probably as heavy, as you are."

"P'raps ye are. Prithee, my lady, will you come with me now and save us both the trouble?"

"I will come with you, but first, you must tell me your name."

He touched his forelock again, and then he began once more to pull at her trunk. "I be called Bleddyn Kennwyn."

The smile she bestowed on him was like a flash of bright sunlight after a storm at sea.

"My name is Ardys Trevallon, Master Kennwyn."

She followed the sweating Welshman onto the deck of the *Plymouth Rose*.

Most of the pirate crew had already transferred onto the *Espada*, swinging across the narrow width of sea that separated her from the *Rose* by the same stout lines they had used to board the merchant ship.

When Ardys came near to the captain of the *Rose*, she spoke, her tone full of icy derision: "You are a base coward, sir, and my fate be on your head."

The arrogant captain of the *Espada* stood just opposite her on his own deck, his black-booted leg up on a wicked-looking demi-culverin, one of the many that lined his ship. His hard stare silenced Ardys.

Bleddyn came up behind her and with a muffled apology lifted her to hand her across to the other vessel. One of the pirate crew came to catch her but Kirkconnell sent him running with a gruff word. Grimly he reached out for her as she came across, his two hands easily encircling her waist as he balanced her on her feet in front of him. He said nothing and held her there, his eyes never leaving hers, and when the wind stirred his thick hair she realized suddenly that he was the handsomest man she had ever seen. She looked away from his intense gaze.

When he released her she stepped hastily back, nearly stumbling, and his hand shot out to steady her. With his strong grip on her wrist she could not but follow him as he led the way across the crowded deck to the stern-castle, a high, ornately carved and painted structure that soared thirty feet above the level of the main deck. She barely had time to look about the huge ship as he pulled her along, but she had a precise mind for detail and little escaped her scrutiny.

The three tall masts reached such a height that she could

not see the tops of them, and the yards and yards of sail, now beginning to fill once more with a breeze that hardly ruffled her hair, blocked her view of the sky almost completely.

The *Espada* was one hundred and thirty feet long from the tip of her bowsprit to the end of her stern; thirty-three feet wide at the beam, and she drew water to a depth of seventeen feet when she was fully manned with one hundred and twenty sailors and sixty land soldiers, together with their victuals, their animals, and their gear. The size of the vessel overwhelmed Ardys, who had never been near such a ship. The mock Spanish fleet of the Armada Day had been splendid indeed, but it could in no way compare with the magnificence of this ship.

Interested in spite of herself, she asked, "That sterncastle, Captain, towering so far above the water line, surely that makes this ship top-heavy and slow to maneuver, does it not?"

The slighter built English ships had made short work of the Great Armada, skimming round these sea-going fortresses like so many sparrows worrying a hawk. The thought filled her with pride, and as suddenly with a pang of fear: she was alone on this vast floating island, surrounded by men who were her avowed enemies, and in the power of a man whose plans for her seemed all too clear.

"It could, aye. But it has never yet been a problem," 'Connell answered.

When she glanced up at him, his dark brows knit into a frown.

The crew returned her stare rudely, and she thought that they did not do their captain justice in their clothing and demeanor. They seemed ragged, poorly-dressed in loose knee britches and ragged-edged shirts that may have originally been silk.

Neither were the men themselves fine specimens of virile manhood: some were only boys, fresh-faced and round-eyed, some old men, gray and wizened and leather-skinned from years of exposure to the salt of the sea air and heat of the sun. Perhaps there were more sailors below, or perhaps there was a sister ship to the *Espada* where the prize crew sailed, separate from this one. These men did not look so fierce, but every one of them was well armed with a one- or two-handed sword and a dagger, and as they ran about their duties she saw how many of them were required to tend the guns. The captain of the *Rose* had estimated well: the *Espada* was armed with nearly forty guns, eighteen of them gaping eighteen-pound culverins. Formidable weapons.

Bleddyn Kennwyn was supervising the crew as they prepared to sever the lines that held the two ships fast. When he shouted, "Away the ship!" in a voice twice his size, the grappling lines were cut and the merchant set free to drift where she would in the calm water. With this hindrance gone, the *Espada* heeled slowly and majestically round, her masts creaking and groaning with the weight of the wind.

Up a short ladder 'Connell pushed her, even as she craned to see the masts again, onto a smaller deck halfway to the top of the stern-castle. There were three doors in the 'castle at this level, and his grip tightened on her wrist as he kicked the center door open and forced her into the chamber.

Kirkconnell slammed the door shut, and leaned back against it with his ankles carelessly crossed, watching Ardys through heavy-lidded eyes.

She took a step forward, closing the distance between them.

"Get on with it," she said. "You have me and I cannot fight you here. My father taught me to choose my battles."

He stood straighter then. "Your father? Was he truly a

fencer, then? And was it from him you got your temper?"

"My father was Fencing Master to the Queen," she said haughtily, "and a better man there never was."

"And he taught ye to fight?"

"Aye."

"Then I owe him thanks! I have had no sport for months. This is well," he said with a smile.

"Sport! What sport is there in kidnapping me?"

"I think ye know, lass. Until now my slapdash sailors and I have merely skirted round the outer edges of Elizabeth's maritime law. All ships that sail the sea are fair prey for us, and we have the advantage of this full-rigged Spanish ship to keep the English sea-dogs from nipping at our hindquarters. We're pirates, yet we sail a Spanish man-of-war. It has been of some use."

"And as captain you must have many comforts," she said, as she stared at the great bed, velvet hung and deeply-pillowed, that took up the entire right-hand wall. There was an oak desk and chair beside it and a lantern swinging overhead.

"Kidnapping an English noblewoman of the court is a serious crime, even by my standards, and not likely to go unnoticed by the English crown," he allowed. "If you are indeed a lady of the court, daughter of the Fencing Master—as I think you must be, to have such advanced technique—then I must make this worth my while. It's as well we are leaving the English shore now, and heading far away where pursuit cannot follow."

Desmond turned from her and shouted, "Tom!" rather loudly in the confined space.

A small door in the wall opposite the great bed opened, startling Ardys, who had borne the captain's last thoughtful, measuring glance with nerves that were near to snapping. With a flicker of relief she saw that here was no new danger; a young boy, barely twelve, entered the cabin, rubbing his eyes as though he had just wakened from a deep slumber. Beyond the youth Ardys saw a small chamber, a closet, really, where the boy had been asleep on a pile of sacking.

Desmond went to him and laid a hand across his shoulders. The captain dwarfed the boy, who had very red hair and fair freckled skin.

"Thomas! Once more I find you asleep in the height of the day." Desmond spoke with some affection. "Battle could have been joined, lives lost, storms fought, and you would have slept on. Come and greet this lady."

He turned to Ardys with an exaggerated bow, waiting, she saw, for her to say her name.

"I am Ardys Trevallon," she said.

"Ardys Trevallon," the Captain repeated, lingering on the words. "For the time she shall have your little cabin, Tom. Do ye sleep with Bled in his cabin next door, or with Father John below if it pleases you."

"But Cap'n!" protested the boy, his voice cracking. "Am I not to be your cabin boy still? I'll not sleep in the day again!"

Desmond ruffled Tom's hair. "By Our Lady, Tom, you will always be my true servant, ye know that. But Mistress Trevallon can serve me in ways which you cannot."

Ardys flushed as Tom murmured, "Aye, sir," and left the cabin.

She said quietly, "I am loath to think that you would deprive yourself of your body servant because of me. Or if you are thinking I will be your servant, sir, you may think again."

"Servant? What, young Tom there?" Desmond crossed to the alcove and shut the door again. "Hardly a servant—more of a companion. I call him my cabin boy. I could not let him work with the crew; you saw how fragile he is. He is a close kinsman of a friend of mine, a man whose good will I need to keep, and so when the father asked me to take the son on my ship, I agreed. But it will do the boy no hurt to sleep elsewhere."

With a glance at her, he pointedly unbuttoned his doublet, shrugged it off, and placed it on his bed. "As for your becoming my servant, madam, rest easy. I think we both understand what I want of you."

Ardys, determined not to lose her composure during this, the final assault, did not look away.

The bed was very wide and luxurious. The Spaniards that built the *Espada* had seen to the sleeping comfort of her captain, and the bed took most of the cabin's floor space. The room was dark and richly paneled, hung with small Flemish tapestries of brilliant colors, and boasting two small lead-paned windows that afforded a view of the wake left by the great ship. Weapons of various kinds were displayed on the open beams, among them a heavy two-handed sword that was larger than any Ardys had ever seen. She felt his eyes on her again.

She returned his stare, determined to be calm, to remember who and what she was. Only her rapid breathing betrayed her.

There was a movement on the bed.

Two bright yellow eyes peered owlishly from the heap of pillows at the head. The velvet coverlet on the bed was a soft orange color, and the immense striped cat that now rose and stretched on it matched it perfectly. It was fatter than any cat should be, and it leisurely began to wash its face with its right paw.

In spite of herself, Ardys laughed with nervous relief.

"This is Great Harry," Desmond said, going to the bed and giving the animal a rough whack that sent it neatly onto the floor where it sat licking itself, completely unperturbed.

66

"He's red and fat like the old King, so I call him that. He catches rats and mice in the hold and the crew's quarters. He was here when we first took this ship, and for untold time probably before that. Since I have been aboard he has not gone ashore, nor shown the least inclination to do so."

"There must be many rats on this ship; he looks exceedingly well fed," Ardys said, bending to stroke the cat's head when it came and rubbed against her legs.

"D'ye like cats, then?" he asked. "I confess to some affection for this old beast."

"God's teeth, I am no witch," she answered. "Many at court believe cats are the devil's servants."

"Then 'tis no wonder he serves me so well," 'Connell said.

She fidgeted a bit, shifting from one foot to the other.

"Have you a husband, Ardys Trevallon?" He asked abruptly, going to the door where Great Harry stood on his hind legs, pawing at the latch in an effort to open it.

Her gaze left the cat and she jerked up to look at him. Once more he was uncomfortably near, only an arm's length away.

"I have no husband." She glared at him. "Nor do I want or need one."

"Then, pray tell me, truly, who taught you to fence? For, by God, you have had a brilliant teacher."

"I told you! My father was William Trevallon, master fencer to the court of Elizabeth."

"Trevallon . . . No, the name means nothing to me. Of course," he said dryly, " 'tis a long time since I have been invited to the court of the English Queen."

"He died less than a fortnight gone." She blurted it out without thinking. Suddenly she saw her father as he had been: healthy, tall, and proud, his rapier at his side. The image of him was so clear it startled her.

Desmond opened the door to the cabin and the cat

scooted gratefully through. The captain frowned at its retreating backside, and turned to look at the girl again. He seemed to be contemplating her anew.

Then with a shake of his head he left her, pulling the door shut behind him. Ardys was alone.

Great Harry sat on the deck and scratched at his ear with one of his hind legs. A flea sprang out onto the planking, and the cat snuffled at it before making his leisurely way to the trap door that led below to the hold.

Bleddyn Kennwyn knocked hesitantly on the door of Kirkconnell's cabin. Ardys's chest was on its end beside him. Kirkconnell was nowhere to be seen. There was no answer, so Bled pushed the door open and began to drag the trunk inside.

Ardys was in the little cabin off the main chamber, furiously pounding at the straw pallet on the floor that of late had been the bed of the boy Tom. A cloud of dust hung in the air around her; as there was no window in the closet she was all but obscured from view.

The captain had left her, for whatever reason, and in his absence she claimed the tiny closet as her own. There was no lock on the separating door, but perhaps if she could stay out of his sight, 'Connell's obvious desire for her would lessen, and she would be safe from him.

Bled's hand on her shoulder made her start, and Bled stood there with her trunk leaning against the wall of the captain's cabin, waiting for her to make some sign where he should put it.

"Tain't enough room in there, my lady," he said when she impatiently took hold of one of the handles and tried to tug it inside the smaller chamber.

"Aye, there is, Master Kennwyn. Here, I'll move this pallet out of the way there. Now lay the trunk down flat, and

68

I'll put the mattress on top of it for a bed. You see, it's narrow and high but it will serve, will it not?"

He helped her move the trunk and the pallet.

As she straightened the pallet, she said, "Your captain, master Kennwyn, did not say where are we bound."

"Home, mistress," answered the mate.

"Aye, home! But where is home?"

"Ireland."

Ardys frowned at him.

"To Carrickfergus," Bled went on. "To put ashore, scrape the hull of gull's eggs, and sell the cargo."

"Gulls eggs—on the hull?"

"Aye. You know, mistress, hard things, that attach and grow," he searched his memory for the proper word. "Barnacles, they be called."

"Oh, aye! But at any rate, surely there is no one in that God-forsaken place wealthy enough to buy this cargo, Bled. In the north of Ireland, surely there be only savages."

Kennwyn nodded. "Aye, p'raps. Many o' the crew hails from there. Cap'n 'Connell grew up there."

"In the North of Ireland? But he's a swordsman, and are not the Irish people brute savages, who fight only with axes and rakes?"

Bled whistled. "If you see the Tyrone, my lady, I pray ye don't call him a savage to his face."

"Tyrone? That name brings dim memories . . . the Queen, angered by the rumors of a secret army amassing in the north of the isle; and the name Tyrone . . ." she paused, thinking.

"Hugh O'Neill, the Earl of Tyrone? You sell your cargo of wool to him? Now I mind Hugh O'Neill's name; not that I've met him, forsooth, but I know the family of Sir Philip Sidney from court."

"Philip Sidney?" echoed Bled, confused.

"Sir Henry Sidney's son. O'Neill lived with them while he and Philip were growing up. Aye, now I remember! The Queen wished to keep O'Neill safe from his Uncle Shane, who wanted him dead for some reason. I do not recall what it was. Philip told me of it—and Lord Burghley, too, knows this Tyrone as well. They consulted over plans for the building of the Tyrone's castle, Dungannon."

"Aye. And the lead that Lord Burghley sent to O'Neill of Tyrone for the roof of his hall of Dungannon was melted down—and molded into gunshot!" Bled laughed.

"But Hugh O'Neill found favor at the English court! He was friend to Sir Francis Walsingham, and to Lord Chancellor Hatton. Why," she looked at Bled sharply, "a Spanish ship, manned by Irish, preying upon English vessels—all for the Tyrone?"

" 'Tis a matter of business, my lady," Bled said.

Kennwyn turned to go.

"Bled, wait," she said in distress. "For your kindness to me, you have my gratitude."

"Aye," said the mate with a nod and a small smile.

When he had gone the dust began to settle onto the pallet, which she now finished smoothing on top of her chest. A high bed, indeed, and narrow, but with her velvet cloak spread over it, soft enough. Not so comfortable perhaps as the bed on the other side of the door, but she would not think of that.

Ireland, and the Tyrone. Not home, not for her: not the Cornish cliffs she had played upon, not the ornamental gardens of Hampton Court Palace. She and her father were not known in Ireland; no one would care for her loss. Her mourning would be private, not part of some public spectacle of funerals and feasts.

Perhaps, she thought grimly, this might be better . . .

Her grief had become more distant in these last hours

since the *Espada* had appeared on the horizon, but it sprang back to her with almost physical force now, as she sat quietly on her makeshift bed. Her mind whirled faster and faster and her heart began to pound as she relived what had gone before. She may have no control over her fate here, but at least she could face it well, with dignity.

Truth to admit, she looked forward to fencing with the handsome captain again. As for the rest of it, she would endure and wait for landfall. On land there was mayhap some hope for escape.

She lay back on the bed, exhausted.

On deck, Desmond placed the golden compass carefully back into its carved wooden box. Taking up the long cross staff and holding it to his right eye, he sighted in on the sun. Pulling the transom piece, which crossed the staff at right angles, he adjusted it so that it fit in his sight between the horizon the vast expanse of the sea and the sun, and read the latitude of the ship. He stood on the poop royal, the highest part of the *Espada*, atop the sterncastle. Leaning down, he marked the course on a chart that lay spread before him on the binnacle, the desk-like compartment where the navigational instruments were stored. The wind stirred his thick hair.

"Steady to her course, George," he said to the helmsman standing next to him.

The captain put his hand on the tiller, the great wheel with its long handles that was the responsibility of the helmsman, liking the feeling of the ship's power in his grasp.

"Aye, Cap'n 'Connell. Bit more to the south is it, then we swing 'round land's end and make for the coast of Ireland?"

"Best stay far from the Cornish coast, George. I have no wish to tangle with the English patrols."

"Aye, ever since the Armada came, there are always patrols in these waters, for sure. Many's still got the fear a second invasion fleet'll come, no doubt."

"I agree. Queen Elizabeth may have sent most of her able seamen home after the defeat of the Spanish squadron—so that she could avoid paying them!—but this English coast does not lie easy yet. A chance sighting of the *Espada* would bring the entire English fleet down on us."

The wool merchant that Ardys sailed on was the first ship Desmond had taken within the actual confines of the English Channel. It would be well to reach Ireland again.

"What think ye of this here ship, Cap'n?" George asked, his steady hands on the wheel.

Kirkconnell squinted at the horizon. "Before you signed on, George, I'd been pirating for a few years along the Irish and Scottish coasts, occasionally down into the Caribbean, around the Canary Islands and across to Africa," Desmond said. "I've served on many ships. This one will do for the purpose, I suppose. The *Espada* is a far better vessel than that small three-masted Portuguese carrack we had before, do ye not think? That was an ill-built, under-gunned tub that leaked! And we did not do particularly well in that ship, either," he reflected, "for most of the vessels we met were not easy enough prey for us when we were new-made pirates."

George laughed, showing gaps in his front teeth. "Aye, p'raps, but we're better pirates now, are we not?"

"Oh, aye. Still, I miss that old ship sometimes, George. This one's clumsy."

Desmond named his first ship the *Jane*, for his mother, when he bought her from Black John Newchurch in Dublin. He paid a trifling sum for her: Desmond had been Newchurch's first mate aboard the *Pride of Folkestone* when the carrack was taken; he'd traded his share of its spoils to Newchurch for the captured vessel itself. The Portuguese ship was returning from the New World laden with gold.

Desmond knew Black John had made the better bargain, but the captured ship had become Desmond's to rule. And Newchurch knew that if his first mate had not left when he did, there might have been a struggle for power on the ship.

Newchurch was glad to be rid of his mate, a potential rival for command, and equally happy to let Desmond's friends go with him when he left. Kirkconnell, Bleddyn Kennwyn, the helmsman-pilot George, the old cook Grimsthorpe, and some few others left the *Folkestone* to sail with Kirkconnell on the *Jane*.

As time passed, more men had joined the *Jane*'s crew: peasants from the Irish and Scottish villages that lay along the coasts; English prisoners escaping from being pressed into that country's navy; a few malcontents from the crews of the ships the *Jane* took.

They had marauded for two years, modestly successfully, but never quite taking the great prizes that sailed in the Spanish treasure fleets.

Desmond looked about him. The *Espada* was a hardier vessel, if unwieldy, and he'd gotten her by sheer luck in August of '96. The *Jane* had been careened on Innishmurray Island in Donegal Bay on the northwest of Ireland; Desmond had been preparing to scrape the hull, fresh-paint the ship, and sell it.

Desmond was restless and thinking of leaving the pirate's life when he saw this great ship moored in the bay. It was old and in disrepair; the masts broken and the paint faded, but it was still afloat. The Innishmurray men were using it as a platform for sorting their fish. There were seagulls wheeling all around and there was a harsh fish stench.

Desmond had seized the *Espada* as gladly as a drowning man catches a line. He sold the *Jane* to pay for the Spanish ship.

The *Espada* was in fact one of the last of the Armada fugitive ships, wrecked like so many others on the rocky coast of Ireland. The scant Spanish crew that still survived aboard her in 1588 were battered by storms and half starved. When the ship's hold filled with water, most of them had drowned. The *Espada* had a gaping hole in her midsection, which the fisherman had roughly patched, and her sails, proudly emblazoned with the cross of Spain, were little more than shreds.

Weeks of repair under Bled's close supervision made her seaworthy once again, and Desmond put to sea in his new ship in the winter of 1597.

Desmond glanced at George's brawny hands, steady at the tiller. The helmsman was a large man, with a paunch that promised to turn to fat in his later life.

"Wind's holding well, George," said the captain, and George, happy with the wheel in his hands, smiled his gap-toothed agreement.

Still, the *Espada* had been a disappointment. She was unwieldy and top-heavy, and Desmond understood well how the English ships had won the day at Gravelines. The *Espada* wallowed when she swung about and no amount of baling would ever completely free the bilge of water.

There had been few prizes during the winter and it was on a reckless impulse that Desmond had taken the *Espada* into the English Channel to seek them, leaving the Northern sea-lanes of the Scandinavian coast where he'd been leading a string of raids.

The *Plymouth Rose* had blundered into the *Espada*'s path just as Desmond was concluding that he was a failure as a pirate, and he had nearly let her go by. But the merchant sat so enticingly low in the water that he reasoned she must be laden with something of value.

The wool in the *Rose*'s hold was quite valuable, and Hugh

O'Neill would doubtless pay well for it; delighted with his good fortune, Desmond felt himself a king.

Then a wench had drawn a rapier and split open his fine Spanish doublet. Christ's wounds!

The ship rolled a bit beneath him and he shifted, snapping back to the present.

Ardys Trevallon. Perhaps he had heard the name before: she came from the English court, and Hugh O'Neill had told Desmond stories by the hour about the people there. Desmond concentrated, frowning as he tried to recall Hugh's booming voice in the firelit hall of Dungannon . . . Trevallon, the fencer. The most skilled fencer in the realm, perhaps in all of Europe, a man who had never fought in any war and yet trained the perfumed dandies of Elizabeth's court in his art. He used the rapier exclusively, although that weapon was not as popular as the more common heavy swords used in most European courts. Desmond and Hugh laughed at the thought of the polite way such rapier-fencers must fight, bound by rules and using steps like dancers.

But if Ardys had learned her fencing from Trevallon, then mayhap there was some validity to his teaching.

She said she was his daughter. It made sense. Skill like hers could be only partly learned; much of it had to be innate. She had finesse that Kirkconnell knew he lacked. He found himself smiling as he pictured her in the stance. He knew his one advantage had lain in his coldhearted approach to their duel.

She'd been surrounded by his men, on a vessel they had taken, and still she had the courage to fight him, alone. Aye, Trevallon's daughter.

Desmond stood by the wheel for a long time, thinking, while the quiet and competent George steered the ship. He should go below, into his cabin, and at least talk with her.

He shook his head, went down the ladders to the lower deck, and knocked at his cabin door, more to warn her of his approach than from any thought of gallantry. There was no answer and he went in, wondering if perhaps she was sleeping.

At first he could not see her in the darkness of the closet, but he heard her faint breathing and when his eyes adjusted he saw her well enough.

She lay on her makeshift bed as she had collapsed, the rumpled green velvet dress folded around her. Her fine dark hair curled around her face as she slept. Gently Desmond moved her hair away from her brow; in her deep slumber she was not disturbed and did not move. The velvet of her sleeves was thin and frayed at the elbows, he saw, as though she leaned on them often.

Ardys's hands were clenched in tight fists, and when he tried to loosen them he found he could not and stopped trying for fear of waking her. He was reminded of the clenched fists of a grimy nine-year-old boy who had seen his father hang and had run from the sight headlong into the dense trees of a northern forest. Desmond Kirkconnell, so many years ago.

She had told him that her father had died less than a fortnight before. Desmond could remember too well the pain he'd felt at the loss of his parents, the bitterness and despair. He had been only a child, unable to understand, bewildered and lost.

But Bessie O'Donnell had found the boy Desmond there in the forest of Northumbria, and kept her comforting strong arms held tight around him. She'd held him when he finally wept, and later she had taken him across to Ireland, where her Catholic kinsman had welcomed them, and he had learned to live again.

There was no Bessie for the lass that lay here now in his cabin, her energy spent, her fight gone, her frown smoothed by sleep. A wave of warmth coursed through him.

Let her sleep. She was in no danger from him.

CHAPTER SEVEN

Ardys awakened hours later, stiff-muscled and with a bitter taste in her mouth. It was black and airless in her tiny compartment; someone had shut the door. She imagined it must have been Kirkconnell and the thought of him near her while she slept gave her an odd feeling, like a chill, yet she was not cold.

She rolled onto her back and stretched, her gown catching under her back before she stood under the low crossbeams of the ceiling. The ship was deathly quiet; it had to be late at night, and the crew all asleep except for the watch. And if they all slept, the captain must be beyond that door, lying in his great soft bed.

There was a sound of growling suddenly; it was her own stomach, and she could not remember the last time she had eaten.

Gingerly she reached out and gave the door a slight push. It swung back on its silent leather hinges. It was lighter in the bigger chamber. Moonlight drifted in through the lead-paned windows beyond Kirkconnell's bed.

Scarcely breathing, she stood and listened as she counted to three hundred. There was a form in that bed, hard to identify but large, and she could hear low, regular breathing. The captain must be deep in sleep.

The wooden floor protested with a loud crack when she slipped into the cabin. She froze with one foot in the air before she took another step, counting his breaths. She was tempted to creep closer, to see him better, and as she did a muffled thump made her stop again, her heart in her mouth.

Great Harry, it seemed, was not so heavy a sleeper as his

master, and had roused himself from his warm spot on the captain's velvet bedspread to investigate the intrusion. The cat came and rubbed against her legs, purring loudly. She did not touch it for fear it would make more noise; and then her empty stomach made its rolling protest again, and the quiet form on the bed stirred and murmured.

Alarmed, she turned and ran lightly to the great door and pulled it open, escaping onto the deck with the cat racing between her legs. The door closed silently and she sped away, half expecting to be followed, half disappointed when she was not.

Desmond rolled over onto his back and sighed, watching the door.

On the deck the night was still, with only the sounds of the lapping waves and the lashings of the sails. There was a suggestion of a breeze, and the ship rocked pleasantly as Ardys inhaled the fresh salt air. She loved the sea at night, since the old days when she and her father had taken their little ketch into the bay beyond Killigerran Head to watch the great shoals of pilchards that came in toward the Cornish shore under the light of the new moon.

Tonight the clouds must be thin, for she could see the stars. There was no moon. At sea the sight of the clear night sky was achingly beautiful, with the flickers of light in untold millions stretching as far as could be seen. She felt small under the vastness, but as she stared up until her neck began to ache she was almost at peace. Her father would be in Heaven, as were all those who had died since the world began, as many souls perhaps as there were stars.

Birth and death, the cycle had gone before and would go on after. Ardys was glad to be alive now. Even, she thought, here, on this foreign ship. Or, perhaps she should be honest with herself: perhaps she was glad to be alive because she *was* on this foreign ship. She wondered how Kirkconnell had come to be here.

The watch stood above her on the poop royal, by the wheel that was lashed for the night to hold one course, but the man had not seen her. He rang the hour with the brass bell: three. Her stomach growled again.

She had to have food, and though she could not know the plan of a Spanish ship she thought that the galley must be somewhere below the main deck, near the middle of the ship. On a calm night like this one a cookfire might still be burning there, and with any luck she would find something warm to eat.

With a care for the watch, she tiptoed across the deck until her right foot stumbled against the hatchway that led below. She swore softly, and briefly massaged the toe she'd bumped before she backed down the ladder through the open trap door, clutching her long skirts about her knees.

An interminable climb, until she missed a rung and fell back, grasping wildly at nothing, coming to rest with a dull thud on something soft on the dark floor.

A hand circled her arm.

" 'ere, wot's this?" A wizened face, ghostly pale, loomed near hers. "The Cap'n's lass! Smelled me stew, did ye, and thought to come an' 'ave a bit?"

An old man, his smiling face a mask of wrinkles, used her arm for support as he struggled to stand.

"Jist a moment, lass, let me get me feet under me . . . there." A sound of scratching and her arm was freed. "Sorry, but ye gave me a fair turn, landin' on me like that in th' midst o' the night. Not that I ain't been waked rough before, mind."

"I'm terribly sorry, but I was hungry, and as you say, I smelled food and thought to . . ."

"He told ye of old Grimsthorpe in his galley, did 'e, the

Cap'n? An' ye've come to see if 'tis true as Desmond said, old Grimsthorpe be the betterest cook what ever sailed to sea. Come on, lass, help me find me flint and I'll light us a torch."

Ardys let the old man, hunched with age, lead her into the heart of the *Espada*, into the galley with its tremendous stone oven, four feet high. Her stomach rumbled again at the warm meaty smell emanating from the black iron cauldron suspended on a swinging arm over the fire, which was indeed still burning, though very low.

"Best quiet that thunder 'fore ye wake the 'ole ship!" Grimsthorpe laughed, wheezing, and showed the spaces where once his front teeth had been.

The heat from the oven was oppressive, even in the cool night, and after he'd ladled some stew into a fine china bowl (from what table, Ardys wondered wryly), they went out again into the passage where the cook had been sleeping on a fur rug. He sat again, joints creaking, and motioned her to sit beside him. His face was so guileless, and his manner so friendly, that she was moved to relax. He would not let her talk, but bade her eat her fill while he watched her with evident satisfaction. His eyes, nearly obscured by the wrinkles, were a bright green, and now that she could see his flowing white hair and beard Ardys decided he reminded her of a woodland elf, a creature of hedgerows and glens. His gaping smile was infectious, and she laughed with him when he pointed to her stomach and did a passing imitation of the growling noise it made.

"Aye, Grimsthorpe, the cook. I keeps the fire aburnin' so long's the wind's mild and weather's steady. Hot food's more better'n cold for the men, sticks to they bones, it does, and makes 'em brave for battle. That's why I sleeps out 'ere in th' passage, to keep watch on the fire, an' to see no one can help hisself to the stores."

"This is the most delicious stew I have ever eaten, Master Grimsthorpe," Ardys said gravely, wiping her mouth on her sleeve. "What's in it? Mutton?"

"I adds to it, a bit o' this, a tad o' that, like, all 'long the voyage. Flavors melt together real nice. They's some wine in there, too, from the original owners o' this ship."

Her belly full and comfortable, Ardys sat back with her hands around her knees and listened to the old man talk, not really hearing, content to be full and in friendly company.

"Tell me, Grimsthorpe, how long have you been a sailor?" she asked.

"Sailor! Bless me, mistress, I ain't no sailor. I be a cook. Happens that Kirkconnell's on shipboard, and so I be too, but if he'd been on land, I'd be his cook on land. 'Tis all one t'me, so long's I be where he wants me to be."

"How long then, with Kirkconnell?"

"Since he were a tad up in Tullaghoge. Knew Old Bessie what raised him, she were a cousin 'o mine. Good woman. And when she's ready to die, she says to me, Grimsthorpe, ye old fool, take care o' the lad, look after 'im and see he's fed. Well! She died hard after, so I could hardly refuse 'er last wish. So where the boy goes, goes I."

She leaned her chin on her knees, trying to imagine Desmond's angular, handsome face on a boy.

"Were you always a cook then?"

"Nay, a soldier I were. An O'Donnell gallowglass, a proper warrior I was, but I got sliced through once too often and me back went hunched, so I figgers, if I be hunched it might's well be over a stew pot." He laughed and she could not tell whether to believe him.

"You, a gallowglass?"

Ardys knew nothing of Kirkconnell's crew, yet the two she had met, Bleddyn Kennwynn and now this old cook

Grimsthorpe, had been kind to her. And above her, in the dark cabin, slept a captain who had been raised by a woman named Bessie and who let a cat sleep on his bed; who had not touched her since that warm, lingering kiss aboard the *Plymouth Rose*.

Life was passing strange.

Grimsthorpe kept talking, and Ardys slept, lulled by the food and his pleasant voice. It was full day when she awoke and made her way back to the captain's cabin.

The door opened before her outstretched hand, and Kirkconnell stood outlined in the light of the window behind him.

"Unless ye prefer to take exercise in a gown, I think it better that you put on a doublet; you may have one of mine if you have not one of your own. Or something of Bled's would likely fit you. Come, do not gape so! It's a new day, and I wish to see if there is anything to be learned from the Fencing Master's daughter."

Alice Trevallon stood next to the wooden coffin that contained all that was left of her late husband, William Trevallon, the Fencing Master. The vicar was murmuring but she did not listen, nor could she see well through the heavy black lace veil that covered her head. Her eyes were dry beneath the veil; there were no tears for the stranger in the box, not even for the sake of propriety.

The clouds had lifted mid-morning yesterday and the weather become clear and hot. The coffin lay on the boards spread across the mud in the family burial ground beyond the garden of Helford House.

Alice was petite in her mourning regalia, dainty still after twenty-two years of marriage and so many children borne and lost. The veil hid her features.

The arrival of the mule-drawn cart, suddenly and without warning, and then the news that filtered over from Falmouth, that her daughter Ardys had been taken prisoner by blood-thirsty pirates, would have unnerved a lesser woman. She was not alone, with her six girls ranged round her in their varying sizes down to her youngest, now five years of age.

The heir of the manor, David Helford, said to her: "He was a good man, Will was."

"Aye," Alice agreed. "He was a good man." She looked at the coffin with a slight frown. "Yet even now, after all the years we were married, I feel I did not know him."

Taken aback, David said, "He did honor to your family and ours at the court of the Queen. He was admired and . . ."

"Oh, aye, admired he was. And I was his wife. I was his wife, and he was with me once a year. His duty! He did his duty by me, got children on me, and then left me again. His leaving is no different now, except that I am not with child," she said bitterly.

"Forgive me, Alice, I do not understand."

"Will's dead, and Ardys lost too, yet I feel nothing . . . nothing for the stranger who never stayed with me, nothing for this daughter who was closer to him than I could ever be. They were inseparable in life, those two, it's mayhap fitting that they should be taken at the same time. I endured their in-difference, their endless swordplay. Will and Ardys were in their own world and I was never welcome. Enduring became my habit. It is no longer so hard."

David desperately searched for some words of comfort. "You are welcome here, you know that, Alice. You and your children must stay here. All your days. Prithee, stay."

Alice looked up quickly. "I had not thought to do other-wise," she said in surprise.

She felt his eyes upon her now and straightened up a little, rearranging the veil.

The vicar finished, closing his Bible, and the iron-barred doors to the crypt swung shut with a dull clang. The company began to walk back to the house, carefully in the mud from the recent rain. David walked at Alice's side. He held out his arm and without hesitation Alice took it, delighted in his gesture. Will was dead, but now David was by her side. Under the heavy black veil, Alice was smiling.

The *Espada* rounded the Scillies, the small rocky cluster of islands off Land's End, in a driving rain about thirty hours after Will's widow began contemplating a new life. The ship kept to a southern tack, however; its master was in no hurry to reach their destination.

Ardys wrapped herself in a coarse cloak of the captain's, and stayed on deck in the rain as long as she could stand to do so, for this was the first day the weather had not been clear, and she was nervous about going back to his cabin now.

Since the morning when he had met her at his cabin door after her midnight conversation with his cook, she and Desmond Kirkconnell had fenced many times. They seldom spoke, except about fencing, and they seldom met unless it was in practice. He was avoiding her at mealtimes, and always went to bed hours after she had retired: there had been no repetition of his brief passion aboard the *Plymouth Rose*. To her secret dismay he was treating her as though she were, indeed, no more to him than a fencing partner.

The morning after she had shared Grimsthorpe's stew, Ardys appeared in her favorite black doublet with her rapier drawn and had taken the stance before Desmond on the main deck.

"Well, Captain Kirkconnell," she said.

"The doublet suits you," he said, his sword hissing from its sheath. "Now . . ."

Across the decks, around the masts, up the ladders to the stern-castle poops, back again to the bow they fought, and the business of the ship went undone while the men watched the exhibition. It was no fluke, the duel that had been fought on the merchantman; this woman could fence. The fighting was fast, but by tacit consent of the opponents no blood was ever drawn.

After, when they were tired and sitting on the hatch cover together drinking a pint of ale, they talked.

"A beautiful weapon," he said, touching her sword. She moved it gently away. "Well balanced and sure."

"I was taught to fence in the Italian manner, where grace and agility are of greatest importance. I love the intricate finger play of the circular parry and the counter-disengagement."

"Aye, but skill is useless without a cool head, a keen eye, and a hard heart."

"Mayhap . . ." she said drinking deeply of her ale and watching him over her cup.

"Have ye heard of the 'sentiment de fer'?" she asked, wiping her lips carelessly on her sleeve.

"I learned to fence to defend myself, woman, not to dance with court dandies."

He leaned back on his elbows, crossed his long legs, and grinned, wiping the blade of his cup-hilt rapier with a corner of his doublet.

" 'Tis the ability to feel the attacker's reactions on the blade itself."

"Why should I worry about reactions? I fight to save my skin, not to make a pretty show."

"Fencing is an art, captain!"

"There again we disagree. Fencing's no art, it's a skill of war."

She pressed her lips together. "Oh? Do not soldiers practice with the lance and the battle-ax? Do not archers hone their skills through hours of repetitious movement and display? In battle, does not superior skill make equal those mismatched by size?"

She glanced sideways at him. "Without my skill, where would you find your enjoyment in fencing with me?"

He sheathed his blade and stood, looking down at her. "Be careful, madam, when ye speak of my enjoyment of you. That is dangerous ground indeed."

Ardys reddened and looked quickly away. Watching a gull wheel overhead, she had stood and walked to the railing, feeling Desmond's gaze on her all the while.

Now, in the rain, she watched the Scillies fade into the distance, knowing the weather would soon send her inside. Her mother and sisters must have buried her father by now: that seemed farther away than those islands, a distant unreality. Well, her father was gone, and her mother—face the truth—had always been a hostile stranger, a displeased shadow hovering behind Will and his daughter. And last night Ardys had dreamed again of Kirkconnell's mouth, warm and insistent, on her own.

She felt his presence behind her before she heard his footsteps. She turned as he came to where she stood at the starboard rail of the main deck.

"You're wet through," he said, shouting to be heard above the rain. "Come inside, Grimsthorpe's brought some stew and says if the weather holds this foul 'twill be the last hot food we'll see for some time."

When she looked up at him the rain ran into her eyes and she had to blink.

"Then by all means, it must not be wasted," she said, her cheeks pink, her wet hair curling in little tendrils around her face. She gathered his cloak closer about her and followed Desmond into his quarters.

The cabin was filled with the smell of Grimsthorpe's stew, and Great Harry left his close inspection of the bowl with reluctance after a cuff from the captain.

"You'll have the leavings, fat beast, but not until we've eaten our fill."

Ardys flicked some of the water from the cloak at the cat and he scurried beneath the bed.

"Let me take that." Desmond said, hanging the cloak over one of the hooks in the wall beside his own. He glanced at her. "Your pardon—do ye need to change your wet clothes?"

"I'm dry enough, Captain. I do not melt, I am not so dainty."

He raised an eyebrow. "Then sit, here on the bed, we'll put the bowl between us and if the ship rocks we can catch it before it spills."

He remained standing and began to spoon out his stew.

She thought: this is the first time we have eaten together, the first time we have been together on his bed.

She was more warmed by that than by the savory stew. The cabin was very quiet.

The bowl was empty within minutes, for out of nervousness she had eaten quickly. The cat licked the bowl contentedly when Desmond set it on the floor.

The rain trailed across the windows and he got up to light the swinging lantern. The flickering yellow light laid a glow on her hair and lit a sparkle in her dark eyes. Desmond sat beside Ardys on the bed, then rose and leaned instead against the front of the carved desk.

He said nothing.

Ardys, to avoid looking into his eyes, had become preoccupied with his hands. Long and slender, like the rest of his
body, yet with an assurance of strength in the grip.

He finally said, "Damn the weather."

"Aye . . ." She could feel the hot blush spreading over her
neck and cheeks. He thinks I am a fool, tongue-tied and
unsure because we are alone in his cabin with this great bed,
but I am not a flighty court maiden. I am Ardys Trevallon and
I am this man's equal when we meet on deck with swords in
hand.

Two steps, she thought, and she could be in his arms. He
would crush her soft mouth with his and kiss her until she
yielded to him. She blushed at the image in her mind's eye.

He went to sit behind the desk, his jaw more tightly set
than it had been a moment before. She looked up, startled,
when he moved.

The very air in the cabin was charged with tension. He
leaned back in his chair and put his booted feet on the desk.

"I vow, that rapier of yours is a beautiful thing to behold,"
he said. "Was it made for your use alone?"

"Made for me, yes. My father commissioned it to an
Italian craftsman, to mark a date." She hesitated. "Tell me,
Captain 'Connell, what is the day?"

"Day?" He considered. "The seventeenth, I judge." He
flipped through the pages of the ship's log that lay on the right
side of the desk. "I should write here more often. I've not kept
the journal up on this voyage."

"The seventeenth . . . Then this is the anniversary of my
birth," Ardys said. "My father gave me the sword two years
ago."

"A fitting gift it was for you, my girl. How old are you,
then? I am no judge of such things." Desmond frowned at the
cat as it jumped up on the bed.

"Twenty, now," she answered.

He considered her, and after a moment he said quietly: "Did you love your father?"

"That's an odd question. 'Tis a child's duty to love its father."

"I am not asking a child."

"Then I answer: yes, I loved my father. He was all that was important in the world. We were partners, in a way, always together. All that strength, gone!" She shook her head. "His grace, his humor, his joy in living, gone, all gone. Ye cannot understand . . ."

"Can I not? Perhaps you are right, for I do not recall much of my childhood, nor did I love my father. I feared him. But my mother, now . . . She was gentle, and good."

He spoke more to himself than to her, watching the rain on the windows. He did not see how she moved toward him and quickly checked herself.

"Sometimes I believe . . ." she said, "that I shall fly apart into tiny pieces, scattered, like . . ."

"Like the bits of a ship that has run aground on rocks?" He smiled almost gently at her. "You will bear it, Ardys. Your life will go on, unchanged."

"Not unchanged, never unchanged. I am not so hard."

"I did not say you were. But your sorrow will lessen in time; ye will heal the same as you have healed when a blade touches you."

Silent tears came; he must have seen them almost before she felt them on her lashes. She did not bother to brush them away, nor did she sob. The tears fell onto the velvet of her doublet jacket, staining it.

"I am alone," she whispered.

"We are all alone. 'Tis a human condition," he said. "When I was but a child, my mother and father were murdered by agents of your Queen. That is what it means to be alone."

She passed her hand over her eyes. "What happened?"

" 'Twas in the rebellion, in the north, in 'sixty-nine. One o' the border lords used our hut for a meeting place for his conspirators—my parents were only present because they lived there. It was far off from any other houses, or roads, and a good place for secret meetings."

"And so?"

"So, when the soldiers came they burned the hut, killing my mother, and took my father for hanging next day. I watched. Lord Berwick, who led the group of conspirators in that region, escaped. 'Twas said he went to Scotland and then to France. By my faith, for all these long years I have wanted to kill him. I will recognize if I ever see him again. He had a nose like a turnip. A very ugly man."

He turned to her, his face now cold and hard. "To be alone is painful, but ye will survive. I did, and I was but a child."

"Where did you go after this happened?"

"A woman that lived hard by us found me hiding in the forest and took me for her own. She had lived there all her life, but her people had told her stories of her O'Donnell relatives in Ireland. She feared the taint of treason would put me in danger, so she decided to go back to Ireland and find her family—she brought me with her, and raised me there, among the O'Donnells. We went to the coast, stole aboard a ship, and found our way to them. They welcomed us as kinsmen . . . She was a good woman, Bessie O'Donnell. Aye, you'll survive. Everyone does. But ye must go home. You are no use to me here."

She blinked. "What say you?"

"You cannot stay. When we reach Ireland I will send ye south, to a place where you can take ship to England again.

When we reach Carrickfergus, I will see you are put on another ship and taken home."

Heedless of the rain, he went back onto the deck.

In his cabin, Ardys stood, stunned. Home! To see her people again, her land, her father's grave . . . aye, home. It was best. Why then did she think only of Desmond Kirkconnell, on the fact that she would not see him again?

A few days later the *Espada* arrived in the wide harbor of Belfast Lough in the northern Irish Sea. It was late afternoon, and the sails cast long shadows onto the rippling surface of the water. The coast was high and rocky, and on the north side of the bay Carrickfergus Castle loomed vast, gilded by the waning sunlight.

The Normans built Carrickfergus at the end of the twelfth century, and technically it was still an English garrison. Now it was the only English post still standing in the northern part of Ireland, and it was deserted most of the time. Occasionally Hugh O'Neill, Earl of Tyrone, used it as a kind of huge hunting lodge.

Elizabeth's troops had fled south during the Desmond Wars of the 1560s, reluctant to be the sole defenders of English interests in a land full of hostile tribesmen, in spite of the thick walls and imposing structure of their fortress. In the fourteenth century, another O'Neill of Tyrone had tried to burn the castle to the ground and failed. Most of the English soldiers did not wait to see if his descendent would be more successful.

The water of the bay was a deep blue-green, and the rocks the waves pounded below the castle walls were the same color, covered with lichen and tendrils of moss that floated hair-like in the sea. The square keep of the castle was forty feet high, with small slit windows near the top for the archers, and on its sides were two half-moon towers about half its height.

Beyond the headland, the keep faced the town of Carrickfergus—now populated exclusively by Irish, their houses built square and high, towers like the castle. Goats grazed at the foot of the nine-foot thick walls of the fortress, and inside dwelt many families of fishermen and soldiers.

In the outer and inner courts Hugh O'Neill of Tyrone kept a cache of supplies and weapons for the defense of his coast, which his people looked after in his absence, and to which he added when he could.

At the outskirts of the town were the borders of the thick Irish forest. As she stood on the *Espada*'s deck, Ardys caught the earthy odor of moss and peat smoke on the breeze that blew from the land into the bay. There were no other sea-going vessels about, but many small ketches bobbed near the crescent-shaped beach. There was some activity now ashore as the fishermen came in with the evening's haul, and Ardys saw brightly dressed women and fur-clad men moving in the distance in the huts of the town. From this distance they looked like gay, fluttering butterflies against the dark background of thatched huts and the gray stone tower houses.

The *Espada* sailors swarmed about in the rigging of the ship, roping up the sails and preparing to drop anchor. For some of them, this harbor was home, and those ashore their family and friends. No wonder they seemed happy.

Desmond appeared at her side but she had not heard him come.

"It is as well that you now clothe yourself as a woman should. These people are of the old ways, and they are suspicious of strangers. Most of us are known to them, but you are not. If you appeared to them in a doublet, with a sword in your hand, they would doubtless think you a witch."

"I am no witch, Captain Kirkconnell, as well you know. And I look forward to being free of your company."

His strong hand gripped her arm and he spun her round, forcing her to look up at him. He held her fast for a tense second, and then let her go abruptly. She stumbled back to the rail.

Kirkconnell ordered the mate to let down the anchor just inside the mouth of the bay where the water ran deep enough for the great ship. A fleet of small boats put out from the shore and approached the *Espada*, ready to transport cargo and crew ashore. The *Espada*'s own ketches were hoisted over the side and into the water, where they bobbed, held by lines to the mother ship.

The unloading of the wool stolen from the English merchant would take some time, for it must be lifted out of the hold by bale and gently lowered into the waiting boats. Ardys saw Bleddyn was managing this as the captain was going ashore.

Ardys wore one of her finer gowns, one of dark blue velvet with a tight bodice trimmed with lace and pearls along the collar and wrists. A scarlet cloak over her shoulders contrasted it, as did the rich color of her hair and her pale skin.

She vowed she would die before she betrayed any weakness, and held her head high.

Her wooden trunk was lowered into one of the *Espada*'s long boats, and Ardys followed it, climbing down the rope ladder, refusing help. Above her the ship towered, the sharp lines of the rigging etched boldly by the setting sun that now flamed red on the horizon.

Kirkconnell stepped down into the boat and sat beside her, not sparing her a glance, shouting more orders to Bled, who leaned over the side of the *Espada* to hear.

"See 'tis done before full dark!" Desmond called. "And

follow us across with the others. I'll send some of the Tyrone's men to see to the ship so that you all may come ashore, in your turn."

"Aye, Cap'n!" Bled's voice drifted to them across the lengthening stretch of sea.

Soon the ketch grated on the sand of the beach as a last push from the oarsmen propelled it to a stop where the water met the shore. Two sailors leapt out and held the boat while the others jumped across to the sand. Desmond stepped out and was up to his knees in the shallow water; wordlessly he held out his hands to Ardys and swung her onto the wet sand, which squelched under her weight. She swayed a bit, unused to the lack of motion after her time aboard ship, and he steadied her.

"For a man returning to his friends, his homeland, you do not look happy," she remarked.

He had let his beard go untrimmed and there were dark patches beneath his eyes as though he had not slept well for some nights.

Desmond said nothing, let her go, and began to stride toward the village. The gates of the castle opened and soldiers came pouring out in a long wave, on horseback and on foot, shouting greetings to the sailors.

Ardys stayed by the boats, drawing her cape more closely about her as the men ran to the beach. Covered with furs of various kinds, unkempt and unshaven, they went to the cargo and left her in peace. They were more interested in the wool that would make their winter clothes than in a common English wench. Most of them were tall and sturdily built, and without exception they were heavily, if crudely, armed. If this was the army of O'Neill they looked fierce indeed, but there were not all that many of them, thought Ardys, estimating about four hundred on foot but only twenty on horse.

Desmond emerged through the crowd beside a huge man with broad shoulders and thick limbs whose step outdistanced even the long-legged captain's. The Irishman had an enormous spade beard that matched his thick red hair, and he was dressed in the manner of his companions, loose trousers to the knee, a fur vest, and a long heavy cloak. But his cloak was embroidered, and fastened at his right shoulder with a golden ornament the size of his large fist, designed as a circle and pierced by a dagger-shaped pin in the manner of Celtic artisans.

The man towered over Kirkconnell and when he spoke, it was in a deep booming voice that would surely carry for miles.

"Ah, Desmond, me lad, 'tis a cargo of wool, then? None too early, for the winter comes soon—I can smell it! We'll talk of the price later, after we've dined."

Their long strides brought them to where Ardys stood by the boats.

"Why, me boy," said the Irishman in mock horror as he fingered one of the bales, "this be English wool! How does yourself come by fine English wool?"

"What other sort of wool would float in the English Channel, Hugh?" answered Desmond with a laugh.

"And this girl," Ardys flinched as the huge man clapped her heartily across the back, "be she a seagoin' shepherdess? I be the Tyrone, lass. Name's Hugh O'Neill."

His lively gaze raked over her as she straightened her cloak.

"Part of the same cargo," Desmond said casually, "but she's not for sale."

Hugh glanced at his friend.

"Ah, so be it," Hugh nodded. "Come, woman, don't stand there gaping! There's a feast all spread up at the castle,

Desmond. We can travel to Dungannon tomorrow, or the day after, when the food be gone and our business be finished."

The great hall of Carrickfergus Castle was on the bottom floor of the square tower, and when Ardys entered with Kirkconnell and the Tyrone she saw that it had indeed been prepared for a feast. The place was intensely crowded and Ardys's skin crawled with the press of unwashed bodies swirling about her.

The torches were lit, and even though there were no windows, the room was bright. The ceiling was thirty feet high, and the smoke of the fires gathered and lingered there like a low-lying cloud. Long shadows flickered and bounced on the walls in the firelight. The hall itself was square, each wall a length of about fifty feet.

In the center was the great hearth, an open fire laid in a round brick structure ten feet in diameter. The heat emanating from it was fierce, and only those directly involved with the pots that hung over the fire ventured any closer than a few yards.

Tables were placed along the outer walls of the room, made of long planks and barrels, with flat benches ranged behind for the diners to sit on. One table was on a raised dais at the side of the room opposite the entryway, and it was to this table that the domineering Hugh O'Neill and the tight-mouthed Desmond Kirkconnell led Ardys Trevallon.

This was not a formal dinner as she was used to, with ceremony and speech to accompany the food. Hugh's was the way of the old chieftains, and as soon as he sat in his place of honor and nodded, the assembled soldiers and guests elbowed their ways to the tables and began to eat greedily.

The fare was simple and abundant: bread and cheese, meat pies, and strong brown ale. There were no delicacies, no dainty pastries or jellies, but as she considered the rough company Ardys decided such things would have gone sadly unappreciated. There also seemed to be few women in the hall. Perhaps they were not allowed to eat with the men. The men tore at the food as though it was the last nourishment they would have for many days. Across from Ardys, a fur-clad soldier wiped his mouth on his hand and then speared another meat pie with his rusted knife while the drippings ran down his face, all the while conversing with his neighbors in the lilting, rolling tongue of the Gaelic tribes.

At least she was not required to make conversation. She sat between Desmond and a large Irish warrior, and neither of these men spoke to her at all. The din of the crowd was such that any attempt to talk would have been a failure, at any rate, and the men fed themselves to the point where she thought surely some of them must burst.

The food was disappearing, and though her appetite was not great she reached for a loaf of dark bread, trying to ignore the entire situation and concentrate on her need for sustenance. The room was becoming warmer, and she shrugged the scarlet cloak from her shoulders, letting it drop unheeded into the soiled rushes that lined the cold stone floor.

"Forgive me, *mademoiselle*, but you have lost your lovely cloak; allow me to retrieve it for you."

The voice was so low and soft that she doubted at first that anyone had spoken, then she felt a light touch at the nape of her neck and the cloak was once more over her.

The eyes that met hers were as black as ebony, deep and wide. A man was leaning over her from behind, his hands still lightly resting on her shoulders, his head level with hers. Around them the noise and smells of the banquet eddied.

Ardys shivered as though she had been touched in some secret, forbidden way.

"I am François de la Roche," the stranger said, smiling and taking possession of her right hand. Bringing it to his mouth he pressed a light kiss into her upturned palm. He straightened and yet did not release it. "I thought to spend a dull evening in the company of soldiers and sailors, talking of war. How pleased I am to find you instead."

Ardys stared at de la Roche, trapped by his gaze. He stood as tall as Kirkconnell, but he was heavier, and had thick black hair to his shoulders. He was clean-shaven, with a wide sensuous mouth, a long aristocratic nose, and high cheekbones. He had a light French accent, and his voice was low and caressing.

This is a man who need never shout, thought Ardys; when he speaks he will always be listened to.

"May I sit with you?" he asked.

"Aye, if it pleases you."

"Oh, it does," he said, smiling. He was dressed in a dark red doublet, the color of blood, with a black velvet cape over it that reached almost to the ground.

When he swung his leg across the bench, she recollected herself and slid to her right to make room for him at the crowded table. Kirkconnell felt her move, and glanced sharply at her, but she did not notice. De la Roche came to sit between them, never taking his eyes from Ardys's.

"De la Roche," said Desmond loudly, forcing the Frenchman to turn.

"Ah! Captain Kirkconnell; I did not know it was your ship in the harbor."

"Aye, 'tis mine. I heard you were still at sea." Desmond poured himself more ale from the decanter he was sharing with O'Neill.

"So I was, my friend, until an hour past. My ship is anchored by the *Espada*."

François turned once more to Ardys, and again she felt the force of his stare.

"You have not yet told me your name." He spoke so quietly that only she would hear.

"Ardys Trevallon."

Beyond the Frenchman, she saw Kirkconnell scowl.

"Ardys Trevallon," repeated de la Roche. "I hope to know you better, *mademoiselle* Trevallon."

He did not seem interested in eating, though he took a trencher when it was offered him and selected a loaf of bread. Rather daintily, he broke off a piece and began to eat.

"I have wine if you tire of this coarse ale," he said, and from a cord at his hip he took a leather flask. It had a thin neck with a wooden stopper, lashed many times with string to prevent leaking.

He uncorked it and held it out to her, letting her pour some into her goblet before he took some himself. They drank and again she saw Desmond watching, his face stormy. She smiled at de la Roche then, her most brilliant, charming smile.

Captain Kirkconnell might be pleased to toss me aside, she thought. Well, here is this handsome Frenchman, who waits to catch me with outstretched hands!

"This wine," she said softly to de la Roche, "is far too fine a vintage for this company."

"That is why I offer it only to you."

The main dishes were gone; the company turned to drinking with more sincerity, and the noise level rose as the ale went down and the mood of the diners grew more jovial.

She watched Desmond's mood grow obviously worse as the evening drew on. Hugh O'Neill left the table to circulate among his men, to exchange jokes and tales of glory. A trail of laughter followed in the Tyrone's wake as he went about the hall.

Ardys warmed to de la Roche's flattery, and she found him devilishly attractive; but when his warm hand found its way onto her velvet-covered thigh she quickly brushed it away. De la Roche caught her hands under the table between his and held them gently but firmly when she tried to free herself.

His warmth and nearness had its seductive effect when combined with the strong wine. When he leaned forward and put his lips to her earlobe while murmuring in French the while she could not help but feel a thrilling pulse, a response from deep within, and when she turned her head his mouth was suddenly on hers.

"Ardys," de la Roche whispered hotly into her ear, "it is wrong of you to use me in this way. Your eyes are on Kirkconnell even when I kiss you."

She hardly heard him, her head to one side, and her eyes on Desmond.

"I will not take pleasure of you when your desire is for another," de la Roche continued, and he laid a gentle finger on the pulse of her throat as though he had seen that other, deeper pulse. "But I am a patient man. I will wait. Before much time has passed you will need me, and when you do, I shall be there for you. Until that time comes, *adieu*."

François rose gracefully from the table, swept her an elegant, black-caped bow, and strode away into the thick of the throng, leaving Ardys face to face with Desmond.

She nearly flinched under his scornful glance, at the anger in his blue-gray eyes.

The shadow of O'Neill passed over them.

"I grow weary, do you not, my friends?" The Tyrone's hearty voice boomed loud enough for all in the hall to hear. The crowd hushed. "Come, we must all to bed; the hour is late and there is business tomorrow."

His voice rose as the scraping of benches began, heralding

the departure of the soldiers to their women and their sleeping quarters.

"Tomorrow the preparations for our departure to Dungannon begin in earnest. Those of you of the foot battalions, assemble on the beach. Horsemen, here, before the castle walls. And captains, come ye to this hall at cockcrow. Now go, all of you! Let it never be said that the Tyrone's Irish weaken themselves with over-frequent, over-long merry-making."

The laughing crowd began to rise and make for the door. When Desmond got to his feet, Hugh's hand stayed him.

"Come, I have accommodations for ye and for your lady," Hugh said.

Carrickfergus was a maze of halls and stairways, and Hugh and Desmond seemed to know them all. Ardys followed the two men, trying to decide whether she should turn and flee. But she was no coward, and would withstand Kirkconnell's wrath. She was quietly pleased that at least she had provoked a response from him.

Hugh took them up a winding stairway into one of the half moon towers, to a pair of tapestry-lined bedrooms, small but clean, connected by a leather-hinged door. A clap on Desmond's back, a measured smile at Ardys, and Hugh was gone.

Ardys's wooden chest stood in a corner of the first room, a welcome sight. She ran to it, forgetting Desmond, opening its lid to see that her rapier was still in its place, held by the hooks. It was there, and she made sure that it was secure.

Kirkconnell took a tallow candle and lit it from the torch he carried in his hand. No fires were lit in the hearths of these rooms, and a draft whistled though the tapestries, moving them slightly.

White-faced, he left the candle, took the torch, and went

into the other chamber without a word.

Ardys stared at the door a moment, her hands still on the lid of the trunk. She had not expected this silence. So he was, after all, indifferent. Well, curse him, then, she'd go to bed.

She began to undress, setting the candle into a pool of hot wax she let drip on the wooden table by the tiny bed. The bed was under the only window in the room, a mere slit high in the ceiling. She thought that this chamber and its companion, locked from the outside, would make an adequate though comfortable prison and wondered if it had ever been used as such.

The bed was covered with a thick fur robe, and a silver mirror and a crucifix decorated its head.

There was no sound from Kirkconnell's room, and she was uneasy in the deep silence of the chamber.

He was not jealous, then, and it had done no good for her to pass the time with the handsome Frenchman. Desmond cared for her only as a fencing partner, and the brief passion that had flared on the *Plymouth Rose* must have been a chance thing, never to be recaptured.

With an impatient shrug she tried to reach the tiny pearl buttons that fastened her bodice from the back, succeeding in undoing the top few only.

The connecting door opened. Slowly and deliberately, Kirkconnell entered her room. He had had a great deal to drink. His doublet was gone. His white shirt was open to his waist, the lace at his neck at an odd angle. The distance between them was nothing, and in two strides he stood inches from her. His eyes reflected the light like the sharp steel of an unsheathed blade.

She could not breathe.

He said: "You have made a fool of me this night."

"Leave me, Captain. I am tired."

He smiled, a cynical, cold smile. "So should you be. You have played at whoring tonight before me, offering your favors to the first man that asked. You appear to have forgotten," he said through clenched teeth, "that you are mine."

"What matters it to you?" she said and turned her back to him, unmindful that her gown was open, her creamy skin visible beneath the cloud of her hair. "What matter what I do, or to whom I offer myself? What care you? You have never . . ."

She stopped, aghast at what she had almost said.

He slowly traced a finger down the bare skin of her back. She trembled imperceptibly.

"Never taken you, have I? I was sorry for your grief. I let my judgment rule, and took you not. But tonight I have seen you as you are. Are ye afraid of me now?"

He reached around her slender waist and spun her so that she faced him. He finished what she had begun with a rough pull at the sides of her gown. Several of the pearl buttons dropped to the floor and rolled away unheeded.

"Do not do this," she said, standing very still. "I am unarmed and cannot defend myself from you."

"No," he agreed. "You cannot."

His warm hands reached her neck, bare now. He stroked her throat lingeringly.

"No defense for you now."

She looked up at him. Light flickered in his eyes, and there was fire in his touch. Surely she would bear forever the traces his fingers played on her skin.

"Curse you!" she hissed fiercely. "Ye are a fool!"

Her words were lost in his kiss, and his arms wrapped her to him as his lips bruised hers, demanding, hard. She was still a moment, lost in it, then she put her hand to his face, and when the kiss ended and he drew away she pulled him back. The dark velvet of her eyes was soft, yielding, and when he kissed her again she arched against him, pressing her body to his as she had the first time on the *Rose*. He could feel every curve.

Swiftly he bent and swept her into his arms, carrying her to the bed, laying her gently down.

"A great fool," she said softly as he whispered kisses on her throat. "So much wasted time."

His lips traveled down her body to her breast. The nipple, rosy and taut, invited his mouth and as he closed on it his hands moved lower still, pushing her gown aside and exploring gently between her thighs. She shuddered and clung to him.

"Aye, Desmond!" she whispered.

The gentle sound of rain against the stone of the castle walls pattered into Ardys's dream and wakened her shortly after daylight. It was only slightly lighter in the chamber, but even the steady rain and tiny windows could not keep the dawn out completely. She turned her head on the pillow and gazed through her lashes at Desmond, whose rhythmic, peaceful breathing was the only other sound in the room.

His right arm lay flung casually across her body. He lay to her right side, on his stomach, his face toward her. His dark hair was a tousled halo around his face, and his mustache, usually so trim, was askew. In his sleep he looked all innocence. Ardys wondered if all men resembled children when sleep smoothed their brows.

For a long time she lay unmoving, marveling at the beauty of his body, the perfect symmetry of shoulder, hip, and thigh. The smooth skin of his back fascinated her; she remembered the sensation of that warm skin beneath her exploring hands, the power of his muscles as he moved over her. Such strength, such fire: yet so gentle that she felt her heart must break from the tenderness of his touch.

Her cool fingers ran down his spine and he stirred, murmuring, but did not wake. So this was how it was between men and women! She reveled in the memory of the night. They had loved with a fierce hunger, as she would never have believed two people could love. And this morning came with its sense of wholeness, of kinship with every woman across the long ages. How strange that what had happened here, in this chamber, happened constantly—all over the world. Surely her happiness far exceeded that of all other women, for they did not lie with Desmond Kirkconnell, nor did they waken to this glorious glow of spent sensuality. She stretched, and felt tenderness between her legs.

His eyes opened and he took in her nakedness with an appreciating glance; raising up on one elbow he smiled at her, still blurred with sleep. He began to trace circles on her stomach with his index finger.

"You wake early," he said, leaning over to nibble on her ear.

"The rain woke me from a most wondrous dream."

"Did it so? Strange sleep, to awaken so refreshed—and yet so fatigued."

They kissed tenderly, and he yawned. Entwined in an embrace, they lay quietly, each feeling the heartbeats of the other.

"You are mine, my lady Trevallon," he said, "let us capture this moment, keep it forever: your hair like soft mist on the pillow, your silken skin next to mine."

"Yes, my love," she said quietly.

Hunger of another sort finally roused them. The time for breaking the fast was gone hours before, but they left the warm bed reluctantly, hating to end the spell of languorous contentment, the enchantment of the past night.

The chamber was a shambles, bits of clothing everywhere; his hose on the foot of the bed, his boots at the door between the two rooms, her gown a sorry velvet heap under the table. They dressed shyly, she pulling a fresh gown from her trunk, he donning his black doublet again. She smoothed the sheets and the fur cover on the bed. Neither of them spoke.

Her dress was a bright red satin, chosen for its flamboyance. She had changed since last evening, and wanted the whole world to know. The dress was fastened at the back with lacings of silk, and she let him tie them for her. Standing before him, the top of her head just reached the middle of his chest.

She grinned up at him, and said gravely: "I will not be able to ride a horse comfortably today. I hope we shall not soon begin the journey to Dungannon."

"Nay, worry not, I have business to finish with the Tyrone before we go. But I warn you, my wanton, that you shall not find riding any easier tomorrow."

"You are lewd, Captain."

"Aye," he agreed with a smile. He took her arm and led her to the door.

CHAPTER EIGHT

Days later Ardys rode in front of Kirkconnell on a sturdy, rust-colored horse, her skirts tucked about her knees so that she could sit astride. There was no saddle on the horse they shared, lent them by the Tyrone. As they rode she leaned comfortably back against her lover, and his arm encircled her waist.

The journey to Lough Neagh had been slow, for the track through the Irish wilderness was narrow and muddy, and the long train of the O'Neill's soldiers had made it considerably worse. Occasionally through the trees she could see the huge lake, shining a deep blue, surrounded by dense black-green forest. Grimsthorpe, the cabin boy Tom, and Bleddyn Kennwyn rode a few paces behind Kirkconnell and Ardys.

The talk between Ardys and Desmond was contented, familiar, and they laughed when the horse stumbled a bit, tossing them together to the bracken-covered ground in a tangled heap. The Tyrone reined in to see them safely mounted once more.

"Why, Cap'n 'Connell, me lad, I've never seen ye look so content!" The Tyrone laughed down at them.

"Aye, Hugh, content—but bruised," 'Connell laughed back, helping Ardys settle once more before him on the horse.

Once when they passed a fork in the track Ardys felt Desmond's body tense, and his grip around her tightened. There was no sign on the fork; she wondered where it led. She turned to ask, but he only smiled and lightly kissed her cheek.

The trek to Dungannon had lasted a few days, and he had seemed happy to ride slowly along in the column of the Tyrone's followers with his arms around Ardys. Wisps of

Ardys's dark hair, red in the sunlight, drifted into his face, the silken curls brushing softly against his mouth.

He pulled her closer, and the rocking gait of the horse lulled them.

Hugh cantered up beside them, an imposing figure on his huge warhorse. The track was narrow, so that he could not ride too long by them. He maneuvered his horse behind Kirkconnell's.

"We'll make Dungannon soon," Hugh said, patting his mount to still its restive movements.

"Then we'll not pitch another camp?" asked Desmond.

"No need. We're close, I can feel it in me—well, I'll not say it before the lady, but I can always tell when my wife is nearby."

The look O'Neill gave Desmond over Ardys's head was pointed, and Kirkconnell winced as though he had been struck. Ardys frowned when she saw it.

"Then you are married, Lord Tyrone?" she asked, surprised.

"Aye! Did they not know of it at the English court?" Hugh threw back his head and laughed. "No matter, they soon shall know of everything the Tyrone does."

O'Neill set spurs to his horse and sped back to the front of the line of soldiers, still laughing.

"Why does he laugh so?" Ardys asked Desmond.

"O'Neill has many secret jests at the expense of the English."

"Of my countrymen, ye forget."

"I do not forget, but you would do well to, here in the Tyrone's country. If you value your life."

"I do not understand. The Tyrone has always maintained good diplomatic relations with Queen Elizabeth."

"And will continue to do so, as long as it suits him. He

married—" Desmond chose his words carefully, "—an English woman, the daughter of one of the high-ranking military men stationed here by your Queen."

"You speak as though he carried her off!"

"He very nearly did, but I have heard it said that she would take no other after she had seen Hugh O'Neill."

"He is a most impressive man," Ardys said, watching Hugh ride at the front of his soldiers.

"Aye, Mabel Bagenal thought as you do, my girl. She has been his wife for many years. Now be silent before you arouse my jealousy with talk of another man."

He was joking, but she could sense some tension behind his words. Silent, she leaned back against him, enjoying the earthy, damp smell of the Irish forest.

It was late afternoon when they at last reached Dungannon. The sun set in a tinge of pink and purple, just visible through the thick trees.

They rode abruptly out of the woods onto a wider track, and Ardys caught her breath. Before them lay lawns and gardens stretching for hundreds of yards in all directions, and at the center of them a grey stone manor house, two stories high with many chimneys, reposed majestically in the evening light. From beyond the house she could hear the shouts of many men, and the roll and crack of musket fire, but no one around her was alarmed.

The long column of men and wagons continued to pour out of the woods behind them, losing some of its military precision as the soldiers came within sight of their destination.

O'Neill's pride in his home was plain on his face as he rode back to Kirkconnell.

"Dungannon, Desmond—what a joy to see it again!"

Desmond laughed. "Ye have not been away that long, Hugh, surely, but aye, it is always a joy to see it."

"It is hard to believe," Ardys said softly, "that a home of such beauty would be here, in the middle of this forest."

"The Irish woods hold many secrets, my lady," Hugh said with a smile.

A great shout went up from the men as the musket fire came closer. Ardys recoiled, alarmed, when scores of fur-clad soldiers came running toward them from all sides: from behind the house, from the woods, and from the direction of the lake, shimmering nearby.

The company was quickly surrounded by Irish warriors.

Desmond steadied his horse and spoke quietly into Ardys's ear.

"Do not fear. These are more of the Tyrone's men, come to welcome him home."

"There are so many of them!"

"And there are thousands more, camped by the lake and in the fields beyond the house."

"It is like an army."

"Aye. That is exactly what it is."

The soldiers fanned out around Hugh and the other horsemen, allowing them to go through toward the house. There were two wings to the main building, facing north and south. Half of it was an old castle, probably Norman-built, which had been the seat of the O'Neill clan for centuries. The other, newer half, artfully blended to match the grey stone of the original building, was a distinctly Tudor design, with high turrets, chimneys, and a great gatehouse of rich red brick.

Shaped like a rectangle, the two long wings were connected by two shorter ones, with elaborate courtyards in between. Ardys thought she heard the splash of a fountain.

They rode through the gate, and she saw the great clock high in the center of the brick, but it was too dark to see the face. It reminded her sharply of Hampton Court, and she shifted uneasily. To see such design here in the north of Ireland was almost insulting, a mockery to the English court from whence she came.

For an instant Ardys wondered where her true loyalty lay, but in that same instant she knew, beyond all doubt, that her allegiance could only be to the man she loved.

The gallowglass and kern melted then into the night, and only a small company advanced to the manor proper. She could smell nearby campfires, but after their boisterous greeting to their leader the men seemed to have fallen silent. An owl hooted in the distance, and she shuddered.

"Cold?" Desmond asked. "We'll soon be inside, where Mabel doubtless has a feast waiting."

"Nay," she said softly. She shifted. "I am here because you are here, and you are more to me than all the world. If that makes me a traitor I am sorry for it, but I cannot change the person I am. I love you."

He ran his fingers across her mouth. "And I you. Ye are my own heart."

A drop of rain on her hand startled her, and she saw that the night sky was streaked with lightning. A brilliant flash lit up the castle, and details of the structure leapt out in sharp outline for a brief second before the boom of the thunder came.

Desmond swung lightly off the horse and reached up to help her down as the rain began in earnest. A gold- and green-liveried footman ran to take the reins of the animal and lead it to the stables, just visible beyond the north lawn.

Through the main door they followed Hugh and his retainers, into the narrow corridor hung with richly colored tapestries, and then into the great hall, where Hugh stopped short and bellowed, "Mabel!"

He shook the rain from his fur cloak. A tall, slender blonde woman appeared and flung herself into Hugh's outstretched arms. She looked to be nearly crushed by the big man's embrace.

"Ye have come back to me, then, my wayward husband!" she cried, her voice full of affection. "And you have grown smaller since you were away! By my troth, I'll soon have more meat on those fragile bones of yours! And here's Desmond as well—welcome back to Dungannon, Captain 'Connell."

Desmond bowed. "Lady Tyrone."

Ardys stood to the side, embarrassed. But Mabel saw her and drew her over with a smile. "Desmond! You have brought your wife with you," she said.

Ardys turned to Desmond, her eyes wide. "His wife!" She smiled. "I am not . . ."

"Hold your tongue, woman!" said Hugh sharply. "This is a guest of Kirkconnell's, a visitor from the English court. The lady Ardys Trevallon."

There was a slight pause, and then Mabel said with delight, "From the court, is she? 'Tis so long since I've had any news of the place! I have not seen my father or my brothers these pretty many months. But come! There is food to be eaten, and wine to be drunk; ye must tell them in England how civilized Mabel Bagenal has made the Earl of Tyrone."

Hugh bellowed to a servant to build up the fire in the great hall.

The table to which O'Neill led them was on a raised dais at the north end of the hall. The room was vast, and could doubtless accommodate hundreds of diners at the many long tables that lined its paneled walls. In the center of the room was an open hearth, like the one at Carrickfergus, and which emitted the same intense heat. The ceiling was high, wood-beamed and carved with beautiful gilt figures of the Catholic saints. There was a small hole where the smoke from the fire could escape, with a wooden shutter over it to stop the rain. A large Arras tapestry, new-looking and brightly colored, not yet dulled by the smoke, stretched for twenty feet along the wall behind the head table.

"Ye've added some things since I last was here," Desmond remarked, looking around and helping Ardys take her place on the long bench behind the table.

"Aye," said Hugh. "A palace fit for my English lady. It pleases me to please her; and withal, it does so impress foreign ambassadors who come here expecting to find mere Irish savages."

There was an edge to his voice, and Ardys glanced up at him uneasily.

"Let no one say that Hugh O'Neill of Tyrone is not a civilized man," he continued. "In truth, this new hall suits me better than the one in the old castle; here the floors are of wood, not earth—much warmer!"

O'Neill burst into laughter once more. Ardys hoped that Mabel was as strong as she appeared to be, to be able to deal with her fearsome husband. Ardys was not really afraid of Hugh, but even so she missed the comforting feel of her rapier at her hip. She had packed it carefully into her trunk when they left Carrickfergus, knowing it would be uncomfortable to ride a horse armed and in a gown. Besides, Desmond was with her.

The high table now occupied, others began to gather in the hall for the meal. A group of nine courtiers, gaily clad in vivid blues, reds, and yellows, came chattering in, followed close by two dour-looking elderly gentlemen in long, black robes. Ardys knew them for Catholic priests. Behind them came a small knot of foreign dignitaries, obvious from their garments.

These last men approached the head table, and Hugh

waved them to sit on the other side of his wife. Ardys sat between Hugh and Kirkconnell, and she could hear the men
talking with O'Neill. It was a moment before she realized they
were speaking in Spanish, and that Hugh seemed quite comfortable with that language. She strained to listen to the conversation, but stopped herself. Why should she care what was
said here?

When all the others were seated, a slight gentleman came
in alone through one of the side doors. He was poorly dressed
in a faded brown doublet and hose that were yellowed and
frayed; and he spoke to no one, though it was obvious that
many of the company knew him. He glanced around the assembly almost furtively, and he stooped when he walked to
the far end of the table furthest from the dais.

He must have felt Ardys looking at him, for he looked up
quickly.

Ardys turned to Desmond and whispered, "Who is yonder
man? He has such a hunted look about him."

Desmond was taking a portion of meat from the tray
before them.

"Him? That is the eldest son of Sir Henry Carberry.
Thomas is his name. He is a permanent guest of Hugh's."

"He does not bear himself like a guest."

"His father is an English landowner, down near Kildare.
One of the O'Neill's soldiers found Thomas wandering alone
in that county. Dangerous for a young man to be out alone
anywhere in Ireland—if he's English. He was in obvious need
of protection, so he was taken and brought to O'Neill."

She frowned at Kirkconnell, not liking what he was saying.
"You mean he is a prisoner here?"

"Do not ask too many questions, my girl," Desmond said.
"He is treated well, he has the freedom of Dungannon, and
Hugh lets him write to his father in Kildare. Leave well alone."

"But why . . ." Ardys began stubbornly, unwilling to let it drop.

Desmond put a haunch of venison on his trencher, ripping off a piece. "The son of one of the Tyrone's kinsman is a hostage in Dublin, kept by the English in their garrison there. Neither side seems willing to make an exchange."

"The son?"

"A child, little more than five years old."

"By God—but that is monstrous!"

"Tell the English that," Desmond shrugged. "Ardys, do ye not know that wars are fought on many fronts, with many different weapons? Be silent and remember where you are. Eat. Mabel is proud of her feasts and she will be offended if you do not."

Ardys took a small bite from a leg of mutton and began to eat, but she kept glancing at Carberry, who sat alone.

The English took prisoners and the Irish followed suit, or the Irish took one first and the English retaliated; it had gone on for years, since the English had founded the first Munster colony in the earlier part of the century. It was an accepted part of life here.

After the well-prepared meal, there was entertainment. An old storyteller, his hands and face as wrinkled as his cloak, shuffled in and sat by the dying fire. Accompanied by a youthful harpist, the man told tales of the Irish past, of battles, saints, and valorous deeds. He spoke in the old Gaelic, which she did not understand. Desmond translated quietly during pauses in his narrative.

The hall was silent, but for the lilting speech of the old man, and Ardys listened, enthralled by the voice.

When he finished, and the harpist played a last sad air, the diners rose and were led to their quarters by pages bearing candles. The rooms Ardys would share with Desmond were overlooking the courtyard, on the top floor of the south side of the house. As they climbed the narrow stairs behind the boy, Ardys saw the many flickering campfires of the soldiers through the windows, in the distance.

After the boy had lit the twelve candles in the sconce in the larger of the two rooms, he bowed and left them alone. Desmond took off his sword belt, and laid it across the massive desk that stood in one corner. She sat on the bed and removed her shoes.

As he unbuttoned his doublet, he said: "Ye are very thoughtful."

She smiled at him, but the smile did not reach her eyes. "There are many things I do not understand."

"Why must ye understand everything? Either a thing is, or it is not. Too much thinking will disturb your sleep."

She looked at him, and suddenly she remembered that they were alone for the first time since they had left Carrickfergus days before.

She flushed and got up, embarrassed by the warmth that coursed through her. Desmond saw the movement and went to hold her, sliding his hands along her back, beginning to unlace her gown, enjoying the sound of her quickened breathing.

"My love," he said as he stroked the shoulder he had bared, freeing her of the gown. "Nothing is important, nothing matters when we are together. Nothing but this."

He tilted her chin up and kissed her.

The golden months of autumn passed into winter; still Ardys and Desmond lingered at Dungannon. For them, time was suspended into a long, sweet interlude of loving. Ireland held them in its warm hand. Ardys reveled in the time with Desmond. Here she had no responsibilities, no duties, no memories but of the touch of his hands and the warmth of his kiss.

Since September, when they had first come to the Tyrone's stronghold, they had spent most of their time dueling and making love. They were superbly matched at both pastimes.

The celebrations of Christmas lasted well over a week at Hugh O'Neill's court at Dungannon. Many banquets, dances, and masques were given in the great hall while outside the cold, wet Irish winter spent its fury on the countryside. The house was fully occupied: the hundred rooms taken by the guests the Earl of Tyrone had invited for the festivities.

This evening the long wooden tables in the dining hall had been pushed against the walls to free the floor space; the fire in the huge hearth had been doused and cleared away, and the torches along the walls had all been lit early, so that the room was a blaze of light. This was to be the final entertainment of the celebrations, and Hugh had seen to the details himself.

Ardys smoothed the black velvet of her doublet and gave her high-piled hair a pat to see it was still in place. Desmond stood beside her, tall and handsome in a black velvet doublet that matched hers from the starched ruff to the white lace at the wrists.

Bleddyn Kennwyn was with them, talking with his captain. They stood in a small alcove beside the great hall.

"Then all is well with the *Espada*, Bled?" Desmond asked.

"Aye, Cap'n 'Connell, she be all scraped and painted and ready to sail again. I left Grimsthorpe and George and Tom to watch over her while I came down to fetch you."

"To fetch me?" Desmond laughed and clapped his first mate on the shoulder. "Does my crew then order me to return to my own ship?"

Ardys glanced up at Desmond and smiled. "Captain, your crew will not understand why you have stayed away this long."

"You are wrong, woman, my crew all saw you. They will know I do not hurry back to their company when I have the pleasure of yours."

"Desmond, you will embarrass me."

"My dear, I have found that to be challenging indeed. But Bled, perhaps ye are right, it is time to go back. This soft life," he gave Ardys a rough squeeze, "is too inviting."

"There be other news, Cap'n," said Bled, reaching for his captain's arm to get his attention back. "One o' the men sighted the *Corbeau* in the North Sea, making again for Carrickfergus."

"De la Roche? I thought he had gone to the Caribbean for the winter; he said he was planning to when last I saw him. And that was at Carrickfergus."

Ardys saw a signal from the Tyrone and hastily drew Desmond away from his first mate.

"Come, Desmond, 'tis nearly time to begin. Bleddyn, if you stand at the front of the hall you will have the best view."

Ardys laid her hand on Kirkconnell's arm as the mate bowed and walked away into the great hall to take his place among the crowd of spectators.

"Forget not our private wager," Desmond said with a grin. "If I slit your doublet first, ye will serve me as the meanest page would for an entire fortnight."

"And if I cut yours first, 'Connell, you forfeit to me the jeweled dagger you showed me last eve, the gold one encrusted with rubies and diamonds!"

"It's a pretty piece, faith, and it would look well in your hand. But ye will have to best me for it, and you know I never give quarter."

"No more do I, my bragging friend."

Hugh O'Neill bellowed for silence. The Tyrone stepped into the center of the room by the hearth and held up his arms to command attention. The gesture was not needed; Hugh was dressed in a flame-red satin and cloth-of-gold doublet, with a long ermine cloak flung over it, and with his red hair and his wild beard no one would fail to notice him. Hugh naturally dominated any gathering, and when he chose to raise his voice as well, the effect was overwhelming.

"My friends!" Hugh shouted, "Ye are all welcome here, to my home, for our modest celebrations of the Christmas holidays. Know ye then that on this, the last day, there are two among us that have generously consented to perform feats of swordplay the like of which have never been seen in Ireland before."

They had rehearsed their entrances with Hugh the day previous, and at this point in the speech Ardys and Desmond stepped out into the center of the room to stand by the Tyrone.

"This is fighting of a subtler sort than we here at Dungannon are used to seeing," Hugh continued. "I bid each of you to remember well what you see here this day, and to make use of it in our war. Know ye then, that this lady is called Ardys Trevallon, and she is the daughter of the fencing master to the court of our beloved sister, Elizabeth of England; and that this gentleman is Desmond Kirkconnell, captain of the *Espada*, a pirate known to you all."

"His sister? When he is gathering an army against her?" Ardys whispered to Desmond.

"For the benefit of the Spanish emissaries, no doubt, who must be kept in the dark as to the Tyrone's true motives even while he takes their gold," said Desmond, also in a whisper.

Hugh stepped away and Ardys and Desmond went into

the stance, the tips of their blades touching between them, high in the air. The rapiers gleamed in the light from the torches as the two combatants stood still a moment, waiting for the crowd to come to silence once more.

Kirkconnell winked at her, and she smiled at him, as she began slowly to circle, her blade ever at the ready.

"I thought it amusing when 'Connell asked for the use of the halls of Dungannon for fencing practice," Hugh said in a booming aside to the Spaniard seated next to him. "But I ceased laughing when I saw these two dueling. Remarkable skill, eh? This exhibition was my idea, the cap to our long days of revels. In the dead of winter there are not many activities out-of-doors, no jousting or archery. Swordplay will amuse my guests better than any more commonplace things."

Ardys whipped her blade to the left and thrust at Desmond's left side in a sudden movement. He parried neatly and the blades clanged together, a whir in the lamplight. He allowed her to press him back to the hearth before he began his attack in earnest, and then they fairly sprinted across the wood floor, first one taking the initiative, then the other.

As the blades whistled and clashed, Mabel pulled at her husband's sleeve. "It would not be well if one of them is injured, Hugh."

Hugh chuckled low. "Worry not, wife. This is a contest neither of them cares to win. What skill! 'Tis a wonder to watch that lass."

Out on the floor, Ardys never took her eyes from Desmond's face. "I know what ye are thinking, Desmond. I know what your next move will be."

"Ye do not know all my moves yet, wench!"

Their fencing fell into intricate patterns discernible only to themselves: parry, riposte, pause; engage, disengage, lunge. Like the steps of a delicate but deadly dance, at once graceful and dangerous.

She feinted to the right and drove in from the left; her wrist entwining with his and they pressed hard, each trying to push the other off balance. His face was inches from hers and she found it increasingly hard to concentrate. Unwilling, her gaze went to his lips and he took advantage and twisted up, freeing her hold. They circled again, and Desmond grinned wickedly at her.

"You are a woman, Ardys," he said, too low for the assembly to hear, "and you are subject to a woman's folly."

She glared at him, refusing to let him bait her into a display of temper, for when she became angry she lost some of her timing, and he knew it.

"Look to your own folly, my lord," she smiled, and bore into him so quickly that he did not see the thrust, ripping the sleeve of his doublet at the elbow. "Ha! First cut to me!"

"A hit!" Hugh called, and they stopped, panting. "The first hit to Ardys! I therefore proclaim her the winner of the match."

"The dagger is mine, Desmond!" Ardys said in triumph.

"I'll make ye pay for this insult later, when we are alone," Desmond said quietly, with a hint of laughter in his voice.

They bowed to the gathering, acknowledging the applause, and they went to stand by O'Neill at the front of the crowd. They were both sweating a little from the exertion. Someone brought them each a mug of ale, and they shared it gratefully.

Ardys drank deeply, her head thrown back and when she turned to hand the mug to Desmond she found herself locked in the dark, compelling gaze of François de la Roche.

Kirkconnell stepped in front of de la Roche, blocking him from Ardys's view.

"Captain de la Roche," Desmond said, his eyes narrowing. "My men informed me that the *Corbeau* was headed into Carrickfergus Bay."

De la Roche smiled at Desmond coldly. "*Oui,* I have anchored there once more. The Tyrone invited me to Dungannon for the festivities; had I known that there would be such exhibitions, I would have come sooner."

The two men were almost the same height, and Ardys, watching, could not help but compare them. Desmond, more slender, lighter of hair and complexion, with his trim mustache, was almost an opposite of the Frenchman, who was dark and clean-shaven. Anger was apparent in the way Desmond held his body, every muscle taut. He would like to run his sword through this man, Ardys thought, and wondered if there was not more to Desmond's hatred than the fact that once she had let de la Roche kiss her.

François did not seem at all threatened by Kirkconnell; indeed, he seemed hardly to notice him. There was an aura of self-assurance to de la Roche; she could not imagine him ever losing his temper. A light sardonic smile played over his full mouth as he spoke to Desmond.

"I did not know you were so much of a swordsman, Captain Kirkconnell."

"This woman," Desmond put his arm around Ardys possessively, "has taught me much of the fencing technique of the English court."

De la Roche raised a well-curved eyebrow. "Ah, indeed?"

Ardys felt Desmond's fingers dig into her shoulder.

"One day, de la Roche, you and I must fence. I have heard you are skilled with a sword."

The Frenchman looked away from Ardys as though bored by what Desmond had said. "Mayhap we shall meet someday, Kirkconnell."

"Why are you here, *monsieur?*" Ardys asked. "Have you business with the Tyrone?"

"A little, perhaps. I supply O'Neill with information—things I know he will be interested to know that I hear are happening in the Channel, or at the English court."

His low voice was like a caress; she was aware of the effect de la Roche had upon her, and knew that Desmond could see it as well.

Hugh and Mabel wandered amiably over and Desmond and François each took a step back to make room for them. The tension between the two pirates lessened a bit.

"So, de la Roche!" Hugh cried. "Here ye are; we have been looking for you, have we not, my wife? You must sit with us at the banquet, and tell us your news: we have heard that you have been in contact with the Spanish merchants in the Caribbean; what is the state of the trade there? 'Connell, surely you and your lady will excuse us."

"Surely," said Desmond tightly, bowing.

De la Roche made an elegant leg to Ardys. "*Mademoiselle Trevallon.*"

Ardys nodded to him and said nothing.

The banquet seemed interminable. Ardys could not eat at all, for the stony set of Desmond's jaw made her nervous, and de la Roche, seated two people away on the other side of the O'Neills, was making his presence the more felt by his very silence. If only the man would talk to Mabel, or to anyone, then he would not seem to be staring so hard at Ardys. Every time she looked up, she met his gaze.

After the meat course, there was a pause before pastries were served. Ardys hesitantly put her hand over Desmond's and he frowned down at her.

"I am much fatigued, Captain. Shall we not retire?"

Desmond seemed hardly to hear her, and she asked again.

"Very well. If you are tired, let us go," he said, rising. "Lady Tyrone, please forgive us."

"Go with our blessings, Captain. Your lady should not be taxed overmuch in this happy time," Mabel smiled from her place beside her husband.

CHAPTER NINE

The chamber they had shared the past months was cold; someone had neglected to light the fire. Ardys put her rapier in its scabbard and returned it to its place in the lid of her chest while Desmond saw to the fireplace. He was easier since they left the banquet, but still seemed tense, and she could not decide if she should tell him her news or not.

The blaze caught, and Desmond stood and unbuckled his belt, taking off his sword. He sat on the bed beside Ardys and took her hand roughly, his unquiet eyes on her face.

"Stay away from de la Roche, Ardys."

She was puzzled. "Have ye any reason to believe I would not?"

"I do not like the way he looks at you."

She said stiffly: "Many men look at me, sir. I cannot help that."

"And I do not like the way you look at him."

She took a step away from him, bewildered by his jealousy.

"Ah, Desmond!" she said, taking his hand again. "Do you not know by now that I can feel nothing, nothing, for any other man? How can you doubt that, when we have shared such joy these past weeks? Aye, I let de la Roche kiss me, once, months ago, before you and I knew each other and even that was for you, to stir your jealousy. Desmond, do not look so angry! I have something to tell you, the most wondrous thing, and I cannot if you frown so."

His hand went to her hair, began to loosen the tight pins to let it come down to her shoulders. "What would you tell me, my Ardys?" His tone was softer, and he stroked her hair gently. She leaned her head on his chest and sighed with contentment.

"I bear our child, Desmond."

His hand was suddenly quite still. "A child?"

"Our child, here, within me." She patted herself. "Could you not guess? I have been giddy so often lately, and I keep losing my meals. Had ye not noticed?"

"God's death," he murmured, moving away. "Are you certain?"

She took a step back, bewildered. "Desmond! Please, do not look so! Of course I am certain, I would not tell you if I were not. One of Mabel's women, a midwife, examined me. D'ye not share my joy?"

"Joy?" He laughed harshly. "This is most—unfortunate."

He turned away and left the room.

Ardys waited in vain for hours for Kirkconnell to return to their chambers. As the night grew old she finally slept, curled up on top of the velvet coverlet, hugging herself.

There was no clock to consult the time when she awoke, but it was light, and cold, for the fire Desmond had lit had gone out. As she blinked and stretched she felt the familiar morning nausea and then remembered last night's pain, the news that she thought would please him; the anger instead that she could not understand.

"He will come to me sometime during the day; I will be patient, I will wait," she said to herself. "When he comes to apologize I will accept gracefully. Nay, he cannot help but be glad. He was surprised, that is all, and unprepared. He will know he cannot help but make me his wife now. He must!"

The small room seemed overlarge without him. The day loomed long before her too, but she must stay here in their chamber. She must be here when he returned.

The lid of her chest was open still as she had left it after returning her swept-hilt rapier to its place, and a sparkle of light suddenly took her attention. Not sunlight, surely, even on the brightest of days this dark room had precious little of that. Curious, she knelt by the chest.

Her rapier was there, secure in its leather scabbard, but the dagger, she saw, had been laid on the top of the contents of the chest. The brilliant jeweled dagger that she and Desmond had wagered on last night was gleaming there. It was hooked to the chest lid in place of her other dagger.

Touching it, drawing it out, she felt its cold beauty, the sharpness of its stones. She shivered involuntarily as she withdrew the weapon from its gilded scabbard. Tucked in the scabbard by the shaft of the blade was a parchment scrap that feathered gently to the floor by her knees. With trembling hand she picked it up, and stood to find better light. She read.

Ardys:
This dagger is yours. You have Wone it fairly from me, and I do give it you Gladly. I have much Wrong'd you, more than you can Knowe. Now I must leave you; but I praye that this Jewel'd dagger shall remind you of Me.
Kirkconnell

He must have come in while she slept and slid the weapon into her trunk. He had come to her for what could be the last time, and she had been asleep!

She cried out, ripping the note to pieces, scattering them all about her. The chest lid slammed shut. Leave her—he could not leave her! Here, in this foreign place, with a child, his child!—within her womb.

A sudden cramp went through her, doubling her over. Instinctively she became utterly still, her hands on her belly, willing the pain to cease. She must not lose the child! If she had his child he would come to her, he would love her again. What had she done, that he would turn away from her?

Her heartbeat slowed, and the tearing pain dulled to an ache. There, the child was safe. She must think, not panic: panic might kill the babe. The early time was terribly dangerous; she knew that from hearing of other women's miscarriages.

Legs unsteady, she stood, a hand on the chest for support, every move careful and slow. Kirkconnell would not have left Dungannon without words with Hugh O'Neill. Likely he was with Hugh now. Surely for the captain of a great ship there would be etiquette to leave-taking, especially from a court. Elizabeth's courtiers did not remove themselves from her presence without her express permission; surely the Tyrone would emulate her in this, it would be a part of his power.

Dress, and find the Tyrone. Kirkconnell would be with him, he must. And when Desmond saw her, he would know he could not go! Forcing herself to remain calm, to move with care, she changed to a dark wine-colored gown of heavy watered silk, tight fitting over her breasts, flaring out in a small farthingale at her hips, wide sleeved, startling white lace at her wrists and neck. Her hair worn long and loose, as she knew he liked it. And the jeweled dagger at her waist, hung by a silken cord. A deep breath, and then she went out into the narrow hallway.

She straightened her shoulders. Trevallon's daughter was not cast aside so easily. Did he think to have his way with her, to make her love him, and then to disappear? Not while she lived. Trevallon's daughter would be the mother of no bastards!

Anger came to her rescue, and each step she took made her the more resolute. Even if he did not love her, for his honor's sake he must give the child his name.

"Lady Tyrone! Happily met," Ardys said when she saw Mabel. "I was coming to the hall to seek Captain Kirkconnell; he must be with your husband. Walk with me."

Mabel paused, outlined before the alcove window in the end of the long hallway.

"My lord is hunting today, Mistress Trevallon." Mabel went to Ardys and stood beside her. Ardys was much shorter than Hugh's wife.

"Kirkconnell left before dawn, alone. He went back to Tullaghoge."

"Tullaghoge? Why Tullaghoge? His ship is at Carrick-fergus . . ."

She remembered her unease when they rode by that fork in the track on the road from Carrickfergus to Dungannon, the stiffening of Desmond's body behind hers. That must have been the road to Tullaghoge. Strange how sharp the memory was, as though it happened yesterday, not months ago.

"I am sorry," said Mabel.

Ardys smiled, though her eyes narrowed. "Well, if he has gone to Tullaghoge, then I must fetch him back. I am for the stables, Lady Tyrone, please excuse my haste."

Mabel's protest went unheard as the girl sped round the corner to the long staircase, out of sight.

Bleddyn Kennwyn waited at the stable. Having said his farewell to the captain, the mate did not feel his duty was yet discharged.

Desmond had ridden off, pale and stiff, and Kennwyn sat on the wet grass, watching for Ardys.

She came quickly across the lawn, seeming to his dazzled eyes to skim over the ground, her dark red dress shining in the pale sunlight.

He stepped up to meet her, and she stopped short, breathless.

"Bled! We must go to Tullaghoge. Help me to saddle a horse."

Bled stood firmly before her, blocking her way. "Nay, mistress, ye cannot go. Ye must not follow him."

"You do not understand, Kennwyn. Curse you, get out of the way!"

Bled reached out and caught her wrist, his grip surprisingly strong for so small a man. "Ye cannot go," he repeated slowly, as to a child.

"But why Tullaghoge? It is not so far, I shall catch him up."

He heard her voice rising, reaching toward a thin note of panic.

"Mistress, I must tell ye—"

"What can you tell me, Bled, that I do not know already?"

"Tullaghoge is the home of the O'Donnells."

Kennwyn had faced the swords of Spanish dons, the axes of angry Scotsmen, and the cannons of the English naval ships. Any one of them he would gladly face now, rather than say what he must to this woman.

"I care nothing for the O'Donnells," she said, trying to free herself from his hold.

"He was raised by the O'Donnells."

"Aye, by a woman called Bessie. This I know. If he has gone to his kinsfolk, there is no reason I should not go with him."

"Ah, there is, my lady."

She stopped struggling. "Then tell me!"

Bled said: "He has returned to his wife."

A small animal skittered through the grass toward the

stable, a mouse perhaps, or a rat. Bled watched it go, unable to look at Ardys.

She was so silent he thought she had not heard. Then her fingernails dug into the sleeves of his wool jacket, clutching desperately. She turned her head to see what he watched so intently before she spoke, her voice a hoarse, incredulous whisper:

"You lie."

He looked at her, the truth in his eyes.

She caught her breath in a gasp, and her hands went once more to her belly. "But our child! There is life here; I swear I can already feel it within me."

She knelt on the damp grass and looked at him, unseeing, tears streaming down her cheeks.

Percy Longhoughton was singularly unattractive—one could not help but notice that horrid nose! But that made little difference to Alice Trevallon, the young-still widow of the Queen's Fencing Master. Percy was wealthy, he was fond of music—he loved to listen to her play the virginals, and he was very attentive.

Alice and Percy were in the hall of Helford House, enjoying a late supper in comparative privacy. Only two of Alice's daughters joined them for the meal; the rest were at prayers or retired for the night to their nursery. Alice sat at the place of honor, for Lord Helford was away.

Percy amused her. She tossed her bright hair becomingly. "I remind you, sir, that I am but recent widowed. You are behaving without chivalry. Pray remove your hand from my knee."

Her smile put the lie to her words. He had the grace to turn red and look away, but his hand never moved.

"What a luscious wench ye are, Alice!" he said ponderously. "Would that I had known ye when I was a younger man."

"Mayhap if ye had, both our lives would have been different," she said.

With a pointed sigh he withdrew his hand and leaned back in his chair, making much of attending to the meal. Fish and veal pastries, and good French wine.

"Alice," Percy said quietly as he lifted his knife to the loaf of warm bread, "May I tell ye a secret?"

"Is it about how you came to be found washed up on the beach below this house a month gone? I have often wondered how you came to be there."

He glanced about. Her girls were deep in childish conversation with one of their small dogs and would not hear.

She leaned toward him and frowned when he took her hand.

"Alice, I have grown fond of you these past weeks. You must never tell another the tale I tell you now."

She nodded, looking serious.

"My name is Percival Berwick, not Percival Longhoughton, but no one must ever hear the name Berwick spoken. It would mean my life," He looked away. "I am a fugitive from your Queen's justice."

Alice started and tried to pull her hand away but he held her fingers fast.

"Hear me, my lady! It was so long ago, during the Northern uprising in 'sixty-nine. I was duped by some conspirators into letting them use the cottage of one of my farmers for their rendezvous. It was exciting, I was young, I was foolish! Ye remember that rebellion?"

"I remember it well," Alice said primly. "The northern Catholics plotted to free Mary of Scotland, to marry her to the Duke of Norfolk and take our Queen's rightful throne."

"Then you know what happened when the plot failed."

"Queen Elizabeth hung hundreds of men in the north. Disloyal, Catholic traitors."

Percy nodded. "Aye, she did. It was her right. But I escaped. I fled first to Scotland, then to France. Now I have come here, to make a new life. Alice, I believe in the Catholic cause. Ye can have me killed for the secrets I am telling you now."

"Sir!" she cried, then looked about and lowered her voice. "Ye are mad to tell me this. You are a traitor!"

"I am not a traitor to my church, Alice, or to my God."

"It matters not. Your allegiance to the Catholic church will never save your head," she hissed.

"Aye, this I know. Since I have told ye this much, Alice, I must tell you all. I have come here, to Cornwall, because it is far from the north; no one will remember me here. I will be safe. I can begin anew, after all these years."

She pursed her lips. "Wherefore do you tell me this, Percy?"

He looked down at their hands, still entwined. "I have come to love you, Alice Trevallon. Do me the honor of accepting my hand in marriage. I will make you a wealthy woman, and provide well for all of your daughters. I pray ye, do not answer now. If you refuse me, I will leave this place and you will never hear from me again."

Alice's pretty blue eyes narrowed. "How wealthy?"

"I managed to save some of my family fortune when I fled the north. I still have jewels sewn in my clothing that are worth more than a thousand pounds."

She sucked in her breath and stared at him.

"Come, daughters!" she called to the girls. As they ran up to their mother with the dog, she stood and turned away from him. Wealth. A way to arrange for all of her girls to have handsome dowries . . .

Her hands on her daughters' shoulders, she smiled and looked back. "My Lord Longhoughton, I shall think upon your offer."

Ardys did not join the Dungannon household at the noon meal, nor did she grace the evening table. She was missed at the service in the chapel just after dusk as well; back in September the O'Neills had commanded that she attend with Kirkconnell, and she had complied ever since, though the Catholic mass made her uncomfortable.

But now Kirkconnell was gone, and she would not leave their chamber. She lay on the bed, on the pillow that she fancied still bore the imprint of his head beside hers. She stared at the night as it crept in the narrow window. Staring, but not seeing. No tears; no easy release from the horror of his betrayal, only her anger now to sustain her.

He had left her.

"It was all lies between us, the tenderness and joy, the giving. A diversion for him, a welcome change no doubt from his wife, but in the end nothing more," she said fiercely to herself. Her mind would not stop; it was as though she had stepped on a steep spiral staircase that only led down.

She had been a fool to believe he loved her. But his lovemaking: surely such passion must be true . . .

"Yet his leaving when I told him I was with child must prove 'twas not true, it was never true. If he had loved me, he would have told me he was already wed, he would have divorced his wife to marry me. Jesu help me, what have I done? He is a Catholic, God's teeth! There is no divorce for a Papist without the blessing of the Pope; it is a thing even Kings cannot do. The old King Henry sought a Papal annulment of his first marriage and was excommunicated for his pains. I will never marry him now!"

Henry had gone on and found another way—he had made himself head of the Church in England—but there were no alternative means for a man who was not a King. Of that, she had no doubt.

She dozed, her hands beneath her cheek, her legs curled as she lay on her side. Where should she go? Not to Tullaghoge, that never! But she was alone in a country where her enemies, the enemies of her Queen and her homeland, surrounded her. The Irish could flay the skin from her back if it pleased them; they were all savages, content only when they were making war.

"He is one of them," she reminded herself. "Aye, the more reason to hate him. With Kirkconnell gone I am only an Englishwoman, from the English court no less, loyal to Elizabeth, and a Lutheran as well. The priests at O'Neill's court tried once to convert me to Catholicism; they left praying for me even while they consigned my soul to a flaming pit."

She was nearer those flames now, she thought, than she had ever been. Best to keep to the chamber, to avoid contact with the Tyrone's household, until somehow she made her escape. Bleddyn Kennwyn seemed to feel sympathy for her; he would surely help her. He must!

She must go, and go quickly: that was certain. Pride as well as good sense convinced her of that. She touched the bedspread absently, smoothing the wrinkles under her. Here, she was Kirkconnell's whore. That was a measure of protection, but the cost to her pride was too great. And when he came back to Dungannon (the thought startled her, but surely he would, he was a loyal friend of the Tyrone) she must be gone. She would not humble herself by waiting to find out his pleasure. She would not have him think she had waited for him.

Her anger was exquisite: it gave her strength. His tender

136

words, the easy grace of their joining, and all the outward signs of love: deceits, merely a mask for carnal lust. And that lust had left her with child.

But she could not hate the child. She would not try to rid herself of it, though she knew there were ways. The child was all that was left of the beauty that had been their passion. The child was innocent; she could not help but love it. No, she would not seek its destruction.

May Kirkconnell rot in his Papist hell!

Ardys rose and began to gather her clothing together; separating her things from the jumble of the cupboard she had shared with the captain, throwing them onto the bed. The top of her chest fell back with a thud when she opened it, and there lay the jeweled dagger, safe in its leather scabbard. Attached to the cushioned lining of the lid was her rapier, its elegant swept hilt gleaming in the dim light. Her eyes narrowed. She would leave Dungannon by night, armed with this weapon she knew well how to use, travel south to Newry or Dundalk, and book passage on any convenient ship to England. Or steal aboard one in secret if she must.

Smugglers plied the waters of St. George's Channel still, though there was no sanctioned trade between England and Ireland. With any luck she could find a ship bound for Cornwall, any part of Cornwall, it made no matter. Or she could take her chance in Scotland. Anywhere, to be far from him, far from her shame, somewhere to bear her child in seclusion and safety.

The hilt of the rapier was cold to her touch. Better that she had killed him or he her: he had ruined her life as effectively as if he had truly pierced her heart with steel. She unhooked the rapier and drew it from its sheath. Each groove and nick familiar, known. Give Kirkconnell his due, she thought grudgingly: he was many hateful things, but he could truly fence. He had taught her new techniques, new ways of approaching an opponent. Among other things! Aye, and now if they fenced in earnest, not for show as they had done last night, she could well kill him. She longed for the opportunity. Were she not with child, she would pursue him, hunt him down and kill him. She smiled at the thought.

The sharp point drew blood from her finger. Run away like a coward, or instead follow him to Tullaghoge and there take her revenge upon him, him and his accursed wife. Run the rapier through him, feel his once beloved flesh part under it, watch his life ebb away, taken by her own hand. That would be sweet, would it not?

"Riposte," her father's ghost whispered. "Do not give ground, always recover, plan the next move, anticipate. Know the weakness of your opponent and use it."

"Ha, Desmond has a weakness, father," she said aloud. "I know too well!"

Yet even as she savored the thought of his death, she knew she could not do it: never could she kill him. The emptiness inside was bitter to bear, but how much more bitter it would be to know that he had ceased to live, her lover and the father of her child.

Ardys's blood ran cold: why not eliminate the wife, and have Desmond for herself once more? Go to Tullaghoge, and wait her chance. No one need ever know how Kirkconnell's wife died, for raids on villages by rival Irish chieftains and by marauding English were commonplace. Harden her heart, do the deed, and come back to Dungannon to await his eventual return. Then Ardys would decide whether to take him back or to order him away. The decision would be hers!

A smile for the rapier; it would be her salvation. She put it back in its place and searched for an appropriate disguise. She must not be recognized as a woman, and that meant she could not wear her own doublets. Search among his, then, for something she could alter somehow to fit.

She pulled open the cupboard and in her haste some of the contents spilled out onto the floor. A small object skidded under the table, and she bent to retrieve it: a painted miniature of a very young and fair blonde woman, rather stout, dressed in an embroidered gown of deep green that matched the color of her eyes.

Ardys stared at the face, so composed and placid in the portrait. If only she had not seen it, she thought uneasily. This was a child, really, not yet a woman, and pretty in an innocent, rounded way.

This was not a faceless enemy; this was a living, breathing person. Ardys was plotting to murder a woman who had done her no harm except in the fact that she existed. Tears of frustration and rage ran down Ardys's cheeks. She could not kill this woman, either. There was no help, no hope of salvation.

God's death! What was she to do? The back of the miniature was gold, and engraved on it in elegant calligraphic script were the words: Shelagh, 1584.

There was a noise, and the shiver of a shadow behind her. Ardys whirled.

There in the doorway stood François de la Roche, his black eyes glittering in the candlelight.

For some seconds he said nothing, merely watching her. She was sure he must hear her heart thudding in her breast. There was no mistaking that look, and she was suddenly afraid of him. How far to her rapier, across the room, in the lid of the chest? One leap, if she could make it, and it would be in her hand. She coiled to spring but he was quicker. His sword scraped almost noiselessly from its metal scabbard and the point was suddenly resting at her throat.

"I have seen you fence, my lady, though not, I think, in

earnest. I admire your skill, yet I have not come to waste my time in dueling."

The blade traced her neck and chin; she raised her head a bit and was forced to look into his eyes. She willed herself to remain still, locking her knees to prevent them buckling under her when a wave of dizziness struck.

"Kirkconnell is a fool to have left you," de la Roche continued, his deep voice rolling over her like a warm, salty wave on a silent beach. "I would never have done such a thing. You will find me more loyal, and I promise you, you will soon forget his clumsy embraces. I will worship you as a goddess, and you will find pleasure beyond your dreams at my touch."

He stepped forward, and again she felt the slight pressure of the blade against her skin.

"You are very sure of yourself, Captain de la Roche."

"And I am equally sure of you."

"Yet you keep your sword at my throat."

"When you have sworn to submit, I shall remove it. I would not injure you, but I will not have you fight me," he smiled, his full, sensual mouth drawing back to reveal his white teeth. "Do not fight me, Ardys. Once I kissed you and you shuddered, do you remember?" His delicate, pale hand gently grazed her right breast. "Even now, through this thick velvet, I feel your heart beating."

She could not think, and could not look away.

Slowly, lingeringly, his blade cut through her gown, from the low bodice to her waist, never scratching the silken skin beneath, and his hand slid confidently under the fabric.

She cried out and tried to push him away, but she could not. He was too strong. He shoved her back onto the bed. She twisted frantically, but he came down on top of her and his weight pinned her down. She fought and screamed and tried to scratch his eyes, but he caught her hands and laughed triumphantly.

"Now you will be mine, beautiful one," he murmured, shrugging his cape off and easing his shirt up while he unlaced his codpiece.

She panted, and kept repeating, "No!" while she tried to squirm away.

He laughed again and then he was inside her, hurting her, thrusting hard and fast, pounding into her. Then he cried out in ecstasy.

He rolled off her, satisfied, rose, and straightened his hose.

"Ah! Did I not say you would forget him?" he said.

She covered her face with her hands, not wanting to look at him. He had defiled her. Her face was warm with shame, and there was pain. The child! What of her child? She must protect the babe! She breathed deeply, to calm herself.

"Come! We go to my ship now. There is nothing you need to carry. I have everything you will need."

"Your ship? I have no wish to go to your ship—I must stay in Ireland," she said quickly, looking up at him.

"Did I ask what you wished? What would you do, stay here in Dungannon alone?" He pulled his cape back on, unconcerned.

"If I must! I will wait for Kirkconnell to return so that I may have my revenge on him. I must see him again!"

"You speak of revenge? What better revenge than to sail with me far away from here? To join with his enemy? To give and take pleasure with another man—even as he does with another woman?"

"Pleasure? That was pleasure? No! And no again! I shall remain here!"

She leapt from the bed and pulled her torn gown quickly

over her head. She turned toward the chest where her weapons lay. She never saw the blow coming.

De la Roche's fist slammed into her jaw and she crumpled to the floor.

CHAPTER TEN

Desmond tossed and turned. He could not sleep. Shelagh was quiet beside him. He moved a bit; she was so stout that he had not much room in their bed.

What was to be done? Ardys would never, of this Desmond was sure, be reconciled to sharing her lover with his wife.

Wives had been set aside before, God knew. Had not the English Queen's father, Henry, divorced Catherine of Aragon, his lawful queen, that he might marry her lady-in-waiting, Anne Boleyn? Henry Tudor had been excommunicated, damned eternally, and in the church's eyes the marriage with the Boleyn was sinful, bigamous, and the child of that union a bastard. Not that it mattered to the child, who grew up to become Elizabeth, Queen of England!

No, there was no answer for Desmond Kirkconnell in that. Even if he cast Shelagh out, he would still be her husband. No escape.

God's blood, he was a man and he must bear the consequences of his actions. He was allied with the O'Donnells and that must be the end to his thought of a life with the beautiful English lass. He had brought this torment on himself; he had chosen to take Ardys, he had chosen to love her.

"How restless you are, my husband," Shelagh whispered anxiously. "Are ye ill?"

"Nay, 'tis nothing. Sleep now, I promise I shall be quieter."

Tomorrow, I must go back to Dungannon.

He lay awake, his blue eyes fixed on the crucifix that hung

on the far wall of the chamber. Shelagh snored softly. Her plump body repulsed him.

Ardys awoke feeling queasy, but as she often did now she paid it no mind and settled back into the thick down mattress, too warm to move. She was tired, and her legs ached as though she had run a great distance. Luxury to lie still, but she must get up and stretch as soon as Desmond woke . . .

Her eyes, so heavy with sleep a moment before, flew open. The creak of timber, the gentle swaying of the bed, the tang of salt in the air. A surge of awareness, and she remembered the events of last night: de la Roche raping her, and his order that she go to sea with him and forget Kirkconnell; her burning shame at her violation, her refusal to go with him. Then his fist, crashing into her chin with such bruising force, and her dizzy spin down into unconsciousness.

The bed in de la Roche's cabin was soft and deep, making her feel almost suffocated. There was no blood, and she prayed the child was well within her. Except for the bruises, she felt as she had before de la Roche forced her. Perhaps all was well with the child.

The room was richly appointed, larger and more comfortable than Kirkconnell's cabin aboard the *Espada*. Red velvet and cloth-of-gold drapes hung at the leaded windows behind the bed, and on the walls, covering the dark stained panels, were tapestries of fine Flemish design, bright-colored and thick. Between the tapestries hung miniature paintings, most of allegorical scenes of mythological beings and forest creatures. Not the simple elegance of Desmond's cabin; she thought it did not compare well.

François must have drugged her and hauled her the many miles from Dungannon to Carrickfergus, where his ship was moored. The name of the ship eluded her, and as she searched her memory her glance happened on de la Roche's midnight-black cape, slung casually over a chair bolted to the deck on the left side of the bed. The color, like everything about him, was dark, sensual, forbidding.

Corbeau, that was the name of his ship. "Raven" in English, and it suited the man well. She experienced again an old feeling of detached observation, as though she watched her life rather than lived it. The storm of her anger at Desmond was past, and in its place the emptiness, the hollow emptiness where her heart should have been. But the child, the child still lived!

And de la Roche. She was in his power. She shuddered.

There was a bruise on her chin where he had hit her, and it throbbed a bit when she sat up in the bed, rubbing it with a slender, bare arm.

Ah, Jesu, she thought: I am naked, and my clothes are nowhere to be seen.

The heavy door swung open abruptly, and François stepped into the cabin, shutting it quickly behind him to shut out the curious stares of his crew. De la Roche's cabin was on the main deck of the *Corbeau,* under the first poop royal.

He came over and stood by the bed, and instinctively she crouched down among the bedclothes, pulling the coverlet to her chin.

"Ah, *mon cherié,* you are awake. Have you slept well?" He reached out, cupping her bruised chin in his hand, and she winced and pulled away. "I have come to apologize for this."

"It is too late for apologies, *monsieur,*" Ardys said curtly.

"*Oui,* but you must understand that I could not allow you to waste yourself waiting for that *couchon* to return to you."

"That was my choice to make. You had no right to make it for me!"

"I have every right. I want you, and he does not."

"I demand that you take me back to Dungannon."

"Demand all you wish, my pet, if it pleases you."

She looked away, out of the window to the sea.

Somewhere out on the deck one of the crew was singing, and he was joined by a few of his comrades. A lilting song, pleasant to hear. She listened for a time, and when she spoke again her voice was steady.

"I told you last night that I do not wish to go with you. What happened between Captain Kirkconnell and me is no concern of yours. And know this: when he learns of your treachery, of your unchivalrous behavior, he will hunt you down and kill you. Unless I do it myself."

De la Roche sat on the bed and took her hand, kissing her upturned palm as he had when they first met. "I do not believe you are so foolish, Ardys, to let yourself believe that. Kirkconnell and I have always disliked each other, and no doubt he would love the excuse to kill me. But think: the ocean is vast; he could not hope to find one ship in its expanse, nor would he try. He is not a fool. He will think to himself instead that de la Roche has solved all his problems for him, for he knew that he could not keep you as his mistress when you learned he had a wife."

"Curse you for the son of a whore!"

"Gently, my girl, gently. Do not provoke my anger. Your rapier is far from your hand."

"Aye, as are my clothes and all my other belongings, I doubt not," she said through clenched teeth.

He leaned toward her, and she strained away.

"Would he not say," the velvet voice went on, "that he was well rid of a woman who did not know her place, who was too proud, too strong."

"It would have been different if I had known he was wed," she said hotly, turning her face to avoid de la Roche's touch.

"Perhaps, but it is done, and now you are with me."

"I will never love you, de la Roche," she hissed.

De la Roche reached for the coverlet, pulling it down roughly to expose her breasts.

"I grow tired of this talk, *cherié*. I do not ask for your love. I do not want it. All I need from you is this . . ."

Kirkconnell played me for a fool, she thought. Yet I carry our child, I have taken part of him with me. My rapier, and my daggers, aye, all my belongings may have been lost, left behind at the Tyrone's castle, but this child is ours, and no one will rob me of it. As long as I have the child, I will be content. I must endure for the sake of my child.

She closed her eyes and lay still as de la Roche raped her again.

Shelagh's gift to her husband, in late celebration of the new year, was a pair of leather gloves lined with brown silk, fancifully embroidered and reaching almost to the elbow, the cuffs stiff and wing-shaped. He was touched, and had no gift to give her; so he stayed a week longer with her at Tullaghoge, delaying his departure for Dungannon. Cursing himself all the while.

Desmond may not have taken the choicest prizes in his last travels at sea, but there was Shelagh's dowry to fall back on in time of need, and it was not altogether a small amount. Her branch of the O'Donnell family had become respectably rich as sheep herdsmen and traders, and they lived in a seven-room stone manor house at the edge of Tullaghoge village, at the top of a rise. Bessie's old house was near the manor, and it was here, in the bogs and fields by the town, that Shelagh and Desmond had played as children. They were betrothed at a very young age and neither thought to question it.

When they married, it was decided that they should live in

a separate part of her parents' big house. A new room was built for them on the east side. Shelagh's mother feared her daughter would be lonely with her husband so often away at sea.

It seemed well done, too, when the pox came and Shelagh lost her baby, her beauty, and her ability to bear more children. Desmond was at sea when that tragedy had struck his young wife. Shelagh's mother had cared for her through it, but the girl had never regained her full health, and her face remained ravaged with pockmarks.

She had also, over time, become obese and lost her good-humored ways. She was not a shrew, far from it; but her moods tended more toward melancholia than merriment, which made her tedious company indeed.

There were few servants and the family was close knit. Desmond was an accepted part of the clan, as he had been when he was a boy. Shelagh's father, James—when he spared time away from the plump serving wenches he peopled his household with—seemed to approve of Desmond's seafaring adventures. There was a potential for great wealth in that life, after all.

When the time came and James died, Shelagh and her two brothers were to inherit the estate, divided into equal parcels of ten acres each, with some livestock. It was a peaceful life the O'Donnells led, troubled only by the tragedy of the daughter's lost beauty and lost child.

Now, in the bitter cold dawn of January the thirtieth, Desmond bid farewell to Shelagh and her parents, waving to them when he reached the wide track that led to Dungannon. He was once again astride the bay horse he had borrowed without permission from the Tyrone's stable, and he traveled alone.

The journey took three days because of the bad weather

and the worse conditions of the road, and he slogged grimly through the snow and mud, at times dismounting to lead the horse across the treacherously slippery terrain.

He arrived at Dungannon on an early February afternoon of rare warm sunshine. The frost-crackling grass under the horse's feet had thawed temporarily, and through the bare-limbed trees Desmond could see the waters of the great Lough Neagh, still not frozen solid despite the long cold spell.

There seemed to be more soldiers about the castle than there had been before, drilling, marching, and target shooting with their long, unwieldy muskets.

Hugh O'Neill had spent the better part of the day out with his captains, riding with them and inspecting his troops. The numbers of his legions grew constantly, for each raid by the English, each skirmish fought with them in the south, brought more angry Irishmen to the side of O'Neill.

Hugh rode to the gates of his great house.

Midway on the path to the gate Hugh and Desmond met.

Kirkconnell reined in rather impatiently; it was not the Tyrone he had come to see. He greeted his old friend warmly but perfunctorily, challenged the Irishman to race to the front doors of Dungannon, and applied his heels to his tired mount.

"Wait!" Hugh shouted and galloped after Desmond, catching him up and matching his horse pace for pace. "All is not as it was!"

The horses' hooves were thudding noisily on the sodden track, bits of mud flying, kicked up behind them.

"Wait!" Hugh called again, urgency in his booming voice.

Desmond glanced at him, and then pulled his beast to a stop as O'Neill did the same.

"That's a fine horse," Hugh said, hardly winded by the gallop.

"It should be," Kirkconnell said with a grin. " 'Tis one of yours."

"Ah? Then glad I am ye have seen fit to return it."

"I would not steal from you, Hugh . . . There is reason for me to return to Dungannon, as well you know."

The Tyrone quieted his prancing horse, which shook its bridle in protest at the too-short run. "The woman, 'Connell . . ."

"Well?" Desmond said, not liking the expression on Hugh's face. "What has happened? My Ardys—she is well, is she not? She is with child—always dangerous for women— Mother of God, tell me she is well!"

"She was well when last I saw her, my friend. But she is gone."

Across the long field, a unit of soldiers turned smartly, their weapons clattering oddly loud in the still afternoon air. Desmond's horse skittered sideways on the stone path and he reined it in expertly.

"What say you? Gone?"

Hugh nodded. "With de la Roche. Hard after your own leaving."

Desmond stared at him. "You lie! Why would she leave with that cur?"

"Nay, I'd not lie about that. They disappeared at the same time. All her belongings are here still. I did not see them go. No one did."

"Then you had no word from her—she did not tell you of any decision to leave? She said nothing to Mabel?"

The Frenchman again, who had looked at Ardys with such hunger in his black eyes. And Desmond had left her to him. Desmond had abandoned her to his enemy!

Hugh said: "Ardys and Mabel were never warm friends, Desmond—your woman was always too preoccupied with

150

yourself to make friends with others! There were no signs of violence in your chambers. Only some—dishevelment."

"Her clothing is there still?"

"Aye."

"And her weapons—what of her rapier, the swept hilt?"

"There, in the top of her chest, in its place, attached to the lid."

Disbelief gave way to fury. With a hardened jaw, Desmond said: "She would never have left that sword behind. Never. It was a gift from her father. She valued it above all things."

Kirkconnell's horse jumped back as he yanked suddenly on the reins. "De la Roche must have taken her against her will! By my troth, I know it! Curse you, why was I not sent for?"

Hugh considered before he answered, having his own theory on the matter. "Her absence was not noticed for some hours. And she had just learned of your wife, remember. A woman's pride can be a frightful thing. Come, Desmond! I thought you had made your choice between your wife and your mistress when you left; Mabel thought thus also. Mayhap Ardys thought the same."

"Ye should have sent for me, you great oaf!"

Hugh was silent a moment. "Because ye are tired, 'Connell, and angered by this news, I will tolerate your insult. But I warn you—remember whose land this is. Watch your tongue, man."

Kirkconnell glared at the Tyrone, then he said tersely, "Forgive me, my lord."

O'Neill inclined his head. "Your man Kennwyn told her," he said, not knowing of the note Kirkconnell had left with the jeweled dagger.

"Kennwyn!"

"You were gone and no sign of your return. If de la Roche did take her, he merely took advantage of your abandonment. Do not expect me to look after your women, Kirkconnell! Your problems with them are your own and of your own making. Kennwyn has gone to Carrickfergus, back to the *Espada*, and—wait, ye thrice-cursed hothead!"

Desmond's bay reared sharply when he laid into its sides. To Carrickfergus, Desmond thought incoherently. May Bleddyn's soul rot in Hell forever, him and his easy tongue! The horse, tired already, responded again to Desmond's wicked spurs.

The crew of the *Espada* were scattered around the beach at Carrickfergus, mending sails and making barrel staves by bending wood over hot fires. They looked up as one man when their captain came thundering out of the woods on a horse that looked near death, its mouth dripping foam and flecks of blood.

"Day to 'ee, Cap'n," Grimsthorpe approached Kirkconnell, reaching up to take the reins of Desmond's horse.

Kirkconnell barely saw him, his vision clouded by the days of hard riding. The ship swung gently in the bay, looking larger than he remembered.

"Where is Kennwyn?" Desmond asked as he dismounted. "Take this animal and see to it, Grimsthorpe."

"Aye, sir. Bled's on board, seeing to the refitting."

Desmond ran to the beach and commandeered one of the ketches that lay on the sand. With quick strokes he brought himself to the side of the *Espada*, climbing quickly up the rope that hung loosely over the port rail. At the deck above he saw Bleddyn peering at him, a look of confusion and alarm on his fair face.

When Kirkconnell reached the top of the rope Kennwyn

watched him heave himself over onto the ship and asked: "What's amiss, Cap'n 'Connell?"

The Welshman was shorter than the captain by several inches, and confronted with the contorted rage of Desmond's expression he stepped back a pace.

Kirkconnell's hands went round Bleddyn's neck and he began to squeeze.

"Where is the girl?" Desmond hissed, his voice a menacing whisper.

"What girl?" Bled echoed stupidly, trying to tear Desmond's hands away. "D'ye mean Mistress Trevallon? I've not seen her these many days, not since the day you left for Tullaghoge. Pray you, Cap'n! I canna breathe!"

"She's gone from Dungannon. You told her everything, and now she's gone. She disappeared with the dark Frenchman because ye told her everything."

Disbelief and horror chased across Bled's features. "I knew it not, Cap'n. I swear on me mother's grave! Christ, I canna breathe! I did tell her where you was—it were no secret, were it? She was at the stables, and I stopped her following you. Ye would not have wanted that! Then I took her back to the house, real upset she were and I bain't seen 'er since. If she's gone, I knew it not!"

Desmond regarded him for an instant and loosened his grip a bit. "On your mother's grave?"

"Aye, Cap'n!" Bled coughed.

Desmond moved his hands away from Bled's throat, and Bleddyn heaved a sigh of relief.

What does it matter now, Desmond thought, what she thinks of me? What matters is getting her back. A wave of bitter fatigue washed through Kirkconnell! He tried to think what must be done, to plan. So far, he had not thought further than finding and throttling his first mate. Desmond leaned over to knock some of the caked mud from his boots.

Across the short stretch of water, on the beach, Grimsthorpe held the reins of the trembling horse, trying to quiet it. From the ship Desmond watched, uninterested, as the exhausted animal shuddered, its knees buckling under it. It landed heavily on its side, and the old cook knelt beside it, soothing, loosening the saddle straps.

"I shall have to pay the Tyrone for his horse," said Kirkconnell tiredly.

"Cap'n," Bleddyn began to reach forward, then stopped.

" 'Twas my fault," Desmond said. "Hugh was right. I left her without a single word, only a note that said nothing of any importance. And 'tis right ye would tell her where I was—she had only to ask. Ye always were an honest man, Bled. Regrettably so."

"What's to be done now, Cap'n 'Connell?"

Kirkconnell squinted toward the shore where the high walls of Carrickfergus Castle soared upward toward the breaking clouds.

"The *Corbeau*," he said, "de la Roche's ship. She was anchored hard by the *Espada*, was she not?"

"Aye, off the port bow, closer to the sea entrance of the bay."

"Then did ye not see her put back to sea?"

"Nay. They left in the night, I bla', before the tide turned. The watch said she stole out ever so quiet-like."

"And the watch did not rouse ye—he did not think it strange, this skulking out of harbor? God's death, what fool was on watch that night?"

Bled shifted uncomfortably, looking at his feet. "There was naught amiss in it, Cap'n. Many's the time we've slipped out quiet under night skies, as you might say. We had no reason to stop the *Corbeau*, neither."

"I asked you, who had the watch?"

"Tom did. The boy Tom."

Kirkconnell groaned. Of all nights, that lazy boy, who just might be a bastard son of the Tyrone's and was therefore beyond the disciplinary lash.

"Christ's wounds," said Desmond heavily, pushing his hair out of his eyes. "Well, fetch him here."

Again Bled shifted his feet. He said: "Tom is gone, too. He went back to his village. 'Tis near somewhere, and when he said he was tired of life at sea, I thought it best to let 'im go. Did I do wrong, Cap'n?"

"Oh, God's teeth, man, this is too much!" Kirkconnell abruptly sat on a barrel full of rainwater, covered with a leather skin. It rocked a little under his weight but he did not notice. He held his head in his hands, for the moment seeming to be in despair, his shoulders shaking.

When the captain looked up again, the mate saw that he was laughing.

"Cap'n 'Connell?"

"What is to do, Bled? Well may you ask. The woman I love is taken by a man I hate, my ship is guarded by a boy who sees nothing and then disappears, the great lord Tyrone will be angry with me because I have insulted him and killed one of his best horses, and I do not know where the cursed Frenchman can be in all this wide sea—can you not see the humor of it, Bled?"

"Nay, Cap'n," said Kennwyn seriously, frowning at Desmond.

"I can. What's to do?" Desmond stopped laughing and shook his head to clear it. " 'Tis one thing certain: I shall find Ardys. That means searching for the *Corbeau*, and she has almost a week's start on us."

He stood again, glad to have made the decision. "De la

Roche will not have my Ardys. Not while I live and breathe and own a ship!"

He went to the rail and looked back at the beach.

"How long to revictual the *Espada*, Bled? For a lengthy voyage?"

Kennwyn considered, stroking his beard. "Two days, mebbe three. She's seaworthy, in better shape than she's been in some time, too. You was gone a long while, Cap'n, and I kept the men busy. And there's plenty o' food, bought from the locals. Some o' the men made friends among the villagers and o' course, a couple of 'em come from here."

"Good. Make it two days. 'Tis pleased I will be to see the last of this place. We've been too long from the sea, Bled, and I confess I am glad to be going out, even now. Have Grimsthorpe help with the provisioning—he knows better than anyone what we need for food. And send two of the men back to Dungannon. Quickly! There are things at Dungannon that must be brought with us."

At Bleddyn's unspoken question, Desmond smiled a trifle thinly. "Ardys's rapier is still in our chamber there, with all her belongings."

"Nay! The lass's sword? I canna believe it," Bled said.

"Aye. That is why I am convinced that de la Roche took her against her will. She would die before she would leave that sword behind." He stretched. "I will sleep on board tonight. In the morning send George to my cabin, and we'll plot a course."

" 'Tis a fiercesome large ocean, Cap'n 'Connell. How will we ever find one ship?"

"Aye, it is. But de la Roche must have his favorite ports. Villages along the coasts where he raids regularly, or where he trades with the townspeople—in France, Portugal, even in the Caribbean, or around the Canaries. All ships stop at the

Canaries for fresh water and food. I will find him, if I have to search every island in this sea, one by one. Now show me what ye have done while I was away."

"The *Corbeau* has black-colored sails," said the mate suddenly as he walked across the deck with the captain.

"Aye, what of that?"

Bled flashed a grin at Kirkconnell. " 'Twill make her real conspicuous. Nae other ship I know has black sails."

Desmond laughed and put his arm across Kennwyn's shoulders, glad to feel the gentle rock of the *Espada* once more, glad to feel the quickening of his blood. He thought of the battle he would wage with the Frenchman de la Roche, and was cheered to be going to the rescue of his Ardys.

At the doorway to Desmond's cabin the two men parted company, Bled to see to the ship. Kirkconnell went inside his cabin, intending to wash and rest from his long ride before taking formal command. The musty wood and leather smell of his cabin was pleasant to breathe again.

On the great bed, the cat Great Harry rolled slowly over, stretched, and yawned, his yellow eyes gazing at his master.

CHAPTER ELEVEN

The *Corbeau* was a small, seaworthy vessel, capable of quick maneuvers and fast sprints over short distances. She had been built and launched in the Netherlands as a merchant ship, but the pirate de la Roche, after he captured her, did not use her so conventionally.

The three-masted carrack, one-decked and low in the water, with a displacement of about one hundred and fifty tons, was perfect for daylight raids on unsuspecting coastal villages along the Spanish and Portuguese seaboards.

In her time, the *Corbeau* had proven useful on smuggling ventures as well. De la Roche plied the waters between England and Spain, or Ireland and England, with equal ease. The ship could be hidden in the tiniest of shallow coves, for she had a depth of a mere thirteen feet, and under the cover of night he often brought her in under the very noses of the shore patrols. And to further camouflage her, de la Roche, at great expense, had equipped her with all-black sails.

There was little cargo in the hold of the ship now: de la Roche had sold his parcel of wool (stolen from an English coastal town), to the Earl of Tyrone for a handsome profit.

It was well that the *Corbeau* was light in the water, for if she had been fully loaded the storm that battered her off the coast of the island of Cuba would surely have sunk her.

If God allows me to return home, Ardys thought, looking out the porthole at the vast dull gray expanse before her, I vow I shall never go to sea again. Never.

Ninety days, as far as she could tell by the scratches she made daily on the panel under the tapestries that adorned the walls of her prison. It must be nearing the end of April, and at Hampton Court the wide rows of daffodils would be blooming, and soon too the lilacs. The thought of flowers, of ground that did not rock beneath her, gave her a measure of strength, and she wondered if she would be able to stand.

Never had Ardys been so far out to sea as she had on this unwilling journey. De la Roche gave her no hint of their destination, nor had he told her their position at any time.

He kept her here, in his cabin, letting her up on the deck for air only rarely, and then clothed in a pair of his breeches and a castoff shirt. His gallant treatment of her when the voyage was young had changed drastically over the long days.

The child within her was growing, and rapidly enough that she had been unable to hide it from him for long. Even though she fought him, he soon knew every inch of her body, and gave her no clothing with which to cover herself. By the end of the first month at sea her condition had become obvious. She had wakened to feel his hands on her belly, on the roundness there, and she had seen anger in his eyes when he saw she was no longer asleep.

"This," he had said softly, his voice barely controlled, "cannot be mine. It is too far advanced."

She had willed herself to be calm. " 'Tis not yours," she said.

"Kirkconnell's, then."

"There has been no one else."

He gripped her cruelly. "Why did you not tell me of this?"

"Does it matter? Did ye ask? There was no chance. I did not ask to come aboard your ship, Captain de la Roche."

He pulled away from her as though repulsed. "Not matter? *Mon dieu,* not matter that you carry the seed of another man's planting? This makes a mockery of my passion for you," he said, reaching for his clothes. "You are disgusting. Your body

159

will swell and become bloated and ugly."

"You knew he was my lover before you took me," she said.

"And I thought to make you mine. You think I could make love to you now, when he has left his mark on you? I thought to humiliate him by taking his woman, and now I find that he is, after all, triumphant."

"You have never made love to me, you have always taken me against my will!" she said hotly. "And I do not understand. How is he triumphant?"

"Then I shall not explain it," he said roughly, pulling on his boots while he steadied himself with a hand on the chair. Then he turned to look at her. "For the sake of the beauty you once had, I will spare your life. But from this day, I will not touch you. My desire for you is gone, *fini*. You shall remain here, in this cabin, until we reach land, and then I shall rid myself of you, and find my pleasure elsewhere."

True to his word, he had not molested her again in any way, and since that day he had made her sleep apart from him, on a pile of blankets on the floor. He saw that she had food and water enough, to drink and to wash herself, but here his concern for her ended. She did not complain, knowing too well how vulnerable she was, and she was content with the feeling of the babe growing.

She was relieved that his violations of her had ended, and glad to feel the child moving within her.

When she allowed herself to think of making love, it was Kirkconnell of whom she thought.

It was always Desmond Kirkconnell, in her dreams and when she was awake.

The storm these last days had almost driven her out of her senses. There was no end to the noise, the cries of the men, and the wash of the waves. Lightning struck the topgallant spire and the mast had crashed to the deck, crushing three men, and de la Roche, shouting to be heard above the wind and the torrents of rain, ordered the deck cleared of all debris.

Tossed about like a child's toy on the immense waves, her sails furled and her sailors lashed for safety to her decks, the *Corbeau* rode the storm, timbers snapping when the crests of the sea rose over her stern, sinking sickeningly into the troughs of the waves, only to shudder and slowly rise again with the next wave, and the next.

Ardys watched the storm blow itself out through the tiny leaded window of de la Roche's cabin, marveling that the *Corbeau* was still afloat. Afterwards, the sea remained sullen and gray, choppy and restless like a child exhausted after a violent tantrum, reluctant to settle down.

Ardys lay on the bed, wrapped in her blankets to cushion the impact when the ship threw her against the walls and floor of the cabin. She had not been able to grip anything long enough to keep herself from being tossed by the violent movements of the ship, and when there was silence between waves she could only watch the window, praying for some sign that the storm was abating.

Pregnancy and enforced solitude had made her careful; she was a prisoner but she had the child to think of and nothing would ever harm the child while she lived. She was healthy, young, and strong, and she would bear a healthy boy! Each time she was sick from the motion of the ship she told herself, "I can bear this! I will bear anything for our child."

Now, however, she found the silence unnerving, and she kept listening for the next wave, for the next squall. She knew that the crew would be busy repairing the damage, unfurling the sails to make sure that they were still sound, mending the mast with one of the spars, lashed with stout rope. If she could go out, onto the deck, perhaps she could convince herself that it was over, and the danger to her babe was past.

De la Roche came in and found her huddled there on his bed. She expected him to order her off, back to her corner of the floor, but he did not. He was wet and his cape was ruined, the velvet matted beyond hope of repair, the edges shredded by the wind.

Ardys was pale, her face almost pasty-looking in the wan light.

"Get up, *Mamselle*. The wind has finally gone. I shall bring food for us both when the fire has been lit in the galley."

She looked up, still feeling a bit ill. "Did ye lose many men?"

"Seven only. I count myself lucky. Three under the mast, two swept overboard, one on the topgallant when the lightning struck it, and one worthless wretch who fell on his own dagger."

"And the ship?"

"Needs some patching, but she will do. We are not far now from land."

He speaks differently, now that he does not want me, she thought. His voice was so seductive before, so low and soft. And now he speaks to me as though I was nothing to him. 'Tis well. Jesu, men have changing hearts!

He began to change into a dry doublet and hose, and cautiously she tried to rise, leaning back against the headboard and heaving herself to the floor. He did not offer to help her, and she swayed a moment, holding her belly.

Not far now from land, he had said.

"Where are we?" she asked as she had so often during the past three months. He glanced at her.

"In the West Indies, coming into the lesser of the Antilles. In the Caribbean," he said shortly when she looked like she would speak.

"Then we have crossed the Atlantic? We are in the New World?"

"*Oui,* and I will soon be rid of you. You and the bastard you carry."

"And just how will you be rid of me?"

"*Chienne!* Must you ask? There is an island, called Desirade. There are people there who will care for you."

"And you?"

"What matters it to you? I will leave you and sail on, to the Mexican coast. There is much treasure there."

An island. Her heart leapt. Fresh air to breathe, solid ground to walk on. Freedom from this man who hated her. Natives, or Spanish conquistadors, she cared not to whom he abandoned her, it made no difference. There would be women among them, there must be, and they would sympathize with her, and God be praised!—when her child came, she would not be alone. Her chances of bearing a strong, healthy child were greatly improved.

Two days after the storm, the *Corbeau* anchored in the natural harbor of the small island of Desirade, in the Leeward group of the Lesser Antilles. A coral reef formed a breakwater, protecting the beach from the direct assault of the sea, and the palm trees that lined the shore were tall and swayed with the wind, their tops full of coconuts and groups of small, chattering monkeys. At the southern end of the beach a freshwater stream ran down from the hills to meet the ocean, and across, to the north, a few hundred yards away, was the island's only town.

While his crew set about lowering the long boats to haul drinking water and provisions back to the ship, de la Roche led Ardys without ceremony onto the deck, having instructed her to dress herself in one of his old doublets, which was loose-fitting, except where she bulged with pregnancy. The crew looked politely away when she came up, blinking in the tropical sunlight.

There was a woman on the beach. Ardys shaded her eyes with her hand to see better while the oarsmen pulled over the short expanse of sea. The woman was colorfully dressed and hugely fat, and she waved and beckoned when she saw de la Roche, calling him by his first name.

"Who is she?" asked Ardys when de la Roche lifted his hand in greeting.

"Marie Quimper. She is an old friend."

The boat scudded up onto the sand and one of the sailors leaped out to hold it steady while the others stepped over and splashed ashore.

The woman ran to de la Roche and stopped in front of him, her wide face wreathed in smiles. She held out her hand, and the Frenchman bowed low and kissed it.

Her bright green dress fluttered in the wind. Like a sail, Ardys thought, smiling when the woman turned to her.

"Marie Quimper," said de la Roche, "this is *Mademoiselle* Ardys Trevallon. She is English, but she speaks French passably well; you may speak that language with her and she will understand."

Ardys stared at the woman, at her flat nose, beautiful bronze skin, and full lips, and realized that Marie Quimper must be a native islander, one of the Indians Ardys had heard about at court. Indians were talked about as savages, but this big, motherly woman could not possibly be a savage.

"Ah! *Mamzelle* has a *bebe*, no?" said Marie in French. "François, my friend, you have done right to bring your *cherié* to me in this time. I will see that she bears you a healthy child."

De la Roche smiled lightly, his lips compressed. He did not correct her.

"I knew this would be the best thing for her, Marie. You have told me of the many children you have brought safely into the world. This is but one more."

To Ardys's deep dismay, the woman gathered her into her large embrace, hugging her to her expansive bosom. When Ardys protested, Marie simply tightened her hold, clucking like a mother hen.

"Not just one more, François! Every *bebe* is important! Do not worry, *ma petite,* Marie will care for you now. No more of the rocking of the ship, *oui?* Only good food, and a soft bed to birth in. All will be well. Come, Captain, will you dine with Jacques and me?"

When Marie released Ardys, she stood unsteadily, getting her breath back. De la Roche watched her impassively, his dark eyes restless and impatient.

"*Merci,* but no," he said to Marie. "When we have provisioned we must go. There is business for the *Corbeau* in other waters."

"You came all this way only to bring me here?" Ardys said, surprised.

He frowned at her. "I find I do not want your death on my hands. And you would surely die if you gave birth on-board ship. That would be an evil omen indeed; it would frighten my crew and curse our voyage."

"But you will come back?"

"Some time, mayhap. Or mayhap not."

Ardys straightened herself up, realizing that this pirate was abandoning her. As Kirkconnell had. So be it. She would survive, for the sake of the child.

"I am grateful to you, Captain de la Roche, for bringing me here," she said carefully. "Do other ships come here, so that I may in time return home?"

"That is not my concern," he said, turning away from Ardys. "*Adieu,* Marie. I want to catch the tide, so I must leave you now."

He kissed the native woman's hand again, and called to his men to row him back out to the *Corbeau*. Ardys watched the black-cloaked figure fade into the distance as the sailors pulled at the oars of the long boats, heading for the ship. He did not look back, and Marie finally stopped waving when he vanished onto the deck.

"Shall I live all my days here on this island?" Ardys asked herself. "What life is there here for me and the babe?"

The child in her womb kicked her, as if to say, do not think of such things now. I live and I need you.

Marie put her arm around Ardys's shoulders. "So thin you are! You must have displeased the captain greatly, *ma petite*, for him to leave you here."

"Aye, I displeased him mightily."

"But all will be well, you will see, François will come back, he always comes back to Desirade, to trade, to take on water and food, and to visit Marie! He will come back for you, when the child has come. When you present it to him he will surely forgive whatever you have done." Marie said heartily.

"I will have to watch you closely," continued Marie. "You are small, and your hips are narrow. We shall not see the ship off; let us go back to my house, and my brother Jacques will welcome you, too. He has been hunting all day, there should be meat tonight."

Marie steered Ardys up the beach toward the village, chattering the while like one of the monkeys that sprang about in the palms while the *Corbeau* weighed anchor and tacked out to sea, her black sails filling with the southern wind.

At the edge of the village was a cottage, white-washed and two-storied (made, it seemed to Ardys, of dried mud), thatched with palm leaves laid crisscross on the roof. A small animal was tied to a tree by the only door, pig-like but brown and furry, with a square snout and hoofed feet. It squealed at

Marie's approach, and the huge woman leaned down awk-wardly to pat its back as she passed by. Not knowing what it was, Ardys kept her distance from it and followed Marie.

There was one room on the main floor of the hut, with an earthen floor and simple furniture made of wood bound with stout rope. A crude ladder led to a loft above. There was a table and chair in the center of the room, a bench against one wall, and some sort of altar at the other. Above it, hung on the wall, was a carved stone crucifix, painted in gaudy colors, nearly a foot high. The face of the Christ figure was lifelike, contorted with pain, and the blood flowing from the hands and side was brilliant crimson.

How sick I am of Papists, Ardys thought, and then real nausea washed through her, making her sweat. She swayed on her feet.

Marie shouted for her brother Jacques but there was no answer so she heaved Ardys up the short ladder alone. One room also in the loft, and one small bed, too small surely for the bulk of this woman, Ardys thought, lying down without protest when Marie bid her. She had walked further today than she had for weeks, and was ashamed of her frailty. I am no fragile girl, she wanted to tell Marie. I am the Fencing Master's daughter and I can stand against any man; I have been to sea and I have been to the stronghold of the Tyrone, I have loved and been betrayed, been kidnapped, raped, and abandoned but I am no weakling. I will survive!

Marie stroked Ardys's forehead, noticing the heat there, soothing her with a gentle touch. Ardys lay stiffly for a moment, and then her eyes closed slowly and she sank into sleep.

She dreamed she was at sea, and when she awoke the room was spinning about her crazily. She retched and gagged when cool water was forced into her mouth. Marie was there, holding her, and behind her stood a large man, dark complexioned and bald headed, worriedly wringing his hands and speaking to Marie in a patois Ardys could not understand.

Marie patted her arm. "There, my child. The dream is gone, and you are safe. This is Jacques, *mon frere*, who is unable to greet you in any language you understand. Drink the water, *cherié*, you need it, for you have sweated much."

The room slowly halted its spin, and Ardys drank greedily out of the hollowed-out coconut shell. The water was bitter, as though it had been mixed with herbs. When she was finished she lay back again, aching in every bone, and then she remembered the child and frantically clutched at her belly.

"*Mais non, cherié*, you have been very ill for a while but your child lives still. Gently, do not rise up. Marie will care for you, you must not worry. That would hurt your *bebe*."

With that reassurance, Ardys relaxed a little and noticed the man beside Marie, who was so like her that he must have been her twin. He looked as concerned as his sister.

"How many days?" Ardys whispered, and Marie leaned closer to her.

"Two. Too much strain for you, too much to say farewell to your lover. Now you must pine for him, but remember his child within you, and be calm."

"Pine—for de la Roche? You have much more affection for him than do I, Marie!" Ardys laughed bitterly. "This child is not de la Roche's, praise be! But ours—Desmond Kirkconnell's and mine; conceived at Dungannon, sometime during the golden autumn we spent there, fencing and making love. It is good to think on those times, it gives me strength."

Ardys was still smiling when the first pain racked her body, as if a rope had been tied round her and pulled tighter. She could not breathe and grasped at Marie's hands to keep from screaming in fear.

"Marie! What is happening? Oh, God, oh, God, no! No! Do not take my child! The child is all I have left! Marie, help me!"

Ten grueling hours later, the babe slid wetly onto the bloodied linen of the bed. A boy, tiny and many weeks too soon, but when Marie pushed a fat finger into its mouth it cried a feeble protest, which Ardys heard through the haze of her pain. Marie gently bound the child in soft cloth, wiping his tiny head and hands, and laid him at his mother's breast with a smile, silently praying to the Madonna to protect this fragile life.

The child lived barely an hour.

CHAPTER TWELVE

May, 1598

The *Espada* had been at sea for almost four months, bitter hard months of high wind and rough weather, with one storm following on the heels of another. The ship was damaged, beaten, and buffeted by the furious seas, but she was still afloat, and there was not too much water in the bilge.

Kirkconnell put in at every village and town where de la Roche's ship might have been seen. They sailed to France, to the Netherlands, to Portugal: Desmond had gone so far as to come dangerously close to Spain, slipping into port by night in one of the long boats to ask if the Frenchman had come through. The answer was the same everywhere they looked. There was no sign of de la Roche or the black-sailed *Corbeau*.

After much inner debate, Kirkconnell decided to head for the southern seas, for the Spanish Main, although it went against his grain to put out into the Atlantic with a scarcely conceived course. He had sailed the open waters of this cold ocean before, and he knew the prevailing winds and the paths any ship must take to the islands of the Caribbean, so he ordered the *Espada* to turn south, in spite of the protests of his crew.

The storms had unexpectedly abated when they hit the open water, and Kirkconnell set the men to repairing the damage to the riggings and the masts.

Desmond stood in the forecastle and sniffed the salt air, trying to guess what the weather held for them in the next weeks. The day was bright, and the sun beat hot on the decks of the *Espada*, where most of the crew was stripped to the waist, glad of its warmth. Bleddyn Kennwyn was nearby, at the rail.

" 'Tis good to see the sun, bain't it, Cap'n?"

"Aye, it is. We should have left the coasts long ago, Bled."

Desmond was stripped like the men, and he stretched, feeling the play of the sun on his back. "But at the time the coast seemed the best place to search, or to begin a search."

Kennwyn said nothing, gazing out to sea. The rigging above them was alive with men, climbing about, lighthearted and gay, their voices drifting down to the deck. On land the business of mending sails could be tedious: merely haul them down, spread them across a convenient beach, and stitch until the fingers were worn and numb. At sea this was another matter, and far more exciting.

Thick needles made of fishbone in their teeth, heavy twine knotted round their waists, the men scrambled up the lines and masts, out onto the cross-bars and to the sails themselves, holding to ropes when possible and to the fabric of the sail when not. One stiff breeze, one missed handhold, could mean a quick, fatal plummet to the deck far below, or into the waiting sea.

A sailor was no sailor if he could not climb up the thinnest mast, shinny down the slipperiest rope. They had seen no action these last months, although they had passed dangerously close to the Lizard and three galleasses of the English fleet had given them chase. The English, having satisfied themselves that the Spanish galleon was heading south, and not towards English shores, let her go.

With the fair weather the crew's restlessness increased, and Kirkconnell put them to mending sails to work off their excess energies. He looked up, and in the stark sunlight the men were etched clearly against the backdrop of tangled lines and blue sky. Like small boys, he thought, climbing trees, daring each other to go higher up or farther out.

"When they have finished that, I will set them to drilling with the cannon and the demi-culverin. Mayhap I shall let them fire a few rounds at nothing, just to hear the sound of the guns, so they will not forget the noise of battle," he said to Bled.

"Cap'n 'Connell," Bled answered, "if we meet another ship, ye must let the crew take it."

Desmond frowned at his first mate. "If it is de la Roche's ship, I will, and that gladly."

"This crew signed on for plunder, for combat and riches. Tedn't fair o' you to deprive 'em of that. They want to fight."

"Tread carefully, Bled," said Desmond, his eyes narrowing. "I am captain here, not you. We search for the *Corbeau*, not for treasure."

"Then," Kennwyn went on, despite Kirkconnell's intimidating look, "ye must tell the crew that. They've been loyal to ye, they've obeyed orders. Cap'n," Kennwyn stood defiantly, his hands on his hips, and matched Kirkconnell's glare. "Give it up! The sea's too big, the Frenchie's gone, and there's naught to be done. Ye've looked; ye've done your best! Wasted victuals and drinking water and men's time on a search that won't bear fruit, made us hug the coast when there's treasure at sea . . ."

"Kennwyn," said Desmond, "you are bordering on mutiny."

"Aye, Cap'n, are ye blind? I only say what the crew must be thinkin'. Ye know I'd follow ye to Hell if ye bade me."

Kirkconnell frowned at Kennwyn a moment longer, then he sighed and ran his hand through his thick hair and looked once more out to sea.

One of the crew was singing a bawdy ditty about an innkeeper's wife, and he was joined in the refrain by several of the other men, the voices totally without harmony.

"Bled, you've been with me these many years. I respect you, and I like you, but I swear to you, if you try to undermine my power on this ship, I will kill you with my own hands."

"If'n I ever did that," said Bled, "I'd hand you me own sword to do it with."

The singing in the upper masts stopped, and the captain and the mate glanced up.

"A sail, a sail! Off the starboard bow! A ship, a ship!" the cry came from the crow's nest, the small platform built at the top of the highest mast for the lookout. The crew was still, breathlessly waiting.

Kirkconnell looked at Bled and shrugged. "Have all the men come down. And see to the guns. I'll tell George to inter-cept."

Kennwyn grinned. "Thank 'ee, sir."

Bled was right. Damn the Frenchman. Here was prey. The *Corbeau* would have to wait.

" 'Tis a Spaniard," came another cry from the crow's nest. "Aye, and alone."

"Run up Spanish colors, then!" shouted Kirkconnell. " 'Twill draw her in. If she's not in convoy, she may need our help."

"Aye," agreed Kennwyn, laughing. "Our help!"

Shouted orders now, and running feet on the deck as the crew scrambled down to their stations, each to take his own position at cannon or culverin or hook. The master gunner handed round ammunition and flints were struck, ready to be put to touchhole. The gun ports slid easily back, and the cannon were run out, ready for firing.

At a signal from Kirkconnell, George changed the course to meet the other ship, and a cheer of anticipation welled up from the crew. They approached quickly, shortening the distance from their prey, bringing her into the range of their guns. The Spaniard lay low and heavy in the water, almost wallowing. And she soon spotted the *Espada*.

The Spanish flag flying at her topsail, the huge cross of Spain on her mainsail, the *Espada* looked to the approaching ship to be a member of her own fleet, and the Spanish pilot pulled the rudder and headed straight for Kirkconnell's ship, looking for safety, to travel with an escort.

The Spaniard was a treasure ship, and towered high above the water line, larger even than the *Espada*. A storm had scattered her convoy, and now, loaded with rough silver ingots stolen from slain Mexican Indians, she was making her slow way across the Atlantic, bound for Lisbon and home.

There was silence on the *Espada* as she drew within hailing distance. Kirkconnell's crew crouched low, out of sight behind the rails; their distinctly English look would give them away to their unsuspecting quarry. Desmond calmly put on his black doublet, and strapped his sword to his belt.

Voices could be heard above the roll of the sails and the lap of the sea: Spanish voices, excited and friendly. The dons were crowding close to their rail, their hands raised in greeting. Kirkconnell wished he had learned to speak Spanish, so that he could draw them even closer. No one on board the *Espada* spoke the dons' language well enough to serve except their priest, who, as always at the onset of any engagement, had blessed the crew and hurried to the safety of his quarters.

The sailor in the crow's nest pressed himself back instinctively as the two ships came within yards of each other. The name on the Spaniard was now plainly visible: the *Madre de Dios*. She swung to; her broadside open to the *Espada*'s fire, and the lookout saw that the gun ports of the other ship had not even been opened.

Too late the captain of the *Madre* saw his mistake: saw the English seamen, the gaping muzzles of the guns.

Kirkconnell, now at the starboard rail, barked the order to board and his crew rose up from their hiding places as one man. The great iron hooks flew across the expanse of separating sea and the men of the *Espada* swarmed over onto the *Madre*. Desmond was the first, his dagger in his teeth, his unsheathed rapier glittering in his hand.

The ships swung and banged together when the men still on board the *Espada* tugged the ropes and brought the helpless *Madre* close enough for the lookout to see the chips in the gilt paint on her keel.

The Spaniards, caught by surprise, fought hard to save their treasure. There was fierce and bloody hand-to-hand combat, the attackers met by the fists and swords of the defenders, and then there was the crack of musket fire as the Spanish captain, at his helm, collected his wits and ordered his musketeers to shoot, never caring that they were as likely to hit his own men in the melee on the deck. The smoke from the weapons added to the confusion, and the noise became almost painful. Several times it seemed that the riggings of the two ships would become entangled, their masts entwined, which could sink them both, but at the helm George pulled hard to port and widened the distance between them.

It was over quickly. Desmond ordered a search of the *Madre*'s holds as he stepped over the bodies of the dead and dying Spaniards.

The storerooms did not disappoint. Desmond and his men went through the food, ale, and water areas to the hold farthest inside the interior of the ship. It was closed with a huge oaken door. It took many ax blows and several minutes to break this door down. Desmond called for a torch before he stepped inside. His anticipation ran high as he swung the door back and went in, holding the torch high before him.

The torch lit the chamber, and a low whistle of astonishment escaped him. The room was filled with silver, piled neatly in shining ingots, lashed to prevent their shifting about. Some of the stacks were as tall as Kirkconnell, and he went to the one nearest the door and pulled one of the squares out, held it in his hand. It was six inches long, three inches wide, and an inch deep, very heavy and cool to the touch.

Untold wealth for the crew of the *Espada*, enough to last them all six lifetimes in great style. After all, it was theirs alone and not to be shared with any lord or King. Enough, in truth, to make them all kings themselves.

Enough, thought Kirkconnell with a wry smile, to keep two separate households, two separate women, in grand style. Ha! As if Ardys would ever willingly share him.

He turned to his crew and grinned.

Ardys collapsed into a fever and hovered near death for some days, and only the diligent nursing of the Quimpers brought her through. When the girl finally recovered, weak, drawn, and thin, Marie forced her to walk on the beach, to lie in the healing warmth of the sun for hours on end, a large hat shading her face. Marie said she believed sweat to be a great physic, purging the body of evil vapors.

Ardys lay full length on the hot sand, her head propped against a piece of driftwood, a light dress, given her by Marie, arranged anyhow about her body. It was several sizes too large, and Ardys seemed the more frail for it. She looked up at the soft thud of Marie's approaching footsteps, annoyed to have her silence shattered.

Marie sat down heavily, sending a small cloud of sand up,

and puffed out her lips contentedly. "How blue is ze sea today! Always it is lovely here, is it not?"

"Lovely," Ardys agreed bitterly. "I've lost my father, my lover, my country, and my son, but aye, the sea is still blue. I wish I had died when my son was born. I wish I had the courage to take my own life."

Marie reached out and touched Ardys's hair where a stray curl escaped the hat, tucking it back under the brim. "It is not fitting for a young woman to wish her life away. Life must go on. It is ze will of God. Giving in to despair is a sin."

Ardys smoothed the sand with her hand, watching the grains fall through her fingers. "Then God has made a dreadful mistake. I cannot believe that He needs my son more than I do."

She sat up. "I thank ye for saving my life, Marie. I do not mean to be offensive to you. You only did what you thought was right, in the sight of your God. But you should have let me die. There is no purpose for my life now."

"Zis is blasphemy! To talk of life as though we had any control of it. I grow angry with you, *ma petite!* While ze sun shine there is hope. François will come back, and zen you can make anozer *bebe.* Ye will be better soon."

Ardys stirred a pebble with her bare foot, the sand scratching her skin.

She said: "Mind ye, I told ye de la Roche was not the father of my child."

Marie moved a little, seeking a cooler patch of sand to sit on before she asked, "Aye, I mind, 'twas another man . . ."

"Another man. A pirate called Desmond Kirkconnell." Such pain, to speak his name. "He had a wife, and never told me. He left me to go to her and now he will never know that our child is dead."

She covered her face with her hands but did not weep.

Dried up inside, she had no tears even by the tiny grave in the lush green undergrowth of Desirade.

Marie patted Ardys's arm in a gesture of motherly affection. "Zen, ye do not wish to see François once more?"

"I do not care if I do or do not. It is all one to me."

"But what do you want to do? You are welcome to stay here wiz us."

Ardys was quiet, thinking. Then she slowly said, "I wish to return home. To Cornwall, to what is left of my family. There is no other place for me now. I can't go back to Dungannon; I could not, not without Desmond, not without the babe! Nor do I wish to return to the English court. There are memories everywhere there, of my father, of his death. I cannot go into a nunnery, more's the pity, but I could retire to Cornwall, and live quietly with my sisters and my mother. Cornwall was my first home. Maybe there is peace for me there."

The *Espada* lay as low in the water as the *Madre de Dios* had, the holds filled to bursting with stolen silver. Kirkconnell had taken the surviving Spaniards' swords and muskets, leaving them with only their daggers and their cannon to protect them, and set them adrift. Without the great weight of the treasure, he thought happily, they would have a better chance of making Lisbon, a better chance of outrunning any other pirates they might have the misfortune to meet.

The *Espada* was intact, hardly scratched beyond some slight damage to the starboard side where the *Madre* had swung into her. Kirkconnell was elated, though he had lost twelve men in the battle, and three more died of their wounds within days. He had the bodies wrapped in old sails, the most suitable winding sheet, said a few words over them, and heaved them overboard, commending their souls to God and their earthly remains to the fish.

The crew set about repairing and cleaning the ship with renewed vigor; for now they were all rich men, eager to sail for home and begin their new lives as men of wealth.

There was a loud groan of dismay when they were informed by Kirkconnell that they were once more heading due southwest, that Kirkconnell had a fancy to see the Caribbean. But for the moment the men were too content with their new-found wealth to begrudge their captain his whims.

"The silver will keep until we reach Ireland—in fact, the longer we stay at sea, the more 'twill be worth when we sell it ashore," Bled said jubilantly.

Bled worried about gambling and laziness, and warned Desmond. The men would have to be watched.

Kirkconnell's dreams of wealth were much the same as his crew's. Find Ardys, bring her back to Ireland, and set her up in her own house, somewhere near to Tullaghoge so that he could visit her daily. If she loved him as he loved her, he thought uneasily, she would see that it was the only way for them to be together, with their child. He must make her see.

CHAPTER THIRTEEN

Ardys's health improved. The color came back into her cheeks, and her hair regained its reddish luster. She could not help but get better under the watchful care of Marie Quimper. Ardys had to admit that it was good to feel her strength returning. If only she had her rapier and could practice, life would have been almost enjoyable there on the quiet, sun-washed island.

But the rapier was beyond her reach, at Dungannon. She must not think of that.

One morning in early June, Marie announced that she would go to the other side of the island, to collect supplies from the harbor town. She hitched her donkey to her brother's two-wheeled cart, and beckoned to Ardys, asking her if she cared to come along. Ardys put on a wide hat and swung herself up beside the other woman, on the short bench behind the donkey.

The cart track ran around the shoreline. The sun beat down and after an hour the two women halted to cool off and drink some water from the skin Marie had filled. Even a slow cart ride in the heat of midday could bring a heavy sweat and pounding temples.

They stood by the road and gazed out to sea. There were other small islands in the distance, and the sea was a clear blue with rippling waves gently lapping the sand.

"Oh, Marie!" Ardys said suddenly as she gazed across the water. "Is Desmond somewhere on this ocean? He sails in a monstrous Spanish galleon. Ye would not believe its size—it towers above the waterline! Does he ever, ever think of me?"

She kicked the sand and brushed her thick hair out of her

eyes. "Nay. He showed what he thought of me when he left me."

She turned quickly and grasped Marie's plump hand.

"I wish his wife would die! Now I have not even his child to call my own, I have no claim on him at all. If I had hopes of regaining his love, I buried them with my poor little son. I buried my hope with my son!"

"Hush, *ma petite!* Marie is here. While there is life, zere is hope. Never wish for death for anyone." Marie held Ardys, felt the shaking of her shoulders as she wept silently. "*Oui,* weep now—it is good to let the sorrow out, for only then will you let it go! Weep, child . . ."

Ardys wept for a long time there in the sun.

She felt the softness of Marie's enfolding embrace, felt the warmth of the sand under her own bare feet, and suddenly smelled the strong salt tang of the sea. The sunshine was beautiful, the sky a clear wondrous cornflower blue with white puffs of cloud.

Ardys blinked and took a deep shuddering breath; her tears slowed. There was a flash of movement at the edge of her vision and she turned, startled: one of the bright green and blue island hummingbirds, its long tail floating in the gentle sea breeze, its feathers brilliantly reflecting the light, hovered a few inches away from her face. She could hear the low hum of its wings, see the glint of its tiny eyes as it stared at her. It hung there before her for a long moment before it zipped off down the beach, making its chittering call.

Ardys laughed with pure joy.

She sniffed a bit, and leaned against the donkey, which accepted her familiar touch amiably, nuzzling her arm with one friendly ear cocked forward. She scratched him between his ears, and he inclined his head towards her as though he enjoyed it. Ardys felt like she was awakening from a long and smothering sleep.

And then, abruptly Marie was running toward the shore-line, her large figure bouncing with the effort, her feet sending up clods of sand.

Ardys saw, too. A ship had appeared on the horizon, bearing in on the incoming tide, making a rapid, expert advance between the reefs toward the small harbor at the end of the beach.

It was a relatively small ship, compared to the vessels on which Ardys had sailed, and looked to be Dutch-built: three-masted, with five large, square sails; three decks all of a level. The sterncastle, the highest part of the vessel, rose only three feet above the top deck. There was no flag or other insignia to be seen.

Ardys's pulse quickened with excitement. No ships had come to Desirade since de le Roche left. There would be news, and she realized she desperately wanted news—about England, about the world! Was her majesty the Queen well? Had the Spanish invaded again?

Ardys tethered the donkey to a bush growing by the road and ran along the sand to join Marie.

As the vessel dropped anchor, Ardys could hear the rusty protest of its capstan as she ran down the beach. About twenty small boats filled with natives had appeared from no-where and were rowing out to greet the visitor. Apparently this ship needed no formal marks of identification to be known to the natives of Desirade. Marie, whose bulk pre-vented her going out in any of the little boats, stood and bounced up and down on the beach, waving and shouting. Marie saw Ardys coming and ran to her, hugging her so that Ardys was swept off her feet.

"*Ma cherié!* It comes, the ship comes! Zis captain, he is friend to me, he take you home, he take you home when I ask him!" Marie was quite out of breath, her face red with exertion and excitement.

Ardys saw the long boats begin to be lowered from the ship.

"Home?" She said the word almost soundlessly. "To England? This ship—can you be so certain?"

The long boats reached the beach and a crowd of natives and sailors, laughing and hugging, immediately surrounded the two women so that Ardys could barely hear what Marie was saying.

"*Certainment!* Captain of the ship, he is *mon ami,* he do anyzing for me, he like my other *frere!*"

Ardys allowed herself to be carried along toward the village with the crowd. She suddenly saw the windswept coast of Cornwall, heard the lilt of her own people's voices again, saw the blue sea off Killigerran Head, that blue that was matched by no other in the world. Another spark of happiness, a tiny coal flaming amidst the ashes of a long-untended fire, flared in her breast.

There, in the crowd, Marie was embracing a man. The natives and the sailors swirled on ahead, leaving them behind, and Ardys stood and waited for the two to catch up with her. This man was as thin as Marie was fat, and foppishly dressed in cloth-of-gold doublet and bright purple silk stockings. His face was like Marie's and his eyes held the same friendly warmth when he saw Ardys.

Marie breathlessly introduced him as Michel Bontemps, and the man made an elegant leg to Ardys and kissed her hand loudly. He had not much English, he explained, so Ardys obligingly spoke in French, liking him and his ready smile.

"I am not a pirate, *mamselle,*" he said, "but an entrepreneur, a tradesman, an importer. I trade all over the civilized world."

"You mean you are a smuggler!" Ardys said, charmed.

He frowned in mock rebuke. "If you must use the word. I travel to France, to the Caribbean, to England, and to Spain."

"But you are like Marie," Ardys stopped, embarrassed by her own rudeness. "Forgive me, but you are an islander; how did you come to have a ship?"

"How does any man come to have a ship? I buy her, of course."

They walked back to the road, where the donkey still stood munching some of the dry grass.

"You say you go to England—do ye visit the western coasts, Cornwall?" Ardys asked, fearing his answer.

Bontemps laughed, a hearty sound. "What smuggler does not? There is a ready market for my French brandy there, and the people have a delightful habit of looking away when a ship comes into one of their coves! I am bound for that coast now, in fact—after I have visited my friends here and picked up my rum at the Canaries."

"Michel!" Marie said to him, interrupting in their native tongue, "could you take this poor child home? She comes from England, and I believe she will ask you."

Michel turned to Ardys. *Mademoiselle,* " he said formally in French, "I would be honored to have you aboard my vessel, if you wish to return to the land of your birth."

Ardys's heart leaped. "Aye! Oh, aye, as soon as you leave, I will be happy to go with you!"

She saw the sadness in Marie's eyes, the tears that were forming. "It is not that you have not been kind to me, Marie," she said quickly, "you and Jacques. But I do not belong here. I will always remember how ye took care of me. And I will always remember that my son is buried here."

Marie smiled. "I will bring flowers to his grave and I will

tell the priests to say masses for his soul. And I will also plant flowers there that will attract ze little hummingbirds."

Marie planted a huge bunch of orange flute-like flowers beside the little grave of Ardys's son. The hummingbirds found the flowers within a day and now there was always movement and life near the site.

On the day she was to leave, Ardys spent a long time there alone. She saw the colors of the flowers, smelled their heady fragrance, and jumped a bit when one of the tiny birds buzzed next to her.

She bent and gently touched the warm and smooth unmarked stone at the head of the grave.

"I must leave ye here, my son, my little nameless one," she whispered. "How sorry I am that your stay with me was so short! But I have to leave you. I have to live, I have to go on. I need my life. Forgive me, little one. 'Tis a beautiful, peaceful place you lie in. Ye can watch these little jewels of birds as they sparkle over you."

She straightened. "I will never forget you, my little boy. 'Tis a promise. Someday mayhap I will find your father and tell him of you, and we will come here together to see where you lie so peacefully in this warm, gentle place."

Michel's trading business on Desirade was completed in five short days, and on Sunday the eighteenth of June his little galley set out to sea once more, carrying replenished stores of food and water, a new cargo of pineapple and coconuts, and one passenger.

Marie stood on the beach and waved until her arm was sore, shouting her blessings. The small ship disappeared from her view quickly, and she turned and walked back to Jacques and her cabin.

CHAPTER FOURTEEN

The Canary Islands, off the western coast of the African continent, were a natural stopping place for all the ships that sailed the Atlantic. They were a convenient source of water and victuals, and those traveling to the Caribbean made a side trip to the Canaries, the last shores they would see before they set their course southeast, into the open sea.

The *Espada* had been patrolling the waters of the mid-Atlantic for weeks when her captain was finally persuaded to make for the Canaries to revictual. Unlike most ships, the *Espada* approached the islands from the south. 'Connell knew his crew were weary, bored from the lack of action, and eager to return to their homes to begin spending the wealth they had stolen from the Spanish treasure ship.

There had been no mutiny. The crew realized that the only way they would arrive home safely to spend its wealth was to follow their captain. It wasn't so much a question of loyalty as it was a question of survival. George, the helmsman and the only passable navigator other than Desmond, was solidly behind Kirkconnell and had told the captain he would not navigate the ship if he were overthrown.

Kirkconnell, still not trusting his men with the truth, did not tell the men that this jaunt into the Canaries was only a necessary diversion, not the first leg of the trip home. He had vowed he would not leave the sea until he had found François de la Roche, killed him, and rescued Ardys. Let the crew grumble, let them dream their dreams of new clothes and new women: he was the captain, and did not answer to them.

Bled could not make him see reason and had given up trying.

The month of June was almost gone, and still no sign of the Frenchman. But find him Kirkconnell would, if it took the rest of his life to do it. Perhaps in the ports of the Canaries there would be news. He glanced up at the crow's nest, high above the deck, squinting into the sun.

"How long 'til we make landfall, Bled?" Kirkconnell called.

Kennwyn leaned carefully over the edge of the narrow platform and shouted down to the captain: "Tonight, mebbe tomorrow, Cap'n 'Connell, if all goes well."

It was well. The sooner they were gone from the islands, the better Kirkconnell would feel. He prowled the decks restlessly, and his crew scrambled to stay out of his way.

What was one woman when he was rich enough to have a dozen, thought Desmond grimly. But for me there is only one woman. She is everything to me. Without Ardys, nothing matters. If I cannot find her, I will never go back to Shelagh, never return to Ireland. The Tyrone can go hang. I have no home, no happiness without my fencing lass.

The day was sultry and windless, the heat on deck oppressive. Best not to drive the men too hard in this weather. Let them rest a little, before we go ashore. Bled might be right. After, I must tell them that we are not going home, but heading out into the Main once more. Desmond stood at the rail and watched for the land.

Aloft, Kennwyn eased his cramped legs, glad that his turn in the crow's nest was nearly over. He could see the islands in the distance, green specks on the horizon that grew larger and larger. Hard to see in this weather, Bled thought sleepily; the heat shimmers off the sea in waves and clouds the view.

Jesu, I could use a drink! One last look round all points, then I'll call for the next man to come an' relieve me. Was it

Bremmer next, or Chasewick? Damned if I mind the one, but it don't make no difference, long as someone climbs up and lets me out of this nest.

Strange how a man's eyes play tricks when he looks too long at one spot on the horizon. Things seem to appear that could not be there at all . . .

"Mother of God!" Bled shouted. "A black sail, a black sail, off the port beam! Cap'n 'Connell, a black sail!"

Bled was hoarse suddenly, his throat constricted, and his voice would not carry. But soon they would all see what he had seen, what he had never thought to see again.

Kirkconnell was at the port rail, leaning on one of the culverin. He stood straight suddenly, unbelieving, and stared.

"Nay, it cannot be. Not the one—surely any ship's sails, from this distance, would look black," he whispered.

"Cap'n 'Connell! Do ye see?" Kennwyn's voice, barely heard.

"Aye. By God, I see," said Kirkconnell softly, his hands on his hips.

He must go into his cabin, and fetch Ardys's rapier. He would kill de la Roche with it, and then return it to her. For some moments Desmond could not move, and when he did he felt himself to be somehow suspended in time, moving slowly. His Ardys. So close now, on board the Frenchman's ship—after all this time, he would see his Ardys again!

The black sails grew progressively larger as the two ships drew closer together. The ship was heading northeast, tacking back and forth to catch the breeze that would maneuver her into the port. Around Desmond the crew began to take notice, and many of them recognized the *Corbeau*. Instinctively they felt for their weapons, and began to see to the great guns. None of them spoke to the captain, standing tall and motionless at the rail.

The day was quiet, the wind soft, the sea a deep, dense blue under a hazy, cloudless sky. Kirkconnell waited. The other ship's crew must have seen the *Espada* by now, but she did not change her course, and indeed seemed now to be on a direct intercepting line. A few hundred yards away, Kirkconnell could see the low decks and the shape of the ship. There was no doubt now. It was the *Corbeau*.

Across the water, François de la Roche stood at his rail, his first mate at his side.

"The *Espada* is a floating castle," the mate said.

"*Oui*. She is easy to recognize. I saw her long before she saw us," de la Roche agreed.

"And she rides very low, does she not? She is heavily laden, and will be sluggish," the mate said.

"She will be no match for us! Here, then, will be the end of Desmond Kirkconnell," De la Roche smiled, his black eyes narrowing. "Another man's seed. We shall see."

At the wheel of the *Espada* now, Kirkconnell spoke quietly to his pilot, George.

"Bring her around, and come up behind, so the broadside guns'll bear on their stern-castle. That'll cripple their steering, and make them easy prey."

"Cap'n," George began, worried, as the *Corbeau* approached faster. "We're too slow moving, with all the cargo below . . ."

Kirkconnell glared. "Do it."

Obediently George spun the wheel.

Calling Kennwyn to his side, Desmond issued his orders.

"Have the men board her, but do not fire into her after the first battery has done its work; I cannot risk more than one broadside with Ardys aboard. Kill every last man on the

Corbeau, no quarter, but not de la Roche. I will keelhaul any man who robs me of the pleasure of killing de la Roche."

The captain of the *Corbeau* gave similar orders, but for different reasons. There would be time enough to sink the *Espada*; first de la Roche must know what she carried in her holds.

"One broadside will be sufficient," said de la Roche confidently to his mate, "then we will board."

In the shimmering silence the two crews listened for the first shot, their tension rising. The *Espada* wallowed to the south of the *Corbeau*, keeping a distance of two hundred yards, and brought her guns to bear.

"Ha! We could almost fit that entire ship into our hold!" Kirkconnell said as he nodded to the gunners.

There was a puff of smoke from the *Corbeau*, and immediately the *Espada's* gunners answered with their own fire. The boom of the cannon's volley came scant seconds after the spit of the fire, splitting the silence of the summer day.

The *Corbeau* made a direct hit: the main mast of the *Espada* went down with a crash and a screaming of splintering wood, the unfurled sails floating like a great lifeless bird to the deck.

Aboard the *Corbeau* there was less damage. The *Espada's* first battery guns were high above the level of the smaller ship, and the cannonballs either sailed over or merely tore holes in the *Corbeau's* canvas.

The two captains signaled the same maneuver, and the ships rammed together with a deafening roar. Grappling irons shot out from both ships, but the Frenchman's crew could not make the high swing up onto the *Espada's* deck, and they found their own decks were soon swarming with Kirkconnell's men.

Desmond leapt down onto the *Corbeau*, his dagger again

in his teeth and Ardys's rapier naked in his hand. All about him the fighting began, swords flashing dangerously close as he made his way to the stern of the *Corbeau*. A wicked slash, a quick thrust, and he cleared his path; those who did not move aside fast enough died.

While the carnage boiled around him, Kirkconnell searched for de la Roche.

If I were in command of this ship, Desmond thought, I would be at the wheel, with my pilot. Let the crew look to the fighting while I try to free my ship, maneuver her away for a clear shot at the enemy vessel.

A few more steps, then a short ladder to the tiller. Brushing the smoke from his eyes, Desmond finally spotted the familiar black-cloaked figure of de la Roche at the wheel. He was speaking urgently in French to his helmsman, and his long rapier dripped red as he pointed at the *Espada* and gave his instructions.

At his feet lay a sailor, dead, but Kirkconnell could not tell if the man was one of his or one of the *Corbeau's*. A volley of musket-fire had obliterated the sailor's face.

Across the stretch of sea, high atop the stern-castle of the *Espada*, Bleddyn had a clear view of the battle. The losses on both sides appeared to be equal, but in the smoke and noise it was difficult to tell when the balance of the fighting shifted in favor of the *Espada's* crew. In spite of the sluggishness of their ship, there were many more of them, and they had the advantage of attacking from above, while the Frenchmen had to wait for them, and had time to think and become afraid.

On the *Corbeau*, de la Roche saw Kirkconnell bound up the ladder, and whirled to face him. There was a flicker of surprise in de la Roche's expression, nothing more. He kicked the corpse of the faceless sailor so that it rolled heavily onto the lower deck, leaving more room, and smiled tightly at Kirkconnell.

The French helmsman clung to his wheel, concentrating on his attempt to guide the *Corbeau* away from the *Espada* while there was still time. Kirkconnell considered a moment, calculating, then threw his dagger. The point burrowed deep into the helmsman's neck, and his head snapped back with the force of the blow. He could not cry out, and he fell onto his wheel with a gurgle of spilling blood.

De la Roche never blinked.

"*Mon ami* Kirkconnell. How enchanting to meet with you in these circumstances."

He shrugged the cloak from his shoulders and hung it carefully over one of the spokes of the wheel; took off his doublet jacket as well and slung it with the cape, taking care that it should not be soiled by the blood of his helmsman. They had, he judged, about ten square feet to fight in, and he turned to Kirkconnell once more, taking a step forward as he drew his short dagger from his belt and brought his sword up. He held the sword in his left hand. The tips of the two blades nearly touched.

"Where is she?" demanded Kirkconnell, glaring at de la Roche with scarcely controlled fury.

"She? There is no woman here," de la Roche circled.

Desmond matched François step for step. "Liar! Where is my Ardys? You took her from Dungannon. Against her will, I have no doubt."

"Ah, I see! The lovely *cherié. Oui,* I took her, but you seek her here in vain. She has been gone for oh, many weeks now."

There was death in the diamond glitter of Kirkconnell's eyes. De la Roche saw it as surely as he saw the sun through the haze of the battle. Veiled by Desmond's dark hair and his sweat, but there nonetheless. François lunged then, a decisive feint and thrust that tore the cloth of Kirkconnell's jacket and scraped the skin of his arm.

Kirkconnell lunged simultaneously, not feeling the prick of the other's blade, but his thrust met only air, whistling harmlessly by de la Roche's left shoulder. The Frenchman pivoted, keeping Kirkconnell to his front, and feinted to the left; but Desmond parried quickly, drove in under de la Roche's arm, and circled the rapier from his grasp. It skittered along the slippery wood of the deck and fetched up at the rail, rocking gently on its basket hilt.

With only the dagger to defend his life, de la Roche backed, trying to draw Kirkconnell closer, but Desmond was not so easily maneuvered, and he kept his sword at the Frenchman's heart.

"Once more," Kirkconnell said. "Ardys Trevallon."

François' black eyes narrowed. "She is dead," he hissed, backing before the sword. Then he gathered his strength and threw his dagger at Kirkconnell's face, a wild shot that missed Desmond's right ear by inches. De la Roche felt the low rail at his back; he could go no farther.

"Why should I lie?" he continued reasonably, a mocking smile on his lips. "If she were on this ship, would she not have been in this battle? Do you not know her well enough to know she would be here among the men, her sword drawn?"

"She is with child," Desmond said, "she cannot fight now."

"Ha! The child you left her with—your brat in her belly killed her!" de la Roche laughed. "She died in child-bed, and the babe as well. Your son and your woman, both dead. I was with her, and she cursed the name of Desmond Kirkconnell to the last moment of her life, to her last dying breath she cursed you, the man who caused her death, despising you, the betrayer of her love, the man who left her for another woman."

Kirkconnell heard no more. Rage engulfed him, filled him, consumed him. His heart pounded and his eyes burned. Almost casually, he slowly brought the tip of his sword to touch de la Roche's chest and drove it slowly and savagely through fabric, skin, bone. De la Roche's eyes widened but he made no sound, collapsing onto the blade that Kirkconnell held steady under the man's weight while the flesh tore.

Desmond watched the dark fountain well up, pulsing hotly, and then he stepped aside, drew Ardys's sword out of the Frenchman's flesh, and lowered the blade, letting de la Roche fall to the deck in the pool of his own blood.

"You killed her," came the dying whisper, and a rasping laugh. "She cursed you with her dying breath."

De la Roche's eyes, fixed open, glazed, and were still.

Desmond stepped back from the body and staggered to the rail, reeling, and below, on the deck, one of de la Roche's men took careful aim with his musket and fired.

From the wheel of the *Espada* Bleddyn Kennwyn saw and shouted a warning, but Kirkconnell never heard. He went down on top of the Frenchman, and Bled saw the blood of the two enemies mingling on the *Corbeau*'s deck.

The gunners left alive on the *Corbeau*, seeing their captain dead, fired their last culverin battery into the hull of the *Espada*, close to the water line. Their culverin did not light properly this time, however, and the flame leapt across some rags to a pile of balls nearby, which exploded. The force of the blast blew the gunners apart, opened a small hole above the *Corbeau*'s waterline, and sheered the two ships from each other.

Straining the grappling hooks, the lines snapped and the sea pushed the ships back together. The bow of the *Corbeau* ripped into the side of the *Espada* with a crash.

The sea rushed into the gap in the galleon's flank with a roar, and the *Espada*, top-heavy and loaded too fully, immediately began to list. On her deck, Bled rallied the men still on board, telling them to forget the treasure and abandon ship, to leap to the relative safety of the *Corbeau*, but the crew scrambled instead to fill their pockets and hands with silver ingots from the *Espada*'s hold, crowding the trap door in the main deck in their mad rush to save their riches, tripping over each other and brawling in their haste.

"The *Espada*'s done, she'll sink, look to the boats!" Kennwyn shouted as the *Corbeau* broke free again and began to float almost gracefully away from the side of the larger ship. "The other ship'll hold you all—there be no time for the silver, leave it, ye fools! What good is silver in a dead man's hand?"

There was no Frenchman alive on the *Corbeau* now, and her black sails luffed fitfully, her tiller untended.

Resolute, Kennwyn stayed at the *Espada*'s wheel, determined to keep vigil for the dying ship, which was rapidly listing to her starboard side as her hold filled with water.

As he watched, Bled saw many of the *Espada*'s men, seeing the relentless drag of the sea, come to their senses and jump overboard, kicking away from the dying ship. The cook Grimsthorpe, his back hunched further by the silver in his belt, leaped into the water and sank, never to come up. The men who were quick enough to jettison their treasure before sinking broke the surface and made for the *Corbeau*, swimming for their lives: Kennwyn knew that when the *Espada* went under, she would suck everything in range down with her.

Bled felt the first shudder as the sea began its taking. He could no longer see the *Corbeau*, which had drifted some degrees to port. He closed his eyes and prayed, tried to think of the green land of his birth, and to call to the soul of his captain, whose blood mixed with that of de la Roche.

With a mighty groan the huge ship fell to her side and began to slide beneath the waves.

CHAPTER FIFTEEN

In the waning days of August, the *Aigrette*, the little three-master owned by Michel Bontemps, put into harbor at the island of Tenerife, the largest of the Canaries.

The weeks of sun, rain, and fresh salt air did Ardys Trevallon much good. She stood on the deck for hours, the wind in her hair, and listened to the sounds of the ship and the sea, not thinking. The color returned to her face, and the hollows of her cheeks filled out once more. She was eating well, better certainly than the crew of the *Aigrette*, for she shared the captain's table.

This was different from the other voyages she had made in the space of this last year: she was going home, and she was not with Kirkconnell or de la Roche. There were no demands made on her body or her heart: on the *Aigrette* she was a passenger and a friend of the captain's, nothing more.

There was no one to impress. For this time she could cease to be herself, cease to be the daughter of the Fencing Master or the lover of Kirkconnell or the prisoner of de la Roche or the valued member of the English court.

"This island is beautiful," she said to Michel as the men of the *Aigrette* dropped anchor in the sheltered cove of Tenerife. Lush, green jungle and bright splashes where flowers bloomed among the trees, and she saw a quiet, white-sanded beach and a small town of neat, thatched cottages, each with a red roof and a little garden plot. Each family with its own house, its garden, its goat, and all around the smell of the sea and the wet palm forest.

"I could live here, take another name, tend plants and

goats, and grow old and fat and content like Marie," she said, and laughed.

"Your laughter is like so much sweet music, *mamselle*," said Michel.

"Ah, *M'sieur*, see those palm trees! I remember how hard it is to climb trees like them—every one of the natives I saw try to do so on Desirade slid down again, landing on his backside."

"With respect, *Mamselle* Ardys, these trees are a different sort altogether, much easier to climb."

She smiled at him. "I do not believe that. These also have no branches, no ridges in the bark, nothing for a grip."

"How can you say it is hard when you have not tried yourself?" Bontemps teased, his button mouth pursed as he gazed to the shore. "You should not make judgment without trial."

"I do not think . . ." She paused. "By God, lend me a pair of your britches and I will try!"

Michel said happily, "I will wager ten gold pieces that you will make the top knot of that tree, there at the south end of the beach, the tall one that leans over—in the time it takes for the small hourglass on my desk to empty."

"This is an opposite to the English way of betting, Michel! If I accept your wager, that means I shall be betting against myself," she said gravely, a twinkle in her eye as she looked across to the tree. "But if I agree with you that it can be done, there is no wager at all."

She stopped, staring down the length of the beach. "Nay, it cannot be," she breathed.

"*Mamselle?*" Bontemps said, turning to look also.

Ardys blinked, tried to convince herself that she was not seeing the man running along the soft sand, his bare feet leaving tracks. Small of stature, red hair, fair beard;

waving frantically at the *Aigrette.*

Bleddyn Kennwyn.

The long boat scraped onto the beach and Ardys was out and running before the sailors were able to pull it from the water. When she made her dash she did not hear Michel and the others shout in surprise, for her forward kick sent the boat spinning back into the shallows.

She did not see the *Espada* in the harbor, but the ship must be nearby, it must. And if the *Espada* was here, then Kirkconnell must be as well!

No time to speculate, Ardys crossed the beach and threw herself into Bled's arms, embracing him as she would a lost brother, laughing and crying at the same time while he held her gingerly, astonished.

"Mistress Trevallon," he began, trying to disentangle himself.

"Bleddyn Kennwyn! I never thought to see you, and surely not here, in the midst of the great ocean! How came you to be here—where is Desmond, and where is the *Espada?* You must meet Captain Bontemps, he brought me here, but first, tell me . . ."

"Bontemps? The man there, by the boat? Aye, please take me to him, I have an urgent request to make of him." Bled was talking quickly, sidestepping her breathless questions.

"Come, then!" Ardys grabbed his hand and dragged him over to Michel, who was seeing to the beaching of the rest of his longboats.

"Michel—pardon, Captain Bontemps!" she came up to him, Kennwyn behind her. "This is Bleddyn Kennwyn, he is first mate on the *Espada,* an old friend of mine."

Bontemps bowed, and saw the raggedness of Kennwyn's clothing and the thinness of his sunburned face which Ardys had not noticed.

Bled bowed painfully from the waist, wincing with strain in his back.

"Cap'n Bontemps," he said, touching his forelock and glancing at Ardys.

"Ah, first mate on the *Espada*? I do not know the ship. Is it anchored at one of the other islands?"

"Nay. Bain't here," Kennwyn said miserably. Ardys started. "I pray ye, don't ask me 'bout the *Espada*."

"Where is she?" Ardys demanded. Kennwyn was weak, she now saw for the first time, and dirty and half-starved. Desmond was not with him, and was nowhere in sight. "Tell me, Bled, please, you must tell me what happened."

Kennwyn looked at the sand. "Sank," he said softly.

"That massive galleon? It could not have sunk—it could never have sunk—not while Desmond lived. Where is Captain Kirkconnell? Oh, God, Bled, where is the crew? Who—who is here after yourself?"

"All dead, but for meself and three other sailors."

Bontemps stepped in, taking Bled's arm, trying to draw him away from the girl. She stood utterly still and silent, and her dark eyes wide.

"Come, *mon ami*, I see you have suffered much. There is an inn near by, we shall share some rum and you can tell me what has happened." Bontemps' business on Tenerife would wait.

The two men turned to walk up the beach, toward the paths that led inland to the town. Ardys moved suddenly, and ran to block their way.

She cried, "Nay. Tell me now. Tell me, Bled, tell me where Captain Kirkconnell is, for Jesu's sake, tell me!"

"Dead, lady." Kennwyn said. "There was a battle, with the *Corbeau* . . . there," he pointed vaguely out to sea.

"The *Corbeau*?"

"Aye. Cap'n Kirkconnell went after de la Roche, and killed him."

"De la Roche—you mean François de la Roche?"

"Is there another? Aye, it was he 'Connell wanted. But the *Espada* took a broadside, and went down, faster'n ye'd ever believe."

Ardys shut her eyes against the blinding sun. She felt the breeze move her hair, the fabric of Marie's castoff dress on her body, the heat of the sand through her light slippers.

"Kirkconnell is dead, then," she said, taking a deep breath and looking at Kennwyn.

"Aye," said Bled. "He ran de la Roche through, but there was a musket shot, took him in the back. I saw from the *Espada*. Oh, my lady, 'tis sorry I am."

She waited while the beach righted itself, ignoring the dizziness that swept her. "I knew. I knew, when I saw you alone. And the ship is not here."

"He died well, Mistress. In battle, like he would've wished. He must have been right glad to have killed de la Roche."

"You must tell me all, Bled. I need to hear it all."

Calmly she began to walk ahead of the two men, leading them toward the town.

"Cap'n Bontemps, I must ask ye somethin' first," Bled said. "I need to get to Ireland. Be there room on your ship? I can work my passage, scrubbin', workin' the rigging, whatever needs to be done . . ."

Michel looked Kennwyn over.

"*Oui.* Of course, I can always use a good seaman. Now put it from your mind," he said kindly. "First we will see that you eat."

"We are not bound for Ireland, Bled, we're bound for England," Ardys said, amazed that she was still on her feet.

"Sooth, will you not go back to Wales, Bled, to Glamorgan, wasn't that your home?"

"After. First I must get to Ireland," Bled said.

"To Dungannon, to the Tyrone?"

He shook his head. "Nay. I must go to Tullaghoge."

"But, why—" Ardys stopped. Then she said, very low: "I understand. Ye must tell Desmond's wife that she is a widow."

Over the meal at the small inn on the north road of the main town of Tenerife, Bled told his story. The pursuit of the *Corbeau*, and the reason for it; the capture of the silver treasure ship, the battle with the French pirate and his crew. The deaths of the two captains.

He spoke in a monotone, between mouthfuls. Ardys listened and did not speak. She heard him say that he had been lucky enough to survive and make it to Tenerife, along with the three others that had clung to one of the spars and kicked their way onto the beach many days before.

"You are eating far too fast, Bled," Ardys said reasonably. "You shall lose all this food and feel worse than ye did before."

Kirkconnell's duel with de la Roche Kennwyn described as best he could. She listened, watching him in the small, ill-lit room. There were only three rooms in the inn, and this one was for the common use of all. The building was made of mud and wattle, supported by thin pieces of wood at the corners, and the side that faced the street boasted one small window. There was no glass, no oiled paper to keep the insects out, and flies and beetles flew all around them, settling on the food and on their hands.

Too many sailors pass through here, she thought. They come ashore to drink and eat and whore, and leave only offal behind them. In the background, not completely disguised by the smell of the meat pie Kennwyn was consuming with obvious relish, there was a faint sour odor of urine and vomit.

When Bled finished, she said slowly: "So he left her, to find me. He could not know where de la Roche would take me, yet he left his wife and came, for me. He lost his ship, for me. Desmond killed de la Roche, and himself was killed, all because he loved me, and could not bear to lose me."

"Aye. That was the way of it," Bled agreed. "The *Corbeau* drifted out into the sea, with those of our *Espada* crew lucky enough to get aboard her afore our ship sank. I hope to find some o' them in Ireland, around Dungannon, though there be little chance o' that. Even if they did make the trip on the *Corbeau*, most of them had no home to go to and would probably make for the first port city they sighted, to sign onto another vessel. 'Tis only reasonable—a man has to make a livin', an' sailors know no other way."

Ardys sat with her chin in her hand, listening. Bontemps asked the proper questions at the proper times.

"Then Kirkconnell is gone, and it is over." Ardys said to them, dead inside and very calm. "Strange, I did not sense his death. I cannot imagine that he could die anywhere in the world and I would not know it somehow. So there is no chance for us, now. I have only my memories. But now I know that he loved me! He did love me after all, he came for me because he loved me and not her, and now I can go home to Cornwall and grow old with that thought to sustain me. I can ask for nothing more. I need nothing more. In a very real way, I am his widow . . ."

"An' that poor cat," Bled was saying. "Drifted by me, trying to swim to the beach. Never liked the water, that cat, wouldn' budge off the *Espada* for nothin'. I tried to grab him, but he only scratched at me, and I couldna' hold onto him, so he kept on goin', and 'twas too far for him, I know. Like a member of the crew he were . . ."

"Ah, how sad," Ardys said, as though from far away. "Poor Great Harry."

"Aye, Mistress."

"How sad," she repeated. "How very sad."

She remembered the first time she had seen the cat, there on Kirkconnell's great bed, in his cabin. How troubled she had been, and how stirred.

Perhaps there was peace in the finality of Desmond's death. Now that she knew he had loved her, perhaps she could find peace. After the pain . . .

CHAPTER SIXTEEN

Mid-October, Cornwall

Alice Trevallon surveyed herself in the little polished silver looking glass with some satisfaction. The small amount of white powder she had applied to her face hid the wrinkles nicely; and she was sure she could almost pass for a woman of thirty. No longer young, but not yet old, either. She patted her hair, piled in curls on her head, drawn back from her brow, ornamented with tiny twinkling jewels, and tucked the stray strands back behind her ears.

Her gown was wonderful, the finest Alice had ever seen, much less worn, living as she had in the country all her life. It was pale orange damask with voluminous over-sleeves and a large, drum-like farthingale that broadened her hips by a foot on each side. A riot of bright embroidery covered the low-cut bodice, and at the neckline was a collar of off-white lace, starched to stand up stiffly. She would have to move carefully down the narrow aisle of the chapel, lest she dislodge some part of the stays beneath. She held out her foot to admire her dainty white heel-less leather slippers, and turned from the mirror with a smile.

"Well, daughter? What think you, how say ye of your mother's appearance this day?"

Ardys said stiffly: "Ye look lovely, Madam. That dress sets off the color of your hair."

Alice considered. "You still look too pale, Ardys. 'Tis well for a woman to be white skinned; certainly ladies born spend no time in the sun! But too white, without artifice, looks sickly."

"You mean if I were white because I had slavered powder on, I would look satisfactory for you?" Ardys asked. "If ye prefer, I will not attend the ceremony. In fact, I would be grateful not to have to be there."

"Silly girl! Of course you must be there! Have you not but recent reappeared among us—from the dead, for all we knew? Are you not my eldest, most cherished daughter? Is this not my wedding day?"

Ardys said, "Yes, madam."

Ardys was a pale reflection of the girl that had left so long ago to go with her father to the court. Even in her new lavender and blue gown, hastily made by the seamstress in Falmouth in five days, Ardys looked wan.

Her mother hesitated. "Ardys, we have not really known each other these many years. I have something—I found something that I think ye will be pleased to have."

She reached into a drawer of her cupboard and brought out some yellowed papers, rolled and tied with a faded ribbon. " 'Tis a letter your father wrote to me, when first he went to the court so long ago."

Startled, Ardys took the letter, handling it gingerly.

"I thank you, madam," she whispered, and went over to stand nearer the tall window, where the light was better for reading. Tentatively she untied the ribbon and gently unrolled the papers. Her father's small, precise handwriting was still clear.

August, 1577

My lady Wife:

Our goodly company did arrive at Greenwich upon the second day of September. We met few Hazards on our way, but the journey was most vexing tedious. I will not paine you with the telling of it. Our spirits were much lightened by the sight of that splendid Palace. I am now lodg'd to the rear of that part that faceth the waterfront, along with most of the other Entertainers and soldiers. Our goode Lord Helford sleeps elsewhere, within the main Building, but I have not seen his quarters. The Day of the Queene's birth, the seventh of September, the entire Court, to the lowest kitchen churl, gathered in the tiltyard to give thanks for her Benevolent Reigne and to pray for her continued Goode Health. She stood, most Sovereign Lady, (it is said she mislikes to sit at all if she need not) upon a raised platform above the multitude, and blessed us all in words most Gracious, for our loyalty. The fencing came at the last of the day, and the Skye had clouded, as it ever will, so that we feared in the rain the Queene would become wet in her goode Person, and some felt the contest should be moved inside the great hall. When Lord Burghley did suggest this to her (and this I have from his manservant, who has become my frende), she laughed Heartily and said that no rain in this world could harm her, shielded as she is by her People's love, and whenever had an honest English rain harmed anyone? (Happily, it rain'd not.) I venture to say that my Fencing pleased Her Majesty. Many men set against me, both singly and in pairs, and with God's helpe (and by my superior skill, I vow), I vanquished them all. After, I saw her well when I knelt before her and kiss'd her hande. Her hands are slender and long and beautifully form'd. She is young still, white of skin and very beautiful. Her bearing is Regal and her gowne flashed with the light of many precious Jewels, such as I have never seen. Her hair is as red as was her great Father's, and she wears it in a pile atop her head, with Pearls fastened in amongst the curls. I include this detail for your pleasure, my lady Wife! I recall not her exact Words to me, so full of awe was I to stand so close to her, but her tone was Kinde and she did enquire of me my name and Household. I answered, rising when she bid me, and then she did ask me of Cornwall: Was it so green as she had heard, and was Spring there so sweet as it is in London. I reply'd (and whence I summon'd the Wit I know not) that Spring was sweetest wheree'er she Dwelt, which answer pleas'd her well. To make an end, my Wife, I am now Master of the Fence to the Court of the Queene, which exalted rank she did then bestow upon me in front of that crowd, to my great pride. I have many duties, but chief among them is instructing the young men in her service in my humble Arte. And so I know not when I shall return unto you, my Sweet Alice. May God keep you and our Childe that must by now have arrived, until such time as I may Return, or until, as I hope, the Queene alloweth me to send for you both. Write me your news!

I remain, your faithful
W.

Ardys stood silently, holding the letter. Her eyes sparkled wetly, but the tears did not fall.

"Thank you, madam, for letting me see this," she finally said. "This letter is precious, like a jewel."

" 'Tis yours, my daughter, with my love. And, I think, with your father's."

In truth, Alice found it an annoyance that Ardys should so suddenly appear at this time. No warning, no message or letter, no time to prepare a welcome that would have been proper: but that was like the girl, always bound to do the thing that should cause her mother the most discomfort. A knock at the main door of Helford House a fortnight gone, and a demand of admittance from the servant who of course did not recognize her. If Alice had not happened to wander through the hall while Ardys argued with the chamberlain,

Ardys might well have been turned away like the slut she appeared to be: ragged, unkempt and dressed in a gown many sizes too large.

Alice had hesitated, then let out a cry of surprise and embraced her, and Ardys had begun to tell a wild, improbable tale of slipping off a Caribbean smuggler's ship the night previous at Falmouth, hiking across the rocks and cliffs to Killigerran Head in the blackness of the dawn.

The reunion of Ardys and her sisters had been warm and touching to see.

Alice tried to feel joy at her prodigal daughter's return, knowing that because she was the girl's mother, such feelings should come naturally. But Alice had little success manufacturing a feeling of motherly solicitude. She was much more concerned with the arrangements for her own imminent marriage to Lord Percival Longhoughton, and felt jealous that she would lose some of the attention due her at this time.

Ardys was spared further questions after the welcomes were said, and was bustled straight to bed with a posset. An exhausted sleep overtook her, and she did not waken for the better part of two days.

After she recovered some of her strength, Ardys offered to help her mother with preparations for the wedding. All week there were celebrations, joustings in the wide, gently sloping field overlooking the sea, banquets in the great hall, and masques in the courtyard. With a thin, hesitant smile, Ardys attended.

Percy Longhoughton kissed Ardys on the mouth, wetly and overlong, when they met. She took an instant dislike to him, with his affected manners and bulging eyes. And God have mercy that any man should be cursed with such an ugly nose. Ardys saw the anger in her mother's rigid stance and endeavored to be polite to Percy, swallowing her comment that if he thought he could ever take the place of William Trevallon, he was a greater fool than even he appeared.

The couple was to be wed by Helford's family chaplain, in the chapel of Helford House, and then they would leave, to live at Longhoughton's newly-purchased estate at Porthtowan. Situated five miles south of Helford House, with a twelve-room manor house and a commanding view of the Channel, Porthtowan was closer to Falmouth, and the house set back from the sea over its own small beach and natural harbor, secluded and hidden by the cliffs along the coast road.

Ardys tried to be glad for her mother.

Percy Longhoughton wrote long and detailed reports to Idiaquez, the Spanish King's secretary, and at preset intervals, when the Spanish ships lay far off the coast in the deepest hour of the night, he would creep down to the cove below Killigerran Head and give them into the hand of waiting Spanish sailors. Few words were spoken, for the messengers were not in the confidence of the King's secretary, and it was best not to take unnecessary risks. Longhoughton wrote in fluent Spanish, never signed his name, and was sure that in the event that the English patrols were lucky enough to intercept his letters, they could never be traced to him.

As Percy Longhoughton, Lord Percival Berwick had naturally spent some time riding about his new estate, and he had taken the opportunity to observe more than Porthtowan's crops and tenant farmers.

He drew careful maps of fortifications, and of the new fortress he had heard was being built at St. Mawes; he knew which ships were put to sea and which were beached for careening and refitting, he noted if the English seamen were paid on time, and what their attitudes were toward their captains and admirals. He watched for signs of discontent and mutiny, sure that they must someday come. No detail was too small to be mentioned in his dispatches. He gloated secretly, thinking what an integral part of Philip's plan for the second Armada he and his fellow spies were.

Away from Helford House, Longhoughton would be even safer. The only thorn that pricked him was the fact that there were no Catholics among the local people; no priest to hear his confession, no masses to attend. He went to the Anglican services at Helford House, gritting his teeth when he felt himself surrounded by the Lutherans—spawn of Satan! It was all for the greater glory of Mother Church, he said to himself, and the needs of one poor sinner could not come before the purpose of the True Faith.

He was fearful that if he should die or be killed among these people, he would not have the comfort of the last rites. When the household was asleep, he would take his crucifix and his rosary from a secret compartment in his jewel box and pray for his soul's safe delivery. He hoped Alice was a sound sleeper so that he could continue his nightly devotions. They had not spoken of his secrets again.

Ha! He thought crudely, I shall see that she is too exhausted by my lovemaking to wake once sleep claims her.

Fragrant flowers filled the chapel at Helford House on the day of the wedding. The autumn was mild this year, and the blooms had not dropped as they usually did; Ardys, with two maidservants, had combed the gardens to find those with the headiest scents and the brightest colors. A long, thin carpet was laid on the aisle of the chapel, and Alice's daughters scattered rose petals down its length in the early morning.

The day had dawned rainy and cool, but the chapel could

be reached from the main house by the east corridor and no one would risk soiling their clothes. By the hour of one, the chancel was filled.

Ardys looked grimly at the crowd. The marriage of the widow Alice Trevallon was clearly something of a curiosity. Will Trevallon was scarcely cold in his grave!

Longhoughton was rich, however. And that counted for much. At least the economics of Alice Trevallon's new liaison were easy to understand.

Ardys knew she was a curiosity because she had lived at the court, and had learned to fence; now, with wild rumors circulating about her life among pirates and savages she was openly stared at. She held her head high and glared at any who met her eye.

An abrupt hush went over the gathering at half past one when a lone man entered the balcony. Ardys recognized him at once. Tall and powerfully built, dark-haired, and clad in a bright scarlet and gold velvet doublet came Sir Walter Ralegh of Devon: Lord Lieutenant of Cornwall, poet, hero of Cadiz, pirate and founder of the first English colony in the New World on Roanoke Island, off the coast of Virginia.

He came alone, unannounced, riding across from Devon unattended by servants. Ardys wondered that the great man would trouble to come to the wedding of a country widow.

At a few minutes after two, the bridal party entered through the main door of the chapel and began the slow, solemn walk up the aisle. Ardys and her sister Elizabeth attended Alice, and the bride was radiant as any young virgin going to her virile young beloved.

Longhoughton followed with the bishop and the ten-year-old boy who was serving as ring-bearer. Sir Walter sat forward and leaned on the railing of the balcony.

The principals stood in a half-circle before the bishop, a

respected man imported from Falmouth for the occasion, assisted by the Helford family chaplain. The words were intoned, the ring slid onto Alice's finger, the blessings given, and the thing was done. The proud groom held his new wife and kissed her, then took her by the hand to lead the way back to the great hall for the wedding feast.

Ardys stood calmly through the brief exchange of vows and followed the couple down the aisle to the door with a fixed, empty smile. Her mother was more of a stranger now than she had been when Ardys was a child, and this Lord, so full of himself, was nothing.

"I missed my father's funeral," Ardys said under her breath, "but truly I have seen him buried today. From the look in my mother's eyes you would think this Longhoughton to be the first man she has ever known."

Ardys glanced out the window and saw that the rain had ceased, though clouds still scudded low across the sky. She did not follow the crowd to the feast. Instead, she went outside, through the gardens and toward the graveyard, not heeding the wet stains the grass made on the hem of her new gown or the mud on her shoes. She had come here often since her return, to sit quietly near her father's tomb.

William Trevallon's body lay in the small mausoleum, locked with members of the Helford family for all eternity. The crypt was white stone, ornamented with sculpted flowers and the Helford coat-of-arms, and stood eight feet high, twelve feet wide, and very deep. It must be rather crowded inside, Ardys thought, knowing that many Helford ancestors lay within the tomb. There was a small plaque sunk into one of the outer walls with her father's name, and a little way to the left of the tomb there were several stone benches set among some rose bushes.

Ardys was tempted to speak aloud to Will's spirit, for she

felt him near, but she did not, afraid her voice would break the stillness of the place. She sat on one of the benches and closed her eyes, breathing the heavy odor of the near-dead roses, listening to the peaceful sound of the sea and the sigh of the wind.

Footsteps on the approaching path startled her, and Sir Walter Ralegh, with a bow and a smile, sat down beside her with a hearty smile. Ardys returned the smile warmly.

"Well met, Sir Walter! You do my mother honor on this day. Here, sit ye down next to me."

He did not speak for a bit, and he placed a hand on her shoulder.

"Ye are thinner, Ardys," he said. "Be you in health?"

"Oh, aye!" she said. "I am well. 'Tis only I am much older than when you saw me last, my lord."

He smiled. "Well met, at any rate. I came to see you, not for your mother's sake . . ."

Ardys inclined her head. "I am not surprised. Nor am I offended to hear you say that. Father would have been pleased that you came," she said softly, gazing at the crypt. "To his grave, I mean! Not to that foolish ceremony . . ."

"I came to see yourself, Mistress Ardys, and to pay my respects to Will. He was my friend; it is only right that I should see his widow remarried," Ralegh said.

Ardys sighed. "I suppose my mother has a right to a new life. Jesu knows she was not happy with the old one."

"Were you?" Sir Walter asked. "D'ye miss your old life—do ye miss the court?"

"I miss so many things," she answered truthfully, looking up at him with a trace of her young smile. "I miss the fencing matches. I recall well the time I bested you, Sir Walter . . ."

He laughed. "I had been at sea many long months, and was not at the top of my form!"

"Aye? I did not know. How very odd. Father told me he thought it was the best ye had ever fenced."

"Did he, now? Then who am I to contradict the Fencing Master?"

He looked out at the sea and then plunged on: "Will is sorely missed at court. The Queen speaks well of him, and of you. She was most distraught when news of your kidnapping by pirates reached her."

"Beloved Lady," Ardys said. "Is she well, does she keep her good health?"

"Well enough, though at times perhaps she moves a trifle more slowly than once she did. Her teeth and stomach trouble her, 'tis said, but she is as dazzling and majestical as she ever was."

"I am glad to hear it. I hope her pains are little. And the court, tell me, is it as it was?"

"As it was. My rival, Robert Devereux, Earl of Essex, rides higher than ever in her favor since I married Bess."

"Bess Throckmorton was one of the Queen's ladies-in-waiting, Sir Walter. You know how she protects and cherishes her ladies. Ye must have known she would be angry with you . . . But surely she has forgiven you by now."

"Mayhap. Yet she has not forgotten."

"What of Essex, then?" asked Ardys.

Ralegh made a face. "He plays the Queen well. Last summer he married Frances, the daughter of old Sir Francis Walsingham. It was a good match for him. The Queen was pleased."

Ardys frowned, remembering. "Frances Walsingham was a timid girl, very quiet. Somehow I do not see her as the type Essex would choose."

"She is the daughter of one of Her Majesty's best-loved counselors. But I agree, if Walsingham had been alive, I do not think he would have allowed the marriage to take place."

"Fathers always die at inopportune times," Ardys said.

"There is never a good time for death, Ardys, unless 'tis the death of an enemy."

She nodded. "I remember when Lord Robert died, how sad the Queen was."

"Dudley? Aye, Lord Robert had his enemies, but he is missed now. The Queen needs him more than ever. She needs people she can trust."

"Essex is not worthy of her trust."

"No, he is not, but she was always over-fond of handsome young men." Sir Walter paused, watching a gull wheel and cry overhead.

"Come back to her, Ardys. Come back to court." With a gentle, callused hand, he turned her face so that their eyes met. "You have nothing here. The Queen would welcome ye, I know it."

"But I have not been bidden to return. And what place would I have?"

" 'Tis false modesty to speak that way, girl. You are the Fencing Master's daughter; you will always have a place at court. Christ's wounds—she has not summoned you because she does not know you are alive! I meself only heard of your return in Devon a week gone, not in London."

"I thank you. But I cannot leave this place."

"Why not, for the love of God?"

"My family is here."

"Pah! Your mother no longer needs or wants you, now she has a man again."

"Ye speak true. My mother never needed me. But, you must understand, Sir Walter, my father . . ."

"You would stay here for his sake? That is sheer folly, and well ye know it. Your father is dead, Ardys! Only his bones lie here, there is nothing else."

"I could not attend his funeral," she said testily, angry that Ralegh spoke the truth.

"Through no fault of your own. Think a moment; he was master fencer, and you were as his right hand. I mind the great tournaments at Hampton and Windsor and Whitehall, when the two Trevallons met all challengers, and were always victorious. Do ye choose to ignore your heritage, the skill your father gave you, the hours you practiced, the years you devoted to the art?"

Another pale smile. "I remember the tournaments well."

"Then ye must see that you are wasting yourself, ye are making mock of his memory, forsaking the Queen's service. Your father would have wanted you to go back, Ardys! There is no master fencer now—that need not worry ye; no one could ever follow Will Trevallon in that office. He has not been replaced."

There was a beetle, scuttling along the stone path, rattling like a miniature armored knight, intent on its business. Ardys watched it until it disappeared into the grass that grew long beneath the rose bushes.

"My rapier is lost," she said at length. Rusted, no doubt, in that tiny chamber at Dungannon, amid the shambles of a love that once had flourished.

Ralegh laughed. "I will give you a new one if the Queen does not. Say ye will come! For my sake, or for the sake of the friendship we shared: you, your father, and I." He slapped his thigh, dislodging a bee that had landed on his bright hose. "By my troth, Ardys, I need the Queen's favor now: I wish to embark on another expedition to the new world; I need her money and her good wishes. I want to make the voyage myself this time. I need her permission to go—although I may go whether I have it or not. I prefer to go with it. It would please her greatly if I brought you back."

"Ah, Sir Walter, finally we have the truth! Ye need me to come back for your own gain!" Ardys said, amused when he had the grace to redden. "But think, it has been many months since I held a sword in my hand."

"Do not ask me to believe that you would forget how to fence."

"Well, I always could best you, my friend."

"Aye," he said, so solemnly that she had to laugh.

The court. The dust in the tiltyard, the clash of steel, the whirl of bright-colored doublets. And Elizabeth at the center of it all: commanding, wise, beloved virgin Queen.

Aye, Ardys thought: aye, I would like to see her again, to serve her again.

Ralegh sat still and quiet. The sea sighed below them while the gulls wheeled overhead.

She stood abruptly and said: "When do ye leave, Sir Walter?"

"Tomorrow."

"Then I have no time to delay. Ye remind me of my duty. Father was the Queen's servant first and always. So should I be, then. I will go with you, and if she wishes it, I will stay. But that decision will be hers."

Ralegh stood and pulled her up into a fatherly embrace, kissing the top of her hair. He saw her gazing at the plaque that bore her father's name. "Of course it shall be hers. And your dear father shall be with ye, wherever you are. What better way to show your love for him than by again living the life you shared with him?"

CHAPTER SEVENTEEN

It never changes, Kirkconnell thought. The seasons seem to swirl around it, winter's snow and summer's rain—always the rain! Yet nothing can touch its beauty, nothing settles on it. I have looked death in the face, and there's a year of my life gone, but Ireland—Ireland is always the same.

He rode slowly up the long road to the gate of Dungannon, enjoying the view of the place, the feeling that he had come home. Time enough to go to Tullaghoge, he had decided. First, he must see the O'Neill.

Desmond reined in when a troop of gallowglass came around from the stable side, armed with muskets and sped on by the shouts of their commander. Their calls cut the silence of the mist-laden morning.

Kirkconnell inhaled the rich smell of campfires, iced-over peat bog, and forest. The air was crisp with cold and he could see his own breath. A fine day for drilling soldiers. The Tyrone should be in good humor: Kirkconnell hoped so.

The gates were open, so he rode into the confines of the castle, the horse's hooves echoing hollowly on the stone courtyard.

It was here that Ardys and I were lovers, sharing such passion for each other and for fencing.

And then when I left I called Hugh a liar, not wanting to believe she was gone.

Kirkconnell's firm hand rested possessively on the ornate swept hilt of Ardys's rapier. He wondered if Hugh would still be out of temper with him. Two maids scurried across the courtyard, carrying a large bundle of soiled linen, and

Desmond noticed them absently. While he was watching them the great doors opened and O'Neill himself strode out into the courtyard; broad, ruddy, and whistling. He stopped when he saw Kirkconnell.

Ill-mannered, Desmond's mount skittered when the Irishman approached quickly and caught its reins.

The Tyrone's hand steadied the horse while Desmond dismounted and bowed stiffly.

"So, come back then, have ye?" said the Tyrone heartily, patting the horse's neck. "Lookin' a little less fit, aren't ye, me lad?"

Kirkconnell nodded. "I suppose I am. I took a musket ball in the back some time ago; it takes time healing. And I've had a long journey."

"Ah," said Hugh noncommittally, raising a bushy red eyebrow.

"I need some toughening," Desmond went on. "I have been idle too long."

"Come to me for that, then?"

"Aye, I have done with the sea."

"So."

Kirkconnell waited. "Well, Lord Tyrone—will ye have me or no?"

Hugh said, surprised: "There be no need to ask that. I always need men who can fight." He pounded Desmond soundly on the back. "Now come in and have a meal. Mabel will be glad to see ye."

The two men walked toward the house while a groom scurried to look after the horse. The Tyrone followed Kirkconnell into the dark passage that led to the great hall.

"What happened to the girl, then?" O'Neill asked presently.

"She is dead. In childbirth. So I was told by de la Roche."

"And what of de la Roche?"

"Dead."

"Ah. Well, I never liked him overmuch. I'll not ask what happened between ye. 'Tisn't any business o' mine." He paused. "But what of the *Espada*?"

"Sank. She was full of Spanish silver when we met the *Corbeau*, and we lost the battle, the ship, and the treasure." Kirkconnell said.

Hugh commiserated. "Aye, worse luck, lad! A ship's a fickle mistress, she'll turn on ye in the wink of an eye."

Mabel was seeing to the morning meal in the hall when they entered, and she ran to embrace her husband warmly. Hugh picked her up and swung her about before he set her back down on her feet.

"Captain 'Connell, returned!" Mabel said when she stopped laughing, her cheeks flushed like a young girl's. "Welcome back to Dungannon, Captain! 'Tis well to see ye again."

"And you, Lady," Desmond said politely, bending to kiss her outstretched hand, wincing when the skin over his back wound tightened with the movement.

The chamber filled with soldiers, standing around the tables talking, taking mouthfuls of warm bread from the trenchers the servants laid out. Some faces Desmond recognized; most he did not. O'Neill's army had grown in the past year. There were several Scotsmen, dressed in the tartans of their clans, and a few dark Spaniards together in a knot by the hearth. There were nearly twenty Irish chieftains, big, burly and fur-clad like the Tyrone. Carberry, the hostage, stood alone as always. Mabel sat, and the men followed suit. Conversation ceased while the simple, heavy meal was consumed.

Hugh sat back and wiped the ale from his red beard with

his furred cuff, watching Kirkconnell.

"God's teeth, I knew that one day ye would kill de la Roche," Hugh said, and Desmond looked up quickly.

"I did not say that I did, Hugh, but 'tis true. I ran him through on his own deck."

"Good. He was too slippery for my liking. Never knew where his loyalty lay."

"With himself, and himself only."

Desmond looked into the great fire that blazed hotly in the central hearth. Dogs lay about gnawing at the bones flung them by the diners. A sudden flash of memory, a feeling of another time, came over him. Laughter; and Ardys Trevallon's warm hand on his thigh under the table, her dark eyes full of mirth and desire. It was some moments before Kirkconnell could speak, and he drank deeply of the ale, willing the thoughts away.

"I recovered and came back on the *Corbeau*," he said. "Sold her at Carrickfergus to a Scots captain named Bracadale. Fetched a fair price for her. Then I sent my crew—what remained of them, which wasn't many—on their way. Some of them will no doubt wind up here. I also lost Bled."

"The little Welshman? 'Tis sorry I am to hear that. When will ye be going to Tullaghoge?"

"I know I must, and I will. But not for a time. Soon, I suppose."

Mabel said: "Tell him, Hugh."

"Be still, woman!"

"Tell me what?" asked Kirkconnell.

Mabel frowned at Hugh, who gave her an angry look.

"Tullaghoge is gone, 'Connell," he said. "Burned to the ground. Raiders. Did a proper job of it: only ashes left. We found almost all of the family's bodies. Most of the servants seem to have run off—though none of 'em have shown up here . . ."

Kirkconnell paled.

" 'Twas a band of cutthroats," Mabel went on uncertainly.

"English marauders," corrected the Tyrone. "Must have been. I am mounting a force to track 'em down and take revenge. Ye're welcome to join. Ye should. They came in the summer, in the night, without warning, and killed everyone there: men, women—we found tracks coming up from the south, from around Dundalk. But Desmond—"

Mabel laid a hand on Desmond's arm, and he looked at her without seeing while Hugh talked.

"They were gone before I heard what had happened and could bring help. I came too late. Desmond," Hugh said harshly, "Shelagh's body we were never certain we found. Found all the rest of the family, for sure, but not her. We found what could have been a woman of about her size and shape in what was left of the family apartments, but there's no way o' being sure 'twas her. The body was burned utterly."

"God's death!" Desmond said. "It must have been her! If it weren't, if she still lived, someone would know of it by now. Someone would have told ye. By my troth," he thought a moment, "none of the women servants were her size. Most of 'em were big, buxom wenches—that's what her father liked around his house, but they were never so big as Shelagh."

"Aye, 'tis true . . . I'll find the butchers, sure enough, and destroy them. Be good training for my troops," said Hugh.

"I shall be glad to be a part of that," Kirkconnell said.

"We must wait till the ground hardens before we move the whole lot of the troops," the Tyrone said. "There's naught but ice-choked bog right now 'tween Dungannon and Dundalk. In the meantime, ye shall rest and heal and regain your strength." There was no mistaking the command. "We will avenge your wife, Kirkconnell. And ye have her family's money now, have ye thought of that?"

"Oh, Christ! Rich am I, then? It's blood money, Hugh. I care not for it. You take it."

Hugh impatiently compressed his lips. "Do not offer me something like that, lad! I might accept. Wait. Don't decide now. Wait at least 'til we've hunted the killers down. Then decide."

The journey from Plymouth to London took the better part of two weeks. Ardys was the only woman in the party, led by Ralegh, who was accompanied by several of his servants and retainers. The roads were muddy in spots, but the going was fairly easy. At first Ralegh had insisted that she ride in his coach, for he was not sure of her strength, but she soon convinced him that the long ride would do her more good than ill, and he had given in.

Ardys bade farewell to home and family with little regret. Alice, come up from Porthtowan with Percy for the leave-taking, was plainly relieved to see her eldest go and was sadly unable to conceal her joy.

In the end, Alice kissed Ardys's pale cheek and wished her well, admonished her to write and to look to her health. Her sisters hugged her and told her that someday she must return and teach them the art of fencing, whispering that it would be a wonderful way to bedevil their stepfather. Percy stood pompously beside Alice, his hands folded across his chest. Ardys glanced at Percy, then winked at Elizabeth, the next eldest, and smiled.

The two weeks of travel passed peacefully: a quiet interlude. The monotony of the daylong rides, and the rhythmic swaying of the warm, sturdy horse beneath her, lulled the ache in Ardys's heart. She found pleasure in small things: a gold and scarlet blanket of clouds at sunset over the trim white cottages of Sherborne; a flock of ravens settling noisily for the night in the trees of the Blackdon Hills, their cries and murmuring growing fainter and fainter; a warm, soft bed and a fire in a snug inn after a day of riding in cold rain. Walter Ralegh's company was a tonic for her, and even more exhilarating with the tankards of ale they shared in the evenings.

When she felt like conversation, he would ride with her and talk of the court, of the Queen and of the Lord Essex and Lord Burghley's son, the little, hump-backed Robert Cecil. Ralegh told Ardys tales of his own adventures at sea, and the journeys others made to the new world for him; his part in the attack on Cadiz and his lieutenancy of the county of Cornwall. His stories were endless and always entertaining, and if he was the swashbuckling hero in them all, that was fitting. She enjoyed listening.

They reached London in the closing days of October and reined up before the gates of the palace at Westminster, only to find that the Queen had made one of her quick decisions and packed the entire court off to Hampton Court for the Accession Day celebrations on November seventeenth.

Ralegh spoke with her Majesty's chamberlain, Henry Carey, Lord Hunsdon, who was still at Westminster with some of the servants, securing the palace and seeing to the storage of the plates and dishes that had not been taken with the Queen's entourage. Carey seemed frantic with worry and told them he had been forced to send his assistant, vice-chamberlain Thomas Heneage, scurrying to Hampton only a few miles and a scant day or two ahead of the royal party to make that palace hospitable again.

Hampton Court had been unoccupied since the month of July. There was much to be done. The entire palace had to be swept, the chambers aired, curtains put back at the proper windows, the huge allegorical tapestries bought from Flanders by Henry the Eighth (at a cost, it was rumored, that would have paid for an entire fleet of ships) rehung in the watching chamber and the great hall where the huge court took its meals in shifts. It was folly to leave these works of art up to fade in the sunlight when the court was not in residence. The bed linens had to be unpacked and the eighteen kitchens re-provisioned. The polishing of the silver, gold, and pewter plates and utensils had to be left for the last possible moment; as did the resettling of all Her Majesty's personal furniture in her private apartments.

The Queen had her favorite bed and chairs and writing desk, and when she moved the court she sent them ahead, so that they would be ready in place when she arrived. Elizabeth was fond of her comforts and it saved money for her to own only one complete set of furnishings and to cart them from palace to palace as she progressed.

Ardys and Sir Walter turned their horses and rode to Hampton Court.

That palace was unchanged. Ardys rode up the long stone path to the gate beside Ralegh, staring at the solid red brick walls, the turrets and chimneys, the familiar grounds. To their left was the tiltyard; beyond, the great maze, and she could see the turret that marked the ground-floor courtyard rooms she and her father had shared. Within those walls, she had watched her father waste and die, and now those memories flooded over her.

Ralegh happened to glance over and saw her stricken expression; he reined up and waited for her to do the same.

"It looks the same," he began.

"Aye," she agreed. "Pray forgive me, I had not thought that the memories of this place would still be so strong. Ye know my father died here."

"No, I did not know." Sir Walter paused. "Well, lass, others have died here too. Queen Jane Seymour died here after giving birth to our good Queen's late brother, King Edward. And the Queen herself nearly died here when she had the pox early in her reign."

"So she did. This place is full of history, and not just mine. 'Tis folly to brood, Sir Walter; it's only a place. And 'tis still a beautiful place." She reined in and smiled at her companion. "D'you suppose anyone has seen the ghost of Queen Catherine Howard lately, running down the long gallery to the royal chapel where her husband Henry Tudor was at service?"

"Who knows? 'Tis said she is often seen there in the evenings. Mayhap she is looking for her head."

"She won't find it anywhere far from Tower Green . . . but we are all older now, are we not? Queen Elizabeth, Robert Cecil—even my Lord Essex may have aged a little."

She looked up at the King's Beasts before the door, remembering. Her favorite had always been the lion, fangs bared, gripping the shield that bore the Tudor heraldic crest. It was there, just as it had been, gray stone, impassive and unmoving.

"I have no wish to see Essex, Sir Walter."

"He is Master of the Horse; it will be difficult to avoid him. You will soon see how it is, how he is struggling for power with Robert Cecil."

"And with yourself, no doubt! But how could Cecil—the little hunchback—be a threat to the great general of Cadiz?"

"Cecil is Burghley's son, never forget. And since Sir Francis Walsingham died, the Queen has been without a chief secretary. Essex hoped to get the post for one of his cronies, a man named William Davison. Elizabeth would have none of him and now 'tis whispered that Cecil will have the title. He has already taken over Walsingham's network of spies."

"Ah?" Ardys raised an eyebrow. "Mayhap I should seek out this Cecil, then, if he will soon become so important."

"Ye will find him a most stimulating man. He is brilliant, with all his father's tact. And he is truly loyal to the Queen."

They walked their horses slowly to the gates, where grooms came out to hold the reins while they dismounted. Behind them Ralegh's servants began to unload their carts, piling cases and trunks on the ground. Through the arched gateway where Anne Boleyn had stayed while her rooms were being readied all those years ago, Ardys and Ralegh strolled slowly into the lower courtyard. The smell of the palace drifted to them, also unchanged: flowers, ale, horses, dogs, cooked meat; perfumes, stone, bread. Each of the Queen's residences had its own peculiar odor, Ardys reflected, but to her, Hampton Court Palace smelled like home.

At least at Hampton almost all the apartments, not just the state ones, had their own latrines. This was a pleasant innovation compared with some of the other palaces where, in the background, there was a persistent, faint odor of urine.

Elizabeth, by the grace of God Queen of England, Wales, Scotland, Ireland, and France was spending her evening at the past-time she most enjoyed: playing cards with Robert Devereux, Earl of Essex, her Master of Horse. She was, not unusually, winning.

The two were seated near a long window in her privy chamber, their game illuminated by the long-shadowed evening light that came through the leaded glass. The cards lay on the small, elegant oak table between them, and their heads were bent close. Robert told Elizabeth that she looked lovely in the glow of the dying sunset, and she smiled and dismissed the torchbearer who at that moment came to light the myriad candles in the chamber. She would summon him again after the sun was fully gone.

Elizabeth and Essex were not alone. Since the early days of her reign, when rumors had circulated that she had allowed Robert Dudley, Earl of Leicester and later Essex's stepfather, into her bed, Elizabeth had been careful with her favorites. She was Queen, and her conduct must always be above reproach, her reputation without stain. Her ladies-in-waiting hovered near her wherever she went, keeping occupied with their embroidery, out of earshot but chaperones nonetheless.

When Elizabeth finally found she could no longer read the numbers on the cards, she called the page and ordered the candles lit. The room was soon ablaze with their flickering light and the rich jewels on her gown sent dancing prisms over the dark-paneled walls when she moved. She shimmered as she leaned forward to discard, holding the large cards carefully in her graceful white hands.

"Ha, my lord! I have you again!" she laughed triumphantly, laying down her cards.

Devereux threw down his cards in an elegant gesture of defeat. He glittered almost enough to rival the sovereign. His doublet was a bright purple, and around his neck, below the ruff and his square chestnut-brown beard, gleamed a circlet of rubies on a thick gold chain.

"Madam! You make a fool of me when we play!" he laughed, enjoying her good humor and glad that they did not play for money, for then he would surely be a poor man.

"Ye did not concentrate on the game, dear Robin," she said, taking the cards and beginning to pile them together neatly on the table. The rings on each of her fingers glowed in the torchlight.

"Concentrate on mere cards when I am faced with such an opponent? It is impossible; I am bested by beauty, my Queen, as always."

His flattery went on, warming her. This light was kind. The white of her thick face powder was not so pronounced, and the brilliant red of her tightly curled wig almost looked like real hair.

There was a silken rustling as one of the ladies came up to the Queen and curtsied.

"Your pardon, madam. Sir Walter Ralegh is without and desires admittance to your presence."

"Ah, Water, is it?" She cast a withering glance at Devereux, knowing that her use of her pet name for Ralegh would bother his rival.

Essex had the grace to flush and looked at the Queen.

He said aloud: "Ralegh is one of your most loyal subjects."

"God's death! D'ye think I do not know that?" Elizabeth flared at him angrily. "I have not forgotten Cadiz so quickly, my Lord!"

Turning to the maid, she said, "Fetch the pirate in. I grow weary and will retire soon."

She stood and smoothed the white brocade corselet that covered her breasts so tightly that a woman with poorer posture or less stamina than the Queen would have been suffocated.

Ralegh strode in with firm step, but hesitated when he saw Essex, who now rose and leaned arrogantly against the window.

"Well, Sir Walter?" Elizabeth said abruptly, offering her hand and with a gracious gesture bidding him to rise. "Why are ye come? Were you summoned by our cousin the Lord Admiral, or do you seek more of our money for another ill-timed expedition?"

"Never that, Your Grace," said Ralegh from another low, elegant bow. "I have instead brought someone back here, to your court. Returned, as it seems, from the grave."

"And whom, pray, could ye have fetched from the grave? Some moldering corpse for my amusement, no doubt! Oh, stop bowing, Sir Walter; you are too tall to keep that position long. Show me whom you have brought."

Ralegh signaled to the ladies, and one of them went to open the door. Ardys stood uncertainly on the threshold, blinking in the light of the chamber, and with tears of joy at seeing her Queen again.

"You may enter our presence," Elizabeth said, not recognizing her.

Ardys obeyed, and by Ralegh's side she curtsied very, very low. She had changed her travel-muddied clothes for a dark blue gown of watered silk with a small white ruff; the fine lace of her under-sleeves covered her hands. Her hair gleamed red and gold in the candlelight.

"Your Majesty," Ardys said, unsure of her welcome now that the moment had come. She did not notice the long, assessing glance with which Devereux favored her.

Elizabeth stared at the girl, contemplating, and then she went forward and drew Ardys up out of the curtsy with a gentle hand.

"Jesu," said the Queen softly. "It cannot be . . . Walter Ralegh, ye are a wizard as well as a pirate. The Fencing Master's daughter, alive!" She patted the girl's cheek fondly. "Ye are welcome back to our court, Mistress Trevallon."

"I have come to offer myself to your service, Majesty. What poor skills I have are yours to command."

"God's death!" the Queen exclaimed. "This is indeed a happy occasion. Come, my girl, and tell us what brings you back to us so miraculously!"

The Queen took Ardys's arm and walked to the padded chairs near the fireplace at the other end of the chamber. To a lady-in-waiting she said, "You there, fetch a page to build up this blaze before the night becomes too chill."

"You have become thinner," the Queen said to Ardys. "Ye may sit, and tell us how it has been with you. We were greatly saddened when we heard you were taken prisoner. We presumed you were killed."

She looked at Ardys and added, "Or, speak not, if it troubles you."

Ardys smiled at the Queen, and settled herself on the chair. "It is easily told, your Grace. I was taken prisoner on the Channel by a . . . by a pirate, and carried off by him to Ireland, to the castle of the Earl of Tyrone."

"The Tyrone! That rogue Hugh O'Neill, who once sat with us at supper and now scorns our laws for all the world to see? How was it at Dungannon—what is the O'Neill's home like? We hear it is very grand for a mere Irishman."

"It is magnificent, your Grace, in a wild sort of way."

"It would be wild, 'tis filled with wild Irishmen. And with Spanish as well?"

"Aye, madam. Captain Kir—the pirate captain—was O'Neill's friend. But, in truth I saw little of the Tyrone's court. I was kept prisoner in a small chamber."

"Were you treated ill?"

"No," Ardys said, hesitating. "But you are right, your Majesty. It does pain me to talk of it."

"Then do not trouble yourself."

" 'Tis of no moment, I will finish the tale. I was taken, after, to an island in the Caribbean. It was a beautiful place where the sun shone always and filled with marvelous birds. There was one such that was so small and moved so quickly that its wings were but a blur, and it made a sound like the buzzing of bees. It shone like a jewel glittering in flight."

"God's great wonder! Such adventure," cried the Queen.

"And there I managed to secure passage on a trading ship, and thence, over time, back to Cornwall."

"Where I found her," Ralegh hastily said from the other side of the room.

Elizabeth turned to him. "You did well to bring Mistress Trevallon back to us, Sir Walter. But we must not tire her with endless questions. It will all come out, sooner or later. You must have seen some extraordinary things in Ireland, too . . ."

The Queen said suddenly, "Tell me, Ardys, do ye fence still? We have an idea."

"Truthfully, I have not fenced for some time."

"But we will wager you retain the skill. We have not yet appointed a new Master of the Fence to our court. There is no man who could match your father's skill."

"No one. I thank your Majesty," Ardys agreed.

"The young gallants of our household," Elizabeth looked pointedly at Essex, who smiled back winningly, "lack the practice of the fencing art, preferring the broadsword, if you please. An antique sort of weapon! If you have truly returned to serve us, we shall let you train them. You must take up your father's post, and teach my courtiers all you know of fencing."

"Majesty," Ardys began, her eyes very round, "I am overcome by this great honor."

"We mean to work you hard! She has bested you before, has she not, Robin?"

Essex took a step forward. "Aye, madam."

To Ardys he made a leg and said, "I would doubtless benefit from your instruction, Mistress Trevallon. Mayhap, with practice, I will be able to rescue my reputation."

He caught Ralegh's glance and continued smoothly, "Ye are to be thanked for returning the Fencing Master's daughter to court, Sir Walter."

"So he is!" said the Queen, rising gracefully in a rustle of starched brocade and motioning Ardys to remain seated. "And we shall reward you suitably, my Walter, for your service to us. When the time comes. But now it grows late, and this girl looks tired," Elizabeth ignored Ardys's protest. "Tomorrow we must speak again. In the meantime, we will inform Thomas Heneage that a new Fencing Master has joined our household, and suitable accommodations must be found."

"Should she not be called the Fencing Mistress, not Master?" Essex asked with a smile.

"This girl wields a rapier as well as any man. Better, in fact, than any man living. She shall have her father's title of Fencing Master, and the honors that go with it. It is our will that it be so. Robin, I will lean on your arm. You, Ralegh, report to Heneage, and see to this girl's comfort."

"Your Majesty," Ardys knelt to kiss the Queen's hand. "I cannot express my gratitude."

"Teach these prancing rascals to fence, Mistress Trevallon. That is thanks enough for us."

CHAPTER EIGHTEEN

In the months that Ardys had been away the style of dress at the Court had become gaudier and more colorful, the result of the influence of the young Lord Essex and his following. Yellow was his color, and it was sported proudly by his many hangers-on and servants, and by all those who wished it known that they were members of Essex's camp.

Those who followed the banner of Sir Walter Ralegh, who was also a favorite of the Queen, wore blue. Like two opposing sets of chessmen: the court was their playing-board, and both sides sought the same prize—the favor of the Queen.

Ardys had been fencing again for a number of days. She was outfitted, according to her new status, with two new doublets of white and silver, made of the best silk and velvet; new flat shoes of the softest black leather; and new white silken hose. And in her right hand, a precious gift from the Queen: a rapier, imported from Germany, its blade over three feet long, polished and shining, its swept-hilt a glorious intertwining design of three swans, their backs forming the guard and their graceful necks, the arcs. It was a light weapon, lighter than her lost swept-hilt, well balanced and quite comfortable to wield.

She tried not to think of her other rapier, now only a memory, part of a life that was no longer hers.

Ardys let the court embrace her, and allowed herself to be swept along in its gay, noisy tide. She went to religious services in the morning, with the secretaries and councilors, hoping that by her renewed devotion to Lutheranism God might forget that once she had attended Catholic masses. She took her meals with the rest in the great banquet hall with its dark panels and its leering cherubim carved into the ceiling beams.

In the afternoons she held classes in the art of the fence. The students gathered at the tiltyard expectantly, waiting for her instructions, and she let them select their weapons from the cache of rapiers kept in a small shed near the back of the field.

Only a few the first day, but soon there were more pupils than she had dared hope. Queen Elizabeth, she knew, was encouraging all the young men at court to attend the fencing sessions—and encouragement from Her Majesty was very like a command. Ardys did not know that Essex also had strongly hinted to his adherents that any man who learned fencing at the Trevallon school would be doing well. Ralegh, of course, was quick to make the same suggestion to his followers, and the tiltyard quickly became a stage where the hostilities of the two rival factions could be acted out under the watchful eye of the Master Fencer.

The first hour Ardys generally let her pupils have at each other freely, to clear the air; and the second hour she devoted to her lectures and demonstrations of basic moves and new techniques. She selected, usually at random, one or more men to fence with her while the others observed. The crowd would gather round the combatants, eager to see the action and straining to hear Ardys's shouts above the clang of the swords and their own excited murmurings.

The third hour the men again took up their weapons and paired off, attempting to copy the movements they had just seen. Ardys went from pair to pair, correcting positions, loosening a too-tight grip, and, when necessary, stepping in to keep the peace when two combatants thrust murderously at one another. It was well that the two court factions dressed in different colors, she thought, so that she could keep them easily distinguished. Perhaps when they had all become more proficient, she would hold a tournament: Essex's men against Ralegh's.

When the Fencing Master came between any two men, they instantly parted. Ardys made her powers known on the first day of lessons when a swaggering youth said loudly that there was nothing to be learned from a wench that could not be learned in bed. She had selected that youth for the second hour's duel and proceeded, effortlessly and thoroughly, to beat him back and back again until the sweat poured from him in streams and he was scarlet with humiliation.

"The first lesson," she called out to the audience, "is this: do not think yourself better than your opponent, regardless of his size. You must assume nothing, take nothing for granted. Remember that a sword is an instrument of death and keep your respect for it at all times."

This afternoon, at the end of the second week of fencing lessons, the sky threatened rain. Ardys was reluctant to move the class inside. The clouds thickened but the rain held off, and she was able to complete the lessons and dismiss her students after three hard hours. They were learning new footwork. It was amusing how clumsy some of them were and they left the yard exhausted but exuberant because the beautiful Fencing Master had praised their efforts.

For a group of men so dedicated to dancing as were these of Elizabeth Tudor's court, Ardys's pupils were surprisingly heavy-footed. Instead of a graceful pivot, their heels would dig deep into the soft sand of the tiltyard and their legs would catch and tangle. Ardys never laughed at them, and tried to help them maintain their own good humor; but at night, alone in her chamber, she would recall some of their ridiculous posturing and chuckle, wishing her father was there to share her amusement.

There must be more footwork tomorrow, she decided now, as she watched them disperse. Most of them went in search of a tankard of beer to rid their throats of the dust.

Alone, Ardys walked slowly to the weapons shed, where she checked that all the swords were stacked neatly in rows, hilt to point; the way she had seen pilchards, small fish, drying once in Cornwall when she was a child. The swirling dust was beginning to settle and the lowering sun cast long shadows, picking its way through a tear in the cloud cover. Ardys hummed, pleasantly tired, liking the ache of the muscles she had not used for so long, and she started back to the gate, her new rapier tucked under her left arm while she pulled off her short black gloves.

At the main gate a figure loomed out of the shadows, tall and bearded: Robert Devereux, Earl of Essex. Ardys ceased whistling and waited for him to pass by, and remembered the terrible heat of the Armada Day so long ago. Her poor father encased in a breastplate because of this man's whim. Only her knowledge of her own rank and the fact that the Queen loved Essex kept Ardys from challenging him.

He did not pass by, and when she began to walk through the gate, he blocked her way.

"I have come for instructions, Fencing Master," he said. He was dressed more soberly than usual, in a gold cape and a doublet striped horizontally with slashes of vivid green.

"This day's exercise is finished, my Lord. Come you tomorrow; there are others who will also be here for their first lesson."

She stopped, annoyed, when he did not move away.

"Have you not wondered why I have not come before today?" he asked, stepping forward so that she had to step back into the yard once more. His eyes were a murky blue, and he was slightly flushed as though he had been drinking something stronger than ale.

" 'Tis not for me to wonder about the doings of a great lord," she said, compressing her lips.

"I cannot be seen to be bested in front of other men. You brought down my man Northampton once, d'ye recall?"

"He does not come to the lessons now, my lord. Allow me to pass, pray you, I am tired."

"I am a great soldier," he went on, his words slurring. "One day I will lead England into glorious battle, and I will lay victory at the Queen's feet like so much treasure."

"Aye?" she muttered.

"But if I am to lead armies, I must be invincible," Essex said. "And so I plead with you, Ardys Trevallon, to instruct me privately, not with the rest of the men. I am not one of them and I must excel in everything I do. Greatness is in my blood. My blood is older than the Queen's, did ye not know? I ask your help. You will find me an apt pupil, I do assure you."

She pretended to consider, her dark hair caught back in its ribbon catching the last of the daylight.

"As ye ask so graciously, my Lord, how could I refuse?" she smiled sweetly, and he did not notice her sarcasm.

Ardys's mind was busy. Perhaps there was a way to bring this man down after all, to entangle him in a web of his own making. Why should she not? Desmond was dead, their babe was dead. Why not occupy herself with revenge? Essex was known for his discreet dalliances. What if he were caught in an indiscreet flirtation? Would that not turn the Queen against her favorite?

Robert Devereux was far too conscious of the precariousness of his position to risk his own downfall by letting his passions run away with him. But Ardys knew, standing so close to him that her richly curved body was outlined invitingly under the clinging fabric of her doublet, that he was tempted. She was a favorite of the Queen's. Yet her duties kept her far from the Queen's company for days at a time, and she did not gossip with the other ladies who served the sovereign, so Essex might feel himself to be comparatively safe. His own wife, Frances, was at his house at Devereux, down the river.

Devereux advanced into the tiltyard and drew his long rapier from its scabbard at his left hip, never taking his eyes from Ardys's beautiful face. She backed and took her own weapon and ran a piece of velvet over the blade to polish it as she allowed Essex to lead her into the center of the arena. It was quiet, and the light was nearly gone; most of the court would be preparing for the evening meal. There was no one about.

The young lord did not seem as drunk as he had moments before, and Ardys noticed that he had no sour smell of liquor on his breath; she wondered if that might have been a ruse on his part to protect his dignity if she refused his request. He was not, in fact, even the slightest bit the worse for drink.

Ardys turned and faced Essex and her heart wrenched when she noticed that he was the same height as Kirkconnell and in the dimming twilight there was a superficial resemblance. Devereux also had an aura of strength, like Desmond, but he lacked the easy grace, the light step of the renegade captain. She looked at Essex closely, and saw the lust in his eyes. Of course that would be what he came for, not for any fencing lesson. She saw his gaze move over her breasts, and she took a slow, deep breath. She was rewarded by his sharp intake of breath and almost laughed aloud. Were all men so easy to manipulate?

They raised their blades, swept them to the side in formal salute, and took up the stance.

240

"We shall begin with a free-style, Lord Essex, so that I may discern where your weakness lies, and where my instruction will be of the most benefit to you."

She smiled and brought her blade up to touch his, tapping it metallically. She did not bother to circle him.

He stood quite still and answered her small movements with his own blade. In the distance, along the walls of the palace, the fire-bearers came to light the torches in the iron brackets.

The night seemed suddenly blacker beyond the friendly reach of the torches' glow, but still neither of the fencers took so much as a step forward to challenge the other. Then without warning Ardys's blade slid the length of Essex's, and he had to parry wildly before she pierced through his rich doublet, beginning her assault.

Her thrusts came from every side. To his dismay Essex found himself sweating, and he had to give ground.

Ardys's smile glittered coldly. She was confident and in control of the match. Kirkconnell's lessons were well learned; she kept her hatred at bay and concentrated on only the fencing, anticipating Essex's inept thrusts, and instinctively attacking his left side where he showed himself to be weakest. She was backing him against the weapons-shed when her blade found the puffed sleeve of his jacket and ripped it through, narrowly missing the skin beneath. He parried too late and caught her blade, in a coward's move, with his gloved hand; and a lucky twist of his wrist drew her face close to his. Before she could move away his mouth fastened eager and hot on hers, catching her off guard in mid-maneuver.

Breaking free, she stepped back and said icily: "In any tiltyard, that move—grabbing your opponent's blade with your hand—could be your death. That is not dueling. That is insolence."

"Not so. Come, I know you are the better fencer; I seek only to stop you before you tire yourself toying with me. Ye have no need to impress me with your skill, Ardys Trevallon."

He leaned toward her slowly, and she knew suddenly that here was Essex's ruin: she had him in the palm of her hand. Through the haze of his desire he would not see her hatred, would not see that she planned his downfall, that she would use her attractions for her revenge on him: the man responsible for her father's death. She could not kill Essex, but she could ruin him. For Will Trevallon, she would act like a lovesick girl. For her father!

She would keep Essex at bay, but that would increase his desire. When she had him so in her thrall that he could think of nothing else, she would accuse him of trying to seduce her, one of the Queen's servants. Elizabeth might overlook many of Devereux's faults, but that sin would be too obvious to be ignored, and she would banish him in disgrace from the court. It would be the end of him.

If Ardys could not convince the Queen that she was pure before Essex tried to force his attentions on her, she might be disgraced as well, however.

It was a risk she would have to take; every well-made sword, after all, had two edges. If she lost her place at court and found herself cast out, she would still have had her revenge.

Essex ran his left hand down the side of her face, through the hair that had escaped the ribbon at the nape of her neck. Then he dropped his sword and peeled his gloves off, and moved forward as she stood silent and still, waiting.

He found the fastenings of her doublet and began to fumble at them. She pushed him off, and unlike de la Roche, Essex stopped and backed away.

Waves of revulsion went through her, and for an instant

she feared she would spoil it all and become ill, but she emptied her mind and let innocence show in her eyes. This was a dance she could master.

In early December of 1598 Alice Trevallon Longhoughton stood in the center of the great hall of Porthtowan House, filled with pride. The masons and carpenters would soon be finished with the room, she judged. Heavy, rough-hewn beams jutted across the ceiling, and on these there would soon be a series of carvings in fanciful shapes: animals and birds on the northern end; pious scenes of angels at the southern. The dark-stained panels for the walls lay about her in layered piles at her feet; they would take some time to put up, she supposed, but the flooring was done, and the large, lead-paned windows were already set in place high in the walls.

Perhaps a fortnight, Alice thought, perhaps less if the work continued to go as smoothly as it had thus far. Not soon enough for celebrating the twelve days of Christmas, more was the pity. In the spring, as soon as the roads became passable, Alice would have a banquet to show off her new home and her new husband. She had never had a home of her own, as she and Will had always dwelt with the Helford clan. Alice was thrilled with Porthtowan, rundown as it had been when she and Percy moved in.

Alice had few friends outside of the Helford family, but no matter. Rich folk made friends easily. Percy certainly did. There were always people coming now to Porthtowan, not only the craftsmen who came to work on the refurbishing, but also the local gentry, who came out of curiosity as they had to Alice's wedding.

She made sure Percy was a generous host, even in his unfinished house. She set a grand table, well stocked with meat and wine, and the neighbors quickly accepted the Longhoughtons into their community. It would not be long before Alice and Percy would be invited to visit in other homes, as equals.

The commotion at Porthtowan never seemed to let up. At the oddest of hours, and more than once in the dead of night, Alice heard the clatter of horses' hooves in the cobbled courtyard. When she felt in the bed for her husband, he would be gone, his side of the great four-poster cold as though he had not been there at all.

At such times Alice wondered uneasily where Percy got his money, for there was no end to it, it seemed. He owned no mine, no ship, and no property other than this estate. He had his jewels, but they were always kept secure in a strongbox by the bed, and even Alice was not permitted to touch them. Mayhap, she thought, knowing little of finance, he borrows against the value of his jewels.

Once she asked him outright, when they were still newly wedded, whence his great wealth came. Had he brought it with him when he escaped the Queen's men? He had merely tweaked her chin fondly and told her not to be so curious, that she already knew all she needed to know of him. A wife should look to her house and leave its support to her lord husband.

Alice was happier than she would have believed possible. Percy was a doting husband, looking to her every need and comfort, and seemed to derive real pleasure from anticipating her requests before she made them. If her day-shoes were wearing thin, trust Percy to notice, magically she would awake to find a new pair beside her wardrobe. If she lost a pearl from one of her collars, another pearl would find its way to her dressing table. When she found his gifts, she would throw her arms around his neck and thank him prettily.

"Who am I, then," said Alice to herself, "to ask questions of my lord? He makes love to me regularly (nay, often) and well, he sets food upon my table, he is building me this beautiful manor house. What matter that once I overheard him speaking with some of his guests in a language I could not understand, only to return to English when he saw I was listening? And if once when I looked in his wardrobe for an old tunic of his so that I could have a new one made of the right size, a rosary fell from one of his pockets, which means he is still a practicing Catholic?"

The rosary, however, did give Alice some worried moments, when she allowed herself to dwell on its implications. Catholics were not unknown in this part of England, of course, though Alice, in her sheltered life, had never actually met one face to face. At least, not that she knew of. All she knew of Papists she had learned from the Lutheran chaplain at Helford House, who had thundered against them from his pulpit in ringing tones, calling them traitors and seekers-after-idols.

She must be loyal to her husband.

"Well, I have no counselors," Alice thought. "I have married a Catholic and there is an end to the matter. Thinking like this only makes my head ache; I shall think of pleasanter things instead."

Alice smiled. She was young yet, and Percy, God was witness, was a virile man. Soon they would have children of their own to match the Trevallon brood. There was a chamber adjoining their bedroom, complete with soft cushioned chairs and a cradle, waiting for the additions to the Longhoughton household. Alice had produced a living child almost every year of her married life with Trevallon, and she had much less time to conceive then, since Will was always impatient to return to court. There was no reason to suspect that she was not still fertile.

Alice left her girls at Helford House when she and Percy moved down to Porthtowan, using the excuse that a house being redone was no place for young girls of sensitive nature. She wanted to be alone with Percy, to begin her new life afresh, unencumbered by the living reminders of her previous marriage. Truth to tell, Alice did not miss the girls one whit except perhaps Margaret, the youngest. Porthtowan would soon be finished, at any rate, and Alice would have to send for them. Percy certainly liked them well enough. Thank God that Ardys had gone back to the Queen, and was not likely to return.

An enthusiastic hug from behind startled Alice from her meditation.

"Contemplating our new hall, eh, my wife? Thinking of the great banquets and dances and masques we shall hold here?" Percy spun her around and beamed down at her, his heavy gold chains at a level with her eyes.

"Off with you, now, there is something for you in our chamber!" a loud kiss on her cheek and a pat on her backside and she went off towards the central stairway with a light step.

CHAPTER NINETEEN

Robert Cecil, newly appointed secretary to Queen Elizabeth, walked quickly across the open courtyard of Windsor Castle to his private apartments. He had a curious hopping gate, and that, combined with his slightly humped back, made him an easily recognized figure, even from some distance.

Ardys watched him, and she could see the small foggy puffs of his breaths as he went along, for the air was clear and very cold. She stood in a small recessed doorway that led to the kitchens from the formal courtyard, cloaked against the wind, and wearing a heavy gown instead of a doublet. She waited for Essex, impatient and in ill humor. She waited for the man she hated, the man whose callous demands on her had increased, not slackened as the winter drew on.

There was no sign yet that he was completely in her power, and until there was she must bear Devereux's attempted pawing. She kept her mind on that: on her revenge, on the day she would go to the Queen and announce that Essex, the beloved, the hero, was no better than a rake, a ruiner of women.

Two months of clandestine meetings: at the shed by the tiltyard, in the stables, behind the mazes in the ornate gardens. Two months, and still she evaded his touch.

When the time comes, she thought, by God, I will have him!

A shuffled step, and Devereux came creeping round the corner of the doorway, stooping to disguise his height, cloaked in dark blue that served to blend him into the gathering twilight.

" 'Tis safe?" he whispered, reaching for her eagerly.

She was glad he could not see her face. She shook her head. "There are many abroad at this early hour, my Lord," she said.

He backed hastily into the shallow recess, pulling her after him. "But if ye were not seen?" he said, his voice tight with desire. Unmindful of the cold, his hands went beneath her cape, trying to fondle her clumsily. She moved back a step.

"Nay. Not seen. But there is risk." Of course there was risk. It was part of the attraction for him.

"Aye. 'Tis never safe for us, Ardys." He sighed in frustration, and withdrew his hands. She pulled her cloak more closely about herself.

"The stable, then," he went on, "inside, in the lofts. After full dark. The Queen has ordered hot water for her feet tonight; she'll sit in her chambers and soak them for an hour at least. And for that hour, I am free." He kissed her perfunctorily. "Do not keep me waiting. I must to supper, but do not fret, soon we shall be together. And this time, my Ardys, we will find full joy."

He was gone before he finished speaking, and his whisper echoed emptily in the wind. Ardys remained in the shadows, rearranging her clothing where his hasty grasp had sought her; and as she did, her hand fell once more on the slip of paper in the pouch that hung suspended by a thin gold chain from her waist.

She pulled the paper out, and peered at it in the light from the cracks in the heavy wood of the door behind her. Tiny, neat handwriting:

Come to my chamber, at twilight. Have a care, No-one must see. R. Cecil.

Cecil, a man she hardly knew—a man not given to furtive

assignations with women. Nervously Ardys shredded the paper into minute fragments, and let the breeze bear them away. She hesitated, contemplating ignoring the summons. Cecil was one of the most powerful men at court: his request could not lightly be refused. She would go.

He held the same post that had been his father Lord Burghley's. Ardys had known the elder Cecil, had liked him because he so obviously revered the Queen and was not afraid to speak his mind to her, even when he dared to disagree with her state policy. He had served Elizabeth faithfully for many years and when he lay dying, the heartbroken Queen had sat at his bedside and fed him as tenderly as any mother would a sick child.

No, the younger Cecil was not the man his father was, though he was shrewd and had his father's wit. But Robert Cecil was ambitious, and fond of fine clothing and jewels. He served the Queen, but it had not escaped court observers that he served himself as well. He did not, could not, love Elizabeth as old Burghley had.

Ardys shrugged. The message from Cecil could not be wished away. It had simply been there, inside the little pouch, when she had donned the gown this afternoon.

Ducking her head more deeply into the protecting folds of her hood, Ardys made her way across the courtyard, following the path Robert Cecil had taken. Haste, she reasoned, would arouse suspicion. This way she appeared to be merely one of those eccentrics who insisted on an evening stroll in spite of cold or wet weather. Cecil's chambers opened directly off the courtyard, under one of the turreted gates that led to the gardens beyond. She paused and glanced about. No movement; she was alone.

Her hand was poised for the knock when the door swung silently open, and without a murmur she slipped inside the anteroom, then into the doorway of the first of his inner chambers.

The room was small but well appointed, with a large writing table, some triangular chairs, and an open court cupboard filled with fine silver plate. A fire blazed in the three-foot hearth behind the desk, and its light played along the walls of the room, which were decorated with fine paintings. The chamber had been arranged by someone with somber taste, for the paintings were all tones of black and gray and brown, muted and understated. The wall panels were also dark-stained. The sunniest of days would not brighten the confines of this room.

Robert Cecil sat scribbling at his desk, the sharp quill of his pen scratching in the silence. He was dressed well, in a deep blue jacket and black velvet capelet, and around his neck flashed the heavy gold chain and pendant that was the badge of his high office.

He looked up when his servant let Ardys in. A glance from Cecil, and the page bowed and disappeared into one of the inner rooms of the apartment.

"Mistress Trevallon," he said, putting aside his pen and rising, pushing his chair back from the desk. He had a small, pointed face, delicate and pale, dark eyes and hair, a neatly trimmed mustache and beard above his starched white ruff. He came round in front of his desk and bowed over her hand.

"Master Cecil."

" 'Tis good of you to visit me," he said pleasantly, pointing to the door through which the servant had vanished, gesturing that they would be overheard. He quietly picked up a long fur cloak from one of the chairs and fastened it round his neck, nodding to her. "Let us walk a while in the gardens, Mistress Trevallon."

"Aye," Ardys said, as he put his finger to his lips and

mouthed one word: *"Silence."* They passed into the outer room.

He opened the door and in the room behind them the fire flared in the sudden gust of wind. He allowed her to pass through, and then followed her out into the dark courtyard, pulling the door closed.

They walked briskly over the cobbles, their soft leather heels making little noise.

"Pray, forgive me," Cecil said as they passed through the wrought iron gate that led into the gardens, and away from the palace. "I trust no one; I do not take risks when I have private matters to discuss. It is more discreet to talk here, in an open field. 'Tis a pity that there are no flowers at this time of year. Come, we will walk."

It was not a request. His eyes were bright when he looked at her, reflecting the scant light of the cold stars. She slowed her pace to match his.

"Have you been keeping well?" he asked.

"Master Cecil, if ye mean only to enquire as to the state of my health, I must remind you that there are more comfortable surroundings."

"Aye. To be sure." Cecil cleared his throat. "I meant to say—forgive me, but I need to know if you are with child."

Her foot struck an unseen rock and he grasped her arm to steady her. They stood still. For a long moment, stunned, she could not speak. Then she wrenched herself away from him.

"What! What are you accusing me of? I am outraged! No, God's teeth! I am not with child!"

He said: "Your meetings with Devereux . . ."

She gasped and glared at him. "How dare ye!"

He held up his hand. "I know everything that happens here at court. Everything. But I do not understand what ye hope to gain by this liaison with him."

"Gain? There is nothing to gain. There is no liaison. We are not lovers. He pursues me, that is all. It is not your affair."

Her breath frosted before her face, and she wished she had worn heavier slippers. "It is not your affair," she repeated.

"Ah, I see. Then you think to make him love you, because you are in love with him."

Her laughter was sudden and loud, startling them both. She began to walk again, her soft shoes now crunching on the frozen ground.

Her voice was still edged with laughter when she said: "I think you do not know so much, Master Cecil, if you can believe that of me. That I could love Robert Devereux is unthinkable!"

"Do you seek wealth, then, or . . . ?"

"Ye know he has none but what the Queen allows. This is pointless. Say what you have to say; or ask me what you must. I grow colder by the minute."

He took another step. "Do you love the Queen?"

"Of course I love the Queen!" she said, as to an idiot. "She is our most sovereign lady and I am her loyal servant."

"Will you abandon your meetings with Essex, if I tell you must?" He leaned forward and held her arm, stopping her from going further. "I mind the day, so long ago now, of the Armada Tourney," he went on rapidly. "I remember when your father, Will Trevallon, lay gasping on the ground. Most of the crowd looked at him, but for an unknown reason I looked instead at his daughter. I saw your face. You were staring at Essex: his back was turned to you and your eyes were so full of hatred that I thought, 'Robert Devereux, the well-loved, the new darling of the court, has made himself a dangerous enemy.' I marked it well."

"That was years ago!" She stood still, facing him, remembering. "Breastplate armor, on a day of such heat! Father was overcome, there for all to see—because of Essex's whim."

"The reason for your hatred does not really concern me. That is for you alone. But Essex—Lord Essex—is my enemy. All know it, though we speak civilly to each other's faces. He seeks to play the Queen in his game for power."

"And you do not?"

"Nay. I do not seek to be her favorite. I could never be. I have not the physical gifts."

Ardys glanced sidelong at Cecil. He was walking slowly and his hunched back seemed more pronounced as he huddled low to keep warm. He was right. He was neither tall, nor handsome; he had no grace but his intelligence to recommend him to the discriminating eye of Elizabeth.

"But you are your father's son," Ardys said.

"Aye. And that is why I shall protect the Queen if I can. I tell you, leave the Lord Essex to me. I will deal with him, 'Tis not for such as you to do so. You will only succeed in ruining your own life if you continue in this folly."

"My life? You speak nonsense, Master Secretary."

"Do I? Why would ye bed a man you despise? There can be no other result from this flirtation. There is only one truth here: if you allow him to keep meeting with you, if you spark his desire, if you allow him to take liberties, you increase the possibility—it is likely that you will become pregnant. Essex can do nothing for you; you do not need his favor. But if you become big with his child, there will be a scandal, inquiries . . ."

"I will shout his name as the father of a bastard," Ardys said.

Cecil held her by the arm a moment, forcing her to look at him. "It will do you no good. It will be your word against his, and he is a great lord and the Queen's favorite. You will be held responsible, not Devereux. Think of the shame you will bring upon yourself."

"I care not! I am willing to risk the Tower, if it will be the end of Essex."

"Do not play at court politics, Mistress Trevallon. Stay in the tiltyard; there you will always be the victor. You will not bring the Earl down. I will tell ye a story: His own stepfather, Robert Dudley, Earl of Leicester, once got a child on Lady Douglas Sheffield, a widow. Before he wed Lettice Knollys. He married the Sheffield woman, or so she said; but he never acknowledged her as his wife. Her Majesty knew of it, but she chose not to see. Lady Douglas went so far as to name her child after Leicester. And years later, when the Queen saw the child, she called him her 'little Robert,' and told his mother he was a very comely boy."

He paused, and saw that Ardys was listening. "Lady Sheffield ended her life far from court, settled, comfortably enough, on an estate in Yorkshire. All forgot her. Certainly Dudley did, and so also the Queen. And Elizabeth loved Lord Robert through it all. She forgave him even for marrying her cousin Lettice later. Aye, she raged a while, and would rage no doubt at Essex. But she did not throw Leicester in the Tower, for all she threatened to. You are a woman; can you not see the flaw in your actions? You would require the Queen to take your part against that of Essex. That she will never do."

"But surely, if she hears he is to blame . . ."

"She sees his handsome face, and his bravery in the field. And he will swear he has known you not. You will be reduced to calling him a liar. He is a great lord, the highest now in the kingdom. You are only the Fencing Master."

Ardys sighed and said slowly, "I cannot understand why she is so taken with him."

"She is the Queen, but she is also a woman. She sees what she wishes to see. It is not your place to war against Essex.

'Tis a war you cannot win. Leave him to me. The day will come when he will bury himself, with his own ambition. He wants to be King!"

There was a shocked pause. Then Ardys breathed, "Treason."

"Aye," said Cecil calmly. "He is young, and proud, and his lineage is very old. Older than the Queen's, whose great-grandfather, Owen Tudor, was only a gentleman of the chamber."

"Aye, that I had heard."

"He thinks it is his right to be ruler here. He believes if he can make Her Majesty love him enough, she will give him England."

"What a fool! She would never do that."

"Of course she will not. We are people of sense, and we know that she would never give up her rightful throne. But Devereux has no sense; he has only his own view of himself, of his own importance."

"He must be stopped. He might harm her!"

"There is no danger of that yet. But ye must understand, it will take more than an unwanted pregnancy to end his supremacy at court. Someday the Queen will see him for what he is. As of this moment, we have no evidence, no charges to bring against him. He has many followers, and he has time. The Queen is an old woman."

"She is not yet so aged!"

"Perhaps not. But she moves freely among the people. It would be easy for an assassin to get to her."

"God's life! Essex would not have her killed. Even I, who hate him, cannot believe that of him."

"Nay. I also believe his folly will stop short of murder. But we must know his movements, we must be ready when he makes his move."

She searched Cecil's thin, pale face for a long moment.

"Jesu, I almost let him touch me," she said quietly, turning away from Cecil with a shudder and beginning to walk back toward the gardens.

Cecil hesitated, watching her thoughtfully, before he followed. He had to hurry to catch up with her, for her healthy strides were longer than his.

Slightly out of breath, he fell in beside Ardys. "There is much I would know about Essex."

She laughed bitterly. "What knowledge have I that you and your spies have not? Or, mayhap I should rephrase . . . What knowledge that ye could use?"

"I understand your motives. You and I are allies in this matter. We both wish his downfall. Is that not so? Am I not being honest with you—can ye not see what I risk in that?"

"I care not for your risk, Master Cecil," she said.

He did not rise to the bait. Instead he said abruptly: "How well were you accepted at Dungannon?"

She whirled, her face pale, bloodless. She had spoken of Dungannon but once since her return, and then only to the Queen. Her memories of that place were sacred, not to be defiled: her love for Kirkconnell, the fencing, the child—her throat constricted with rage.

"God's death," she said through clenched teeth. "I will not ask ye how you know that I was at Dungannon. But I swear to you that if you value your life, you will be careful how you speak to me now."

"Very well," Cecil was unperturbed. "What went on at Dungannon months ago is of no import. I need to know if you would return to Ireland to gather information for me. About the Tyrone. And about my Lord of Essex."

She gazed ahead, at the grim stone walls of Windsor Castle. How high the battlements were, how forbidding. The wind swirled around her coldly but she did not feel it. Cecil stood quietly, waiting.

She said nothing. Ireland. Dungannon. The dark-paneled room, the laughter, the loving. To return, to touch the places she and Kirkconnell had been together. Would that not be a little like touching Desmond again? The bed they had shared, the table where they had eaten. Perhaps there was something of Kirkconnell there still. She closed her eyes, seeing the chamber vividly. The velvet-covered bed, the small window, the hearth, the wardrobe, her trunk. His wife was still at Tullaghoge, but what matter? He had loved her, Ardys, and nothing would change that. He had died for her.

She remembered her unsheathed rapier, lying where she had left it in her trunk.

"I think," she said slowly, more to herself than to Cecil, "that I could go back. Aye. I was welcome enough. And I am ashamed to remain here now that ye know what I have done with Devereux."

"No one will ever know."

"But did you not have others spying on me?"

"Not on you. They followed Essex only. And I made certain that when he had an assignation with you, he was not followed."

"If no one saw—if you did not see—how could you have known?"

"I remembered what I saw the day your father fell. It was not hard to guess, when you were away from your chambers at strange times."

"You are an excellent judge of human nature, Master Secretary."

"We serve the Queen with the gifts we have. Again I vow: no one will ever know. Pray believe me and remember that with what I have told you tonight you could also ruin me."

She paused at the entrance to her chambers. "Ye speak truth. Aye, I will go back to Ireland if by so doing I may serve the Queen. I left something at Dungannon that I would like to retrieve."

CHAPTER TWENTY

The voyage to Ireland was long but uneventful. Ardys sailed directly from London, as there had been unusually heavy snow inland, which prevented her from traveling the more common route, overland to Bath and then across St. George's Channel. Her ship took the northern passage, around Scotland and the Western Isles, then down onto the North Channel off the coast of Ireland.

Cecil, the master planner, made the arrangements for Ardys's passage; and it was he who told the Queen the purpose for the Fencing Master's defection from court. He told Elizabeth the truth, or a modified version thereof: that Mistress Trevallon had consented to return to Ireland to investigate the activities of Hugh O'Neill, whom Cecil suspected was dealing with the Spanish. Essex's name did not enter the conversation.

The Queen blustered that she was not pleased to again lose her Master of the Fence, but she was persuaded of the wisdom in her secretary's plan. Ardys, who had lived at Dungannon, was likely to gather more useful information about O'Neill than a conventional spy. Most men in Cecil's network were reduced to posing as servants, and were therefore denied access to many parts of the fortresses and courts they infiltrated. There was no need for Ardys to so degrade herself.

Elizabeth made her decision when Ardys assured her privately that she was willing—nay, eager—to go back to Dungannon.

While Cecil saw to the preparations for Ardys's journey,

he allowed the rumor to be spread that she was returning to Cornwall to visit her ailing mother. Ardys bore Devereux's passionate farewell, for if she turned away from the Earl now, he might become suspicious. To lend veracity to the tale of family illness, Cecil arranged for Ardys to travel on the river barge down to Greenwich, there to board a ship that was headed for Falmouth. She was set aboard the ship with suitable flourish as befit her station at the court, and just before the three-master pulled out into the Thames, dressed in black doublet and hose, she was rowed back to the shore, and vanished down an alleyway.

Ardys had waited tensely in the dark close for more than an hour, and when the tap on her shoulder finally came, she was hard put to keep from sudden trembling. If she was discovered, the plan was ruined. Robert Cecil was risking much. A muffled stranger led her to a small two-masted carrack some distance from the main dock at Greenwich. Smugglers manned this vessel, or so Cecil had assured Ardys when he gave her the details of her journey, and they were en route to Newry, to trade, illegally, with the Irish.

She kept her distance from the men on the little ship, and let them believe that she was a youth intent on business with the Tyrone. During the eight-day voyage, Ardys had ample time to reflect on the scope of Robert Cecil's influence, for she was left unquestioned and unmolested.

Newry was a bustling village of several hundred inhabitants, the largest coastal town in the north of Ireland after Carrickfergus. There, a white horse was saddled and waiting for her at an inn owned by an Englishman. When Ardys tried to pay for the animal, the innkeeper had assured her that he had already been handsomely rewarded, and she need not trouble herself. Ardys, curious, asked the man why he would stay in this place, so far beyond the Pale, so deep in enemy territory, but he had only smiled. It was also obvious that he had been informed that his contact was a woman, for all her doublet and hose, and he had been warned against any actions that might give her sex away. She must ride to Dungannon alone, and would be safer in her male disguise. The innkeeper, in a low whisper, explained the routes she must take northwest through Armagh into O'Neill's country, and he gave her the names and descriptions of the local people whom she could trust along the way to give her shelter or a meal.

Cecil, Ardys knew, was behind it all. She marveled at the vast network the little secretary must control, for if he had so many servants in Ireland, he would surely have them throughout all the courts of Europe.

Francis Walsingham, before him, had created a vast network of information gatherers during the last years of his life, for Sir Francis had believed that only by keeping his sovereign abreast of even the most insignificant diplomatic events could he protect her.

Walsingham, who had a passion for detail, had sat at the center of a spider's web of intrigue that extended over most of Scotland, France, Spain, the Netherlands, and beyond into the dark forests of Eastern Europe: collecting the data his agents sent in, reading their messages, decoding their warnings. He digested their reports like so many web-wrapped flies, and Elizabeth had relied on him for accurate reports.

Walsingham had died, and now Robert Cecil spun the spider's web. He knew more about the current state of the world than the Queen would ever need to.

Much of the land between Newry and Lough Neagh was thick peat bog and forest, dense and green, and Ardys rode her sure-footed Irish horse slowly, mindful of the treacherous muck under its feet that could be hard one moment and soft the next. She wore an old, stained fur cloak over her male attire, armed herself with a broad sword, tucked her hair under the brim of a large hat, and kept her head down when she rode through villages or stopped for food. She was fortunate to have the contacts provided by Cecil, for she could not understand more than a few words of the Gaelic the Irish natives spoke. She was constantly alert to the danger of ambush, for she remembered Kirkconnell's casual tale of the way Thomas Carberry had come to be a prisoner at Dungannon. If she was caught by a marauding band of Englishmen, she would be killed as a spy for the Irish and she would doubtless suffer a similar fate at the hands of any roving Irish.

On the second day of her ride she reached Poyntz Pass, a narrow track that wound through the steep, hilly country near Tanderagee. It began to rain, a cold downpour that occasionally mixed with sleet and snow.

"The closing days of February," Ardys whispered grimly to her horse, "are not the time to be riding through the wilds of Ireland."

Her mount plodded resolutely through the cold mud, slipping and then regaining its footing while Ardys hung onto the reins and pulled her cloak around her more closely in an attempt to keep warm. The fur of the cloak, matted and wet, smelled like the animal it had once been. Nay, there would be no ambush. The natives of this miserable, wet island were wise enough to stay by their own hearths while the winter winds keened high around them.

Twice Ardys rode uneasily through the remains of villages that had been burned to the ground. There was nothing left in them but a few thin dogs that had slunk off into the forest at her approach. She could not tell how the villages had come to be so decimated, but she guessed that it had been the work of English raiders. The destruction was too thorough: thieves would have taken what they wished and departed; rival Irish clans might have killed all the inhabitants, but they would surely have kept the valuable cleared land about the huts for their own use. In these villages, though, not only the buildings were gone but the fields as well were blasted, blackened and dead. It was senseless waste, and Ardys shifted uncomfortably on her horse, knowing such could be the work of her countrymen.

Ardys rode into sight of Dungannon on the fourth day. She glimpsed the Lough's southern shore at noon, though she could not see well in the ceaseless rain, and she turned the weary horse onto the eastern track by the water's edge, thinking to make the Tyrone's castle by sundown.

It did not take that long. She rode out of the forest unexpectedly quickly, and stopped short.

Dungannon stood in its private valley as she remembered it; bordered on three sides by dense forest and trodden-down fields and on the fourth by the wide path that led down to the Lough. Its gray walls, dark-streaked from the rain, reached toward the low hanging clouds, blending into the tin-colored sky. There were no troops in evidence, no soldiers camping on Mabel's lawns; and Ardys hesitated, wondering what to do now that she had actually arrived.

The horse whickered impatiently, shaking the bridle, tired of the rain. She spoke to it softly, patting its neck. There was only one thing to be done: she must ride boldly to the front gate and demand to see the Earl of Tyrone. She knew what she must say when Hugh came out, but her throat constricted and she found it hard to breathe suddenly, not caring for the rain or cold, remembering that once in this place she had loved and been happy.

Her memories were so dear to her; was it not wrong to come back to Dungannon in this way? Was it not profaning the love she had for Kirkconnell, to spy on his friend?

It was too late for that. The horse would stand no more, and Ardys was soaked and bone-weary; she must brazen it out. She nudged the horse's flanks and cantered up the main track to the gate, rehearsing in her mind the speech she would make to the Tyrone that would explain her presence.

She sought her lover, Kirkconnell (for Hugh would not know that Desmond had died), and would not leave Dungannon until she had seen him. When the Tyrone told her, as he must, that Kirkconnell had disappeared, gone back to sea, Ardys would break down and sob and say that she had nowhere to go, no one to turn to. The Tyrone was goodhearted; he would take her in, allow her once more into his household. Hugh would assume that Desmond would come back for her and make her his mistress again.

It would be a very long wait, Ardys thought wryly, and she could well stay at Dungannon for many months without attracting suspicion.

There was a flaw in the plan, but that could not be avoided. If, by some ill chance, O'Neill knew of Kirkconnell's death, he might send Ardys back to England with all speed, for she had no claim to stay in Ireland; she was not the man's wife, and could not inherit his property. That she knew all too well. Mayhap, while she was at Dungannon, Ardys would have a chance to go to Tullaghoge, to visit that other woman, who now owned everything that was Kirkconnell's. She had a feminine curiosity to see Kirkconnell's wife.

No one answered when Ardys shouted at the gate. No scurrying step within the hall when, with dawning dismay, she dismounted and rapped on the door. Then she noticed that the cobbled courtyard was muddy from the rain, but there were no tracks about to show that anyone had walked across it. She listened, and there was only the sound of the rain dripping from the turrets: no voices, no laughter. Dungannon was deserted.

Ardys pushed the heavy door open. It swung back on its leather hinges with a sigh, and she held her breath for a moment, looking into the dark hallway, toward the great staircase, which she and Desmond had descended so often. She glanced back at her horse, which had wandered under one of the courtyard gates, out of the rain, and was contentedly chewing on a long weed that grew between the cobblestones.

Even if the Tyrone's home was empty, as it appeared to be, Ardys still needed rest and food, and she must change into dry clothing. She might find that, she thought with an odd feeling in the pit of her stomach, in the upper chamber she had shared with Kirkconnell for those three months.

She stepped into the hall, not liking the dank smell and the unlit torches along the walls. Master Cecil certainly had not planned this. The floor was clean enough, and there was no evidence of the dogs that usually roamed freely about Dungannon. Perhaps there were still some servants about, some retainers who could tell her where the great lord of Tyrone had gone.

Her footsteps echoed soggily, for her knee-high riding boots were wet through, and she made her way carefully through the long passages toward the hall. If any people were in Dungannon, she would surely find them in the great chamber. And as Ardys drew closer, she heard a high, sweet tenor voice, singing a soft, tender ballad—in English.

Mabel turned slowly as Ardys entered the hall. A tall, young minstrel stood behind the lady of the house as she sat in the place of honor, alone, at the long table on the raised dais. A sullen, smoky fire burned low in the huge hearth, and the room was not warmed. Mabel was eating, her needs seen to by a pair of brawny pages in grimy yellow doublets and patched hose.

The lady gestured to the young man she saw hesitating in the doorway, and Ardys approached the table. She'd been wrong about the dogs, for a mastiff lolled indolently at Mabel's feet, tongue out, waiting for scraps. More than a year had passed since Ardys had seen Mabel Bagenal, and the year had not been kind to Lady Tyrone.

Her eyes were sunken and red-rimmed, and she had gained a deal of weight. She stood behind the table, and her height made her somehow grotesque, a giant of a woman, growing fat where once she had been reed slender. Her long hair was tangled, and had lost its luster, as had her skin, which was pale and blotched.

Ardys wondered if she herself had changed as dramatically as this poor lady had, and for a moment a rush of pity silenced her. Should she reveal herself as Ardys Trevallon, she wondered, or remain an anonymous youth?

Better, perhaps, to keep her identity hidden, until she found out what was amiss at Dungannon.

"Bring you a message from my lord husband?" Mabel asked in a querulous voice, stretching out her hand.

"Nay, madam," said Ardys cautiously, using a deep voice. "Rather, I seek him."

Mabel's eyes were wild, and her high laugh cut through the sweet song of the minstrel, who looked up in surprise and set aside his lute.

"Seek him? Here? Nay, you have been misdirected, fair youth. The O'Neill of Tyrone is not here. He has not been here for a month or more; he has gone to kill more English, while his English wife dines alone at his table. More English lives for his whip and his sword! Ye kill, did ye not know, for sport, men do: ye keep tally sheets, to make sure both sides lose the same number of lives. In the autumn the English killed all the O'Donnells, and were ahead in the game, and now that the ground is hardening once more my husband goes forth to balance the totals again."

Ardys frowned at Mabel, uncertain. The woman seemed near to madness. Why? There were always raids in Ireland, had Ardys not passed through the burned-out villages? Why should the destruction of . . .

"The O'Donnells?" Ardys said. "Did you say the O'Donnell clan was killed?"

"Certs, the O'Donnells! The entire settlement at Tullaghoge, gone! The raiders fell on them during the night. They threw a woman's body from a window, an old man told me, an old man who looked into the dead eyes, himself beaten and left for dead because he tried to cover the poor corpse with his cloak."

"Stop!" Ardys shouted. "Of whom do ye speak? Tell me, I must know! Tell me, I beg you!"

"Shelagh," cried Mabel. "Kirkconnell, O'Donnell that was. It had to be her. I never knew her, though I knew her husband. He was a handsome lad, but a bad one. Last year he brought his strumpet, here, to my house, and I let them stay because my husband commanded it. The Englishman Wilfrid Ashbourne killed Shelagh, killed them all. While Shelagh's husband was at sea, Ashbourne rode up from Dundalk. He was bored with slaughtering the people of his own district, so he came here, he came to Tullaghoge."

"Lady Tyrone," the minstrel said softly, putting his hand on her arm. "Ye must calm yourself. Sit. Here, drink a little wine. Calmly, my lady."

Mabel settled quickly, gulping at the proffered goblet. The minstrel, who was a fair boy of eighteen, thin and handsome, looked up at Ardys apologetically.

"You must forgive my Lady," he said. Ardys stared. "Since the Tyrone left a fortnight ago, she has not been well. This winter has been hard, and then when she saw the killing . . ."

"Killing?" Ardys said, confused. "What could she have seen of the O'Donnell murders here, at Dungannon?"

"There was a prisoner here, an Englishman," the minstrel said uncertainly.

Ardys closed her eyes and swallowed. "Carberry." She swayed a little on her feet.

"Aye! Thomas Carberry, he'd been here for years."

"He was our guest!" Mabel shouted, pounding her fist on the table. "And when my lord husband decided the time had come to go down to Dundalk to kill the raiders, he took Thomas out—poor, unhappy Thomas! And he tied him to a tree, and with his whip he flayed the skin from Thomas Carberry's body, all the skin, and still Thomas did not die! Thomas Carberry, because he was English, because Hugh must stir up his troops with the sight and the smell of blood before they went into battle. Ah, God!" Mabel began to sob loudly. "I saw it, from one of the windows, I saw the flies that settled on the red bloody thing that was once a man, the thing that writhed and screamed and was still alive, and I shouted to Hugh to stop it, to kill Carberry and have done, but he would not, he would not listen to me, to me, his wife! He laughed at me, and left Thomas to die, there in the cold sunlight, oozing blood. And I saw the men's faces, all those faces, hating the English, all the English—I am English, but I have loved their leader! I did not know what he was when I wed him, I swear before God I did not know! When Hugh courted me, he came on a great white horse and he was so strong and comely, and he said he would carry me away from my father if I did not agree to marry him, and I agreed because I was a fool

268

and thought myself to be in love. Then that night he came to my bed with blood on his hands, Carberry's blood, I vowed that he would not touch me again; not if I must die for refusing him, he will never touch me again!"

Frightened by her raving, the minstrel grasped Mabel's face and tilted her head to pour wine into her throat. She coughed and spat, and spat again, choking on the warmed wine while Ardys stood quietly and watched, and tried to piece together the story so that it made sense.

When Mabel had quieted once more, Ardys said to the minstrel; "Where is O'Neill now?"

"Do ye not know? He has gone to Dundalk, with all his men, to kill Ashbourne, to avenge the O'Donnells and the village of Tullaghoge."

Ardys turned and fled from the room, through the passages that led by the kitchens, past the chapel, up the stairway. She ran without thinking, away from the shrill voice of the madwoman with her tale of blood, on and on, her feet pounding on the tiled floors. Then a door was before her: dark-paneled wood, a familiar door. She leaned against it, gasping, fighting the nausea that filled her. Her chest heaved as she labored for air, and she took several deep breaths, waiting for the terrible pounding of her heart to slow.

She tried to think . . . here was news for the Master Secretary! A midnight slaughter by the English, and the Tyrone's horrible revenge on an innocent hostage. The revenge that had caused Mabel Bagenal to lose her reason.

There was nothing more to be learned here at Dungannon, that much was certain. But could Ardys bear to wait for Hugh to return? Not in this place, not with Mabel the way she was.

Nay, Ardys would gather a set of clothing, and her rapier, her beloved rapier, and go back to England. Damn Cecil and his mission! She would not stay in this land of death. Even Shelagh, Shelagh who had been Desmond Kirkconnell's wife, was gone.

Ardys pushed at the door. Warped, it would not give. With a cry of frustration she kicked it open and ran inside, only to pause, frightened, surrounded suddenly by her past. The chamber smelled of sunlight and leather and wood, of old velvet, and smoke from many fires. She went to the hearth, and steadied herself there, the tears flowing. Time had not passed in this chamber, though the room looked as though it had been tended recently. She could feel Kirkconnell here, and she half expected him to come through the door now, with desire in his eyes and warmth in his touch. It was a long time before Ardys was able to move.

Her trunk stood at the foot of the bed. It was closed, and looked as though it had been dusted. Like a sleepwalker she went to it, and with a curious feeling of detachment, she opened the lid.

There was the jeweled dagger, hooked to the lid, and there on the top of the trunk's contents was her other, less ornate, dagger.

Her swept-hilt rapier was not there.

Ardys gasped, and pain suddenly racked her body, pain like that she had felt when she lost her father, and her child. Frantically she pawed through the chest, spilling her gowns and hose and doublets onto the floor. The rapier was gone.

She searched the room, pulling harshly at the male clothing she found in the wardrobe, lifting the heavy mattress from the bed. Nothing. Here was more betrayal, then! Her rapier, the swept-hilt given her by her father, stolen. The only link she had with both of the men she had loved so well, gone. She sank to her knees by the bed and buried her face in the soft velvet coverlet. Dear God, she fancied that the scent of Kirkconnell still clung there, to the fabric. She wept as she had not since she learned of his death, gasping and sobbing.

Later, when exhaustion overcame her, she fell asleep, and did not awaken until many hours had passed. The chamber was very quiet, and she rubbed her swollen eyes and stretched. Her throat was dry, and there was no water anywhere on this floor of the castle. The rain barrels were kept below, near the kitchens.

She rose, and was about to leave the chamber, when it occurred to her to search the drawers of the small table by the bedside. Mayhap there was some item there that had belonged to Desmond.

The narrow drawers opened easily; long ago, Kirkconnell had rubbed them with a candle to grease them. The upper drawer was empty, but in the bottom drawer there was a faded piece of parchment that crackled when Ardys touched it and drew it out. She knelt on the bed to get the scant light from the window, and read:

November 1599
Hugh of Tyrone:
This is Writ by a Priest for Me because I have not the Skille to Write. I am much Greiv'd to return here and find yourself gone. I came to Tullaghoge to Tell the Lady Kirkconnelle of her Husband's sad Death, and I do likewise Inform you of it before I goe to my Home. Captain Kirkconnelle was Kill'd by the Frenchman de la Roche on the ship Corbeau, during a Great battle at sea. Because he serv'd you, and counted you as his Frende, I thought it mete that you be told. His widowe Shelagh is well, with her own people to Care for her. Now I goe back to Glamorgan, for in truth I

canst not bear this land without the company of mine own Captain.

Bleddyn Kennwyn

Ardys held the letter, wondering how long after Bled's visit to Tullaghoge the widow Kirkconnell had been killed, and if it was possible the Kennwyn had himself been murdered in the same raid. She sighed wearily, longing to lie down and sleep for days on end, but she could not, not in this place, not in that bed.

The memories that enveloped her at Dungannon were not warm and embracing, as she had thought they would be; instead there was only pain here, and heart-wrenching emptiness. She felt trapped, and now she must escape, or lose her mind, as Mabel had. She took only the jeweled dagger from the chest, and left the chamber.

Hugh O'Neill would know where her rapier was, if anyone did. To hell with Robert Cecil and his schemes and plots! Ardys had come to Ireland to fetch the prized weapon she had left behind, and by God, that she would do. Nothing mattered—not Essex, not Cecil, not the Tyrone's troops, not even the thrice-damned King of Spain himself—nothing mattered but that she grasp her swept-hilt rapier once more.

A hasty meal in the kitchens of Dungannon, for she had no wish to speak with Mabel or the minstrel who seemed to be her keeper, and Ardys remounted her tired horse and was gone.

She raced directly south for Dundalk, not caring for secrecy or the exhaustion of her mount, stopping only when night made it impossible to follow the narrow trails.

Ashbourne was at Dundalk. O'Neill would be there also. The horse lathered beneath her as she whipped it.

How bloodthirsty God was, taking Desmond, the babe, and even Shelagh, leaving only Ardys alive.

CHAPTER TWENTY-ONE

Breathing hard, covered with mud, sweat and grime, Ardys knelt on a hillside overlooking Wilfrid of Ashbourne's English-style manor house at Dundalk. The thick shrubbery of the dense forest around her concealed her. The horse she had abandoned hours before, for it had simply refused to go further. Ardys had walked the last seven miles to Dundalk.

She had been unsure of her direction, but when sound of a battle had drifted through the forest she had followed the noise of cannon shot and musket fire. She found the wide trail left by the Tyrone's army, and followed that to Ashbourne Place with ease.

Ashbourne's manor house was comparatively small, built of white stone, with a thick outer wall nineteen feet high and a tall central tower. From her vantage point two hundred yards away, Ardys could see the inner courtyards, and watched the last desperate struggles of the manor's inhabitants. It must have been a short siege, she thought; there was no moat or bailey to slow an enemy's entry. An arrogant way to build a house in an occupied country.

The clearing was a peaceful spot to build a home, there in a small shallow valley, green and lush, not rock-strewn field or dense forest as was so much of the Irish countryside. Ardys could understand why Ashbourne would have chosen this site for his house, but if he believed that he would be safe from the Irish with only the forest to protect him, the man was a fool.

Irish soldiers, fur-clad, howling, and fierce, were surrounding the little castle like bees around a hive. Ardys started when she saw the huge red-haired figure of Hugh O'Neill, unmistakable even at this distance, amid the swirl and smoke of battle. She did not recognize any of the others.

It was almost over; she had arrived in time only for the final killing. The gallowglass had gained entry to the stronghold and invaded the inner tower where Ashbourne had been hiding with his family and servants. The front gate in the outer wall swung open abruptly and the rest of the Irish troops poured inside, filling the elegant courtyard. Soon the place was aflame, tendrils of smoke curling up into the low gray sky. The manor was too soaked with rain to burn brightly.

The defeated English were herded out into the clearing before the castle, and made to stand in a ragged line before the Earl of Tyrone. There were not many of them. Ardys felt pity for them, worn out and terrified for their lives.

Ardys did not expect to see the two Irish mercenary soldiers walk calmly and methodically down the line, stabbing each of the survivors with a single fatal thrust in the breast. Even a woman and a child among them suffered the same treatment, the woman screaming when her child was torn from her arms. Ardys put her hand over her mouth to stifle her own scream, and the sickness that rose in her throat.

The prisoners were dispatched quickly, without ceremony, and Ardys saw the once-shining blades of the Irish broadswords glowing dull red with drying blood. A last man was held apart while the others were slain, and forced to watch. When they had all been killed, he was taken and tied facing a tree, his arms around it as though he held it in an embrace.

The tree was at the edge of the forest that concealed Ardys, and she knelt further down, wondering what would happen to this poor trembling man. A crowd gathered about the tree as Hugh O'Neill stepped up with a great, knotted whip. He shouted something in Gaelic that Ardys could not understand, but she heard the name "Ashbourne" and realized that here was the man responsible for the killing of Shelagh O'Donnell and the others in Tullaghoge.

"An eye for an eye," she said softly, shuddering.

Hugh handed the whip to a big, yellow-bearded soldier and nodded, the signal to begin. Without hesitation the man drew back and lashed the tied prisoner across the shoulders, and a strip of the prisoner's flesh came away under the stroke. The condemned man cried out, but the whip whirled again, and more of the skin of his back came off. While Ashbourne sobbed for mercy, his blood, dark and thick, began to flow freely down his legs, to form a pool on the ground.

Ardys watched, unable to look away, gripped by the terrible scene below. This must be a flaying, where a man was skinned alive under the cruel cut of a barbed whip, and left to die, peeled like a ripe fruit. Thomas Carberry, the gentle prisoner at Dungannon, had died this way—no wonder that Mabel, who had seen, had lost her reason.

Ardys swallowed hard, and stood up. This was too much to bear. No man, no living being, no matter how terrible his crime, deserved to die in this slow, cruel way. Death Ashbourne surely deserved, but this—nay, this could not be endured! The soldiers stood quietly, watching as the whip did its deadly work, and a cloud of flies began to gather as well, hovering in a mass over the screaming man.

It was the flies that spurred Ardys into action. She drew the jeweled dagger from its leather sheath, gripped it in her hand, and ran lightly down the hillside, reckless of cover. None of the soldiers saw her, intent as they were on the gruesome spectacle.

Ashbourne must die. So be it. But let it be quick then, his

death is enough. Ardys had seen too much of death, and she knew that only death would avenge the souls of the slaughtered O'Donnells; she would not rob O'Neill of his revenge.

Robbing him of the pleasure of torture, however, was another matter.

She stopped beside a tree not twenty feet from the red mass of livid flesh that was Ashbourne, forcing herself to be calm, to sight accurately and gauge the distance well. She had never had much success at the art of knife throwing, but now she must try, or be haunted the rest of her life by this Englishman's terrible screams.

She held her breath and threw the dagger, pausing only long enough to see it embedded in the mass of Ashbourne's back, bringing him a merciful, quick death; then she turned and ran up the slope back into the cover of the forest.

The crowd of soldiers was hushed and still for some minutes, staring at the now-dead man tied to the tree. Hugh swore under his breath and then Desmond Kirkconnell, who had been standing at the entrance to the castle, happened to glance up, toward the woods.

CHAPTER TWENTY-TWO

Kirkconnell walked quickly through the ranks of the men and whispered something to O'Neill. The Tyrone nodded and motioned his men to stay back. This flaying had been for Kirkconnell's sake, for the avenging of his poor, pockmarked wife and her people. If now some boy had stolen Ashbourne's death, it was Kirkconnell's right to kill the thief.

Desmond's long legs carried him quickly up the slope and into the dense forest. His prey was a fleeting glimpse of dark doublet and dirty gray hose, flitting ahead between the trees.

Ardys ran until her heart threatened to burst. She glanced back once and saw that only one tall, slender man followed her, gaining on her with each step. She plunged through the tangled undergrowth and could feel her hunter growing closer, could hear the pounding of his boots on the wet earth and the sound of his breathing. She was tired from her ride but still she ran on, desperate to save herself, knowing that if she were caught she would die.

A hand grabbed her shoulder and she fell, twisting hard and awkwardly onto her back on the ground. The tall man towered over her; she heard the hiss of his sword as he drew it from its sheath at his side, and then there was a flash of sudden sunlight through the green canopy of the trees. He raised the sword, poised for the killing thrust as she lay so still and waited; and then in a quick flash of sunlight she saw the glimmer of the steel, the triple S of the swept hilt, that intricate design that she knew bore the initials "ST."

She screamed then, long and loud, startling the man above

her so that he paused a moment and stared.

She did not move or speak.

Kirkconnell stood with the sword raised, one booted foot on Ardys's stomach, pinning her to the ground; and then he dropped the blade to the ground.

Ardys lay panting as he lifted his foot from her body. He stood motionless, looking at her, and then the brief flash of sunlight was gone, and his face was hidden in the gloom once more.

She whispered, hoarse and panic-stricken: "Desmond! I cannot see you!"

"Ardys?" he whispered.

"Aye, my love! You live, ye are alive! Bled told me you had died killing de la Roche!"

"Wounded only, but Bled did not see it all. Ah, my love, why are you here? Whence did ye come?"

He knelt by her, lifting her head gently from the dirt, holding her face between his hands, studying the line of her cheek and the curve of her brow for a long moment before he kissed her.

They kissed for a long time, like those lost in a desert and parched, dying for water, and then his hands found the opening of her doublet and tore that free. She gasped as his lips gently found her tender skin. Arching her back, she grasped his back and held him to her.

Ardys reached for him and suddenly their frantic hands were victorious: their clothing was thrust aside.

Desmond hesitated, looking down at her as she lay in the wet bracken.

"I fear I shall hurt ye," he said.

She answered quietly: "Please, my love, I need you!"

He drove into her and she welcomed his invasion; gloried in it, her body meeting his with joy and laughter until they reached a pinnacle of delight together, crying out with the shared victory.

They lay, flesh to flesh, for such a long time that a bird came and settled on a branch not three feet away, unaware of their presence. It was a thrush, and its sweet warbling song finally broke them apart. When they moved it flew away into the forest, scolding.

She sat up and laughed, trying to pat her hair into some order where it had escaped her hat. He held her and would not let her go.

"My love," Desmond said tenderly, his voice still shaking while he stroked her hair, "you have never looked more beautiful."

She turned to him, smiled gently, warm in his arms, nuzzling, but then she sat up and slapped him hard across the face. "Bastard! Ye abandoned me—to go to your wife!"

He rubbed his cheek and scowled. "She is dead, what can it matter now?"

"Not matter! I will never forgive ye for leaving me, never!"

"Then I will not ask it of you. But I promise, on my mother's soul, that I will never leave you again. My Ardys! When de la Roche told me you were dead—"

Her eyes widened in surprise. "De la Roche told ye that?"

"Aye. Before—" he hesitated.

"Before you killed him."

"Aye. But how could you know?"

"Bleddyn told me."

"Bleddyn? But he thinks I am dead; he sent a letter to Hugh telling him."

"I have seen that letter. I met Bled on Tenerife, and he told me of the battle with the *Corbeau*," Ardys said.

They were silent, kneeling together, hands clasped, aware of the brittle, easily broken peace of their reunion, not yet eager to know the details of the months they had spent apart. She reached for her rapier, and he handed it to her, hilt first. She closed her eyes as she held it and felt the familiar grip, the perfect balance of the weapon.

He began, "De la Roche also said that the child . . ."

She looked up at him, her eyes wet. "Our son, Desmond. He was born too early, and he died. I lost our son."

"We lost him, as I lost you. But we are not dead, and we are together now," he said, and kissed her cheek gently. "We will make more children, my Ardys."

"You will marry me before that happens," she said, flaring again, wiping her eyes and pushing him away. "I thought you were dead: I was content with my memories; and now I will not let you go, I will never let you go." She brandished her rapier. "I will kill you first, I swear I will."

He stirred awkwardly, not wanting to meet her narrow-eyed gaze. "I should have told ye about Shelagh."

"She is dead now. You are right. There is an end."

"I never loved her. I married her, I suppose, because I felt it was my duty—and I left you, whom I do love—I went back to her for the same reason."

"Did she love you?"

"Aye," he said softly, and looked at her.

Ardys touched Desmond's face gently. "I suppose she could not help but love you, even as I cannot. De la Roche told you I was dead: until the moment I saw you again, so I was."

"And I! The world was dark and silent without your laughter. I lived; I slept and ate and moved, but I was not alive. If I had been at Tullaghoge, perhaps Shelagh would be alive still, and her death would not weigh on my conscience."

"Why should it? You did not kill her, Desmond—do not take on another man's guilt. That mocks God! If you had been at Tullaghoge, then aye, perhaps she would be alive. Or perhaps you would be truly dead, too, and we would never have met again. 'What if' is a child's game! We must thank God for what is."

"I grieve for our son," he said quietly. "And I grieve that I was not with you when he was born and died."

"Well, 'tis done. I have had a long time to grow used to the fact, my love. You have not. He was born too soon. Poor little babe."

He sighed. "Aye."

The day grew old and still they sat together, there on the rich brackish earth of the Irish forest, holding each other. The sorrows they had faced were still with them, and could not easily be set aside. It was only when the woods were dark with the twilight that Kirkconnell rose, and pulled Ardys to her feet. He held her close before him, his face in her hair, and wept silently. She felt his warm tears and said nothing.

"Come," he said quietly, steadying himself. "We must go back, and join Hugh, and then ride as fast as we may to Dungannon."

Ardys looked up at him. "Dungannon."

"There is a priest there," he went on. "I vow I will not make love to you again until you are my wife. Marry me quickly, Ardys. I cannot wait long."

She smiled. "Nor can I."

CHAPTER TWENTY-THREE

Ardys Trevallon married Desmond Kirkconnell five days later, on March 5, 1599, in the chapel at Dungannon. Present at the ceremony were the Earl of Tyrone; his wife Mabel, quiet but still a trifle wild-eyed; several of the honored captains of Hugh O' Neill's army; and a number of Spanish envoys whose names the Tyrone would not divulge.

Ardys wore the bright scarlet velvet gown she had worn the day after she and Desmond had first made love. Its color brought out the glow in her eyes and the red highlights in her hair. Kirkconnell was elegant in a black velvet doublet, with white hose and lace trimmed shirt. All through the mass he held her hand.

A Catholic priest performed the ceremony in the Catholic manner, but Ardys did not trouble herself over that. She loved Kirkconnell more than she loved the Church of England, and if she had a few unquiet moments when the priest placed the wafer in her mouth, she did not show it.

When it was done and they had kissed lightly for the first time as husband and wife, they rose and led the procession back into the great dining hall for the wedding feast.

Irish musicians strummed lyres and harps, and Ardys saw the minstrel who had been Mabel's keeper hovering near the head table. Perhaps he is devoted to Mabel, Ardys thought, or, more likely, Hugh has paid him to keep charge of her.

Good red wine flowed freely, and the company grew merrier. Ardys and Desmond ate lightly, for their appetites were not for food, but they could not refuse this banquet in their honor. Ardys sat between Hugh and her husband, flushed with laughter, wine, and happiness.

O'Neill drained the tankard in his thick hand and laughed at the antics of the jesters he had hired at great expense to amuse his guests; then he leaned back and belched and turned to the woman at his side.

"Tell me, Mistress Kirkconnell, how d'ye come to be in Ireland again?"

Ardys reluctantly turned from contemplating the way the firelight flickered on Desmond's thick, mahogany-colored hair.

"I was sent back, my Lord of Tyrone, to spy upon you," she said with a winning smile.

There was silence for a few beats. Then O'Neill slapped his thigh and roared with laughter. His huge laugh filled the hall, and the musicians abruptly ceased their strumming. The Tyrone seemed almost convulsed by a great jest, and Ardys, aware always that Desmond was by her side, was not afraid.

"Robert Cecil sent me," she went on, and Hugh went into fresh gales of laughter when she said the name.

"Cecil! The little hunchback sends a slip of a girl to spy on the Tyrone!" He banged his fist on the wood table and the rest of the company echoed his laugh.

Kirkconnell slid his arm around Ardys's waist and whispered, "Be silent, my love."

"I'll not stop now, husband," she whispered back. "I have come for information; what better way to gather it than through honest questions?"

She turned again to Hugh. "Cecil wants to know if you are dealing secretly with Robert Devereux, the Earl of Essex."

Hugh wiped a tear from his eye and took another swig from the tankard. "Devereux? That puffed-up stripling? I hear that he is the lapdog of the Queen and that he can do naught but play at cards and dance . . . Cecil believes that I would stoop to dealings with such a man? Well, I must excuse the hunchback; he does not know me as his father did. God's Wounds! Deal with Essex?"

"Essex wants to be King," Ardys said. "Ye must not underestimate him."

"King of England? What care I if he is? There is a King in Ireland already, and he sits before you. Steady, Ardys, I have no open quarrel—as yet—with your Queen. But you may return to Cecil and tell him that O'Neill has no time for dealing with young fools. If Elizabeth sends any man, I care not who he may be, into my Ireland, I will chew him up and spit the bones back across St. George's Channel. Tell little Cecil," the Tyrone went on, "all that you have seen of my strength: the numbers of my soldiers, my gallowglass, my weapons. Tell him of the Spaniards you have seen at my table—for I doubt not that your Queen knows of King Philip's interest in my kingdom—and tell him the day shall come that England will regret its interference in Ireland; will regret the Munster Colonies and the slaughters of the Desmond Wars. Tell your Queen to stay off my island, or she will come to dread the name of Hugh O'Neill. Make her listen; warn her that Ireland has always been and will always be the ruin of any man she sends to invade."

Ardys considered, then nodded: "I will tell Cecil all you have said. That I promise. But I do not believe it will do any good, my Lord."

Hugh sighed. "Nay, it will not. The English will come, one day, because they must. And I will meet them, because I must. There can be no other way."

That night, after they had made love with tender urgency, Kirkconnell held Ardys's naked body gently, reveling in her softness.

When he felt her stir, and knew she was awake, he said: "Where shall we go, my love? I have no wish to remain in Ireland now; I do not have the heart to fight for Hugh, or for anyone, when I am so filled with happiness."

She moved closer against him. "And I do not desire to return to court. I can send a letter secretly to Cecil; there is no need for me to see him to tell him all Hugh has said."

"And the Queen?"

"I will ask him to tell her I have married. But I am not one of her ladies-in-waiting; she cannot mind too much."

"I believe," Desmond mused, "that we should attempt to find Bled. He thinks I am dead, and I would like to assure him that I am not."

"Then shall we go to Wales?"

"Aye."

Ardys propped herself up on one elbow and her rich dark hair spilled over her shoulders.

"Husband," she said lingering over the word. "There is a place I would like to visit with ye first."

He lay back, letting his hand stray across her breast. "Anywhere, my love."

"Cornwall. To my father's grave. I wish he could have known you, Desmond. And one day we must go together to the grave of our son, so far away on the island of Desirade."

Kirkconnell drew her down into his arms. "Aye. I would like to pay honor to the other Fencing Master, and I need to stand with ye and acknowledge our son. Your father we can reach; our son will be harder to come to," he said. "Very well. We shall go to Cornwall first, and then to Wales, and from there—well, we shall find a way."

CHAPTER TWENTY-FOUR

The roses around the mausoleum at Helford House bloomed very early in the spring of 1600. They had almost reached full blossom in late May, and when Ardys and her husband walked slowly down the path to the burial ground, she was amazed at their heady fragrance.

They rode here directly after they left the small Irish sloop at Falmouth. Ardys knew that she must soon bring her husband to meet her family, but first she wanted him to see the place where her father, Will Trevallon, lay. Desmond stood alone by the stone bench while Ardys went to the crypt and touched the engraved plaque, weeping silently a little that her father could not meet her husband and see her joy. Her white satin gown billowed in the soft ocean breeze.

She said a few words, so softly that Kirkconnell could not hear, and then she drew her rapier from its sheath at her side, kissed the blade, and set it down, holding her hand out to him. Desmond went to her, and put his hand over hers on the name "Trevallon" etched in the stone of the crypt.

The sky was a brilliant deep blue, and there was a gull crying overhead, breaking the stillness of the afternoon. Desmond held Ardys, comforting her while she mourned her lost father, who would never be there to bless her marriage.

After a while, she bent, picked up and resheathed her rapier.

"My mother remarried, last October it was," Ardys said later, as they rode toward Porthtowan.

They shared a big black horse, and she leaned back against Desmond comfortably, as she had so long before, in Ireland.

Surely, by now the whole family would be at Alice's home; she must have sent for the girls to come and live with her and Percy, for it was not right that the Trevallon daughters should live on at Helford House while their mother had a large home of her own.

It was a long ride down to Porthtowan from the graveyard at Helford, and it was nearly dark when they reached the house.

"My mother's new husband is a wealthy man," Ardys said as they came to the door. "They will have ample room here."

"We shall go back to Falmouth in the morning, and be off for Glamorgan," Desmond said. "We need stay here but this one night."

"I hope you will not disgrace me before my mother and sisters," Ardys said teasingly, though her voice still quavered a bit. "They do not know that I married a pirate."

"You married a pirate; your mother married a wealthy merchant. I see little difference in the two occupations."

Ardys laughed. "But truly, be kind to my mother. He is so ugly, her husband; it must be difficult for her to bear. He has such an enormous nose, all flattened and twisted. I have never seen the like."

The horse whinnied in protest when he pulled sharply back on the reins.

"What did ye say the man's name was?"

"Percy Longhoughton," she answered, wondering why Desmond was suddenly breathing hard. "Is the old wound troubling you?"

He looked at her quickly and smiled. "Nay. 'Tis nothing."

They arrived at Porthtowan at dusk, and let a liveried groom lead their mount away. Ardys knocked loudly on the great double door and a servant answered and showed them into the new-finished hall where Alice, her children, and her

287

husband were all at family supper.

Kirkconnell walked in with Ardys and felt her hand on his
arm, but he could see nothing beyond Percival Berwick,
hated and remembered, seated at the head of the long table.
Alice rose dutifully, and held out her arms to her eldest
daughter, "Ardys! How sweet that you have come back!
Percy, look, here is my other daughter, Ardys, returned—
Elizabeth, do not crush your sister so, you will ruin her lovely
gown!"

Ardys laughed and swung her sister round to face her
handsome, frowning husband. "Elizabeth," she said, as
Kirkconnell forced himself to look away from Berwick and
smile, "this is my husband, Captain Desmond Kirkconnell."

Elizabeth blushed prettily when Desmond took her hand
and kissed it gallantly. The rest of the Trevallon girls, right
down to little Margaret, received the same homage, and then
Alice and Percy stepped from behind the table and came to
greet them.

He does not know me, Kirkconnell thought. He could not;
it was so long ago, I was just a boy. My wife's mother has married my greatest enemy—by Mary's tears, I wish it were not
so. I have sworn to kill this man, but I cannot harm the
mother of my wife—how can I hurt my love for my revenge?
Calmly, then, I will wait, and watch. Berwick does not belong
in Cornwall; he had gone to Scotland, and now he has come
here. Why here, to the west country of England—and
changed his name? But of course he must change his name,
he is an attainted traitor and his life is forfeit. Aye, forfeit. If I
kill him, would I not be doing my Ardys's beloved Queen a
great service?

"Welcome to Porthtowan," Percy said heartily, grasping
Desmond's cold, outstretched hand. "So our Ardys has mar-

ried a captain, and such a fine man, too! Come, sit, and eat with us."

"Elizabeth, do not stare at your sister's husband so rudely," Alice said, sitting again. The children slid down the bench, making room, and the Kirkconnells squeezed in.

Servants brought plates of rich food. Kirkconnell ate a little and tried to make conversation for the sake of his wife. At the other end of the long table Elizabeth still stared, and Ardys poked Desmond in the ribs and whispered, "Be careful that you do not smile too much on my younger sisters. They have already fallen in love with you."

Desmond smiled thinly at her.

Ardys complained of fatigue after dinner and begged permission for herself and her husband to retire for the night. They were shown to a chamber overlooking the cobbled courtyard, facing the sea, and the page lit the candles and left them alone.

Ardys undressed, pulled on a long linen sheath, and went to bed, waiting for Desmond to follow. He went and stood at the window, and stared out into the night.

The moon rose bright, and cast a ribbon of light across the dark rippling water in the cove. He was profiled in the window; she could see his long nose, mustache, and firm chin. After a time Ardys rose, pulled a woolen cloak over her night shift, and padded across the chamber on bare feet to stand beside Kirkconnell. Her touch at his shoulder made him flinch.

"Desmond," she said. "Ye must tell me what is wrong. Please, Desmond, I cannot bear to see you like this. What torments you?"

He touched her arm and then abruptly turned from the window and held her so tightly that she could hardly breathe. She felt his racing heart, the tenseness of his body through the velvet of his doublet. His stiff white collar scratched her forehead.

"Ardys," he said slowly, "have you ever hated a man so much that you would kill him when you saw him?"

"Aye," she said softly, from the circle of his strong arms.

"My mother and father . . ." he began. She looked up; his gaze was far away.

"Were killed in 'sixty-nine, in a raid by the Queen's soldiers—?" she prompted.

"Aye. A raid. Because there were meetings at their hut, meetings of men who conspired to overthrow your Queen and place Mary of Scotland on her throne. I was very young; I do not remember how old I was, but I remember well enough the faces of the men, and that of their leader. He was lord in our village; he controlled the lands for—oh, for miles around. I thought he controlled the world."

"He was not taken?" she asked.

"Nay. He escaped. He was a Catholic, you see—"

"You are a Catholic, my husband—"

He went on as though she had not spoken. "And he rode away, into the forest. Bessie, who raised me, told me he went north into Scotland, but after that she knew not whence he traveled."

He stopped, and she waited.

"His name was Percival Berwick. He had a terribly deformed nose," Desmond said finally, in a strangled voice.

Ardys looked up into his unquiet eyes. "Oh, God."

"Ardys!" He held her for a moment at arm's length, searching her face. She looked at him, and he saw only love and understanding in her eyes. "Ye must understand. My father and mother were killed. How can I let him go, when they died because of him?"

She put her hand to his cheek and he turned his head to kiss her fingertips.

"You must do what you have to do," she said finally. "I only ask ye not to tell me of it. In my time, I have done many things that now I am ashamed of. I beg ye—leave me with my secrets, and I shall leave you with yours."

She clung to him for a moment, and then backed away. "I am going to bed, my love."

It was unfortunate that the moon shone so bright this night, thought Percy as he hurried down to the cove. His ermine cloak, old now, was dingy and gray, blending into the night. Someone could have seen the Spanish barque, even though it hovered far out, on the horizon; or someone might have seen the small boat that was rowed silently up to the narrow beach below Porthtowan. It could not be helped, but Percy felt uneasy.

Damned inopportune that Alice's daughter had arrived today with that glowering husband of hers. Odd, the captain seemed somehow familiar.

Two Spanish sailors were waiting for him, there on the beach, near the large stone that marked their meeting place.

"You have information?" the smaller of the two asked, tapping his booted foot against the stone impatiently.

"Aye. All the information is complete and up to date—tell King Philip's secretary, Master Idiaquez that I have served him well."

"That is for him to decide, once he has read these papers." Handing the packet to his companion, the Spaniard turned back to Berwick with a pouch. It chinked softly.

Berwick opened it and poured some coins out into his hand. "Jesu! These are Spanish doubloons! How can I spend these here? These are no use to me! Where are the jewels you always pay me with?"

"There are no more jewels for the likes of you, Señor. Take these coins and be happy you have them."

"That was not our agreement!"

"Take it up with Idiaquez when you see him. There is nothing to be done. We go."

The sailors pushed the ketch out to sea and rowed back to the waiting ship.

Percy grunted and began to walk back up the beach. "Spanish doubloons. I will have to exchange them somehow—maybe through one of the French smugglers . . ."

Porthtowan loomed large on its hillside, the new roof of the great hall higher than the rest of the house. Percy walked slowly, fingering the coins, toward the cliff path that led up to his house.

"Lord Berwick."

Percy stopped in mid-stride, one foot held up.

"Berwick," said the low voice again.

"Who," Percy cleared his throat, trying to think of an excuse to explain his presence on the beach at such an hour. And no one knew his real name here! "Who is there?"

Kirkconnell stepped out from the shadows and stood before Berwick. Outlined in moonlight, his face was not clear to see.

"Ah! Ardys's husband! Have you come, like me, for a stroll in the moonlight?"

"Mayhap." Kirkconnell stepped closer, and Berwick stepped nervously away.

"I often come here when I cannot sleep—you may ask my wife."

How much had this man seen? Perhaps if Percy offered to pay him, he would keep silent. Not a good solution, but the best he could think of.

"I could never sleep in your house. I wonder that you can. In fact, I could not sleep at all if I bore the name of Berwick."

"Berwick? Berwick—I know no Berwick, my name is Longhoughton."

"You were a traitor when you lived in the forests in the north, and ye are a traitor still, here on this Cornish coast. Do you think I care for your politics? Do you think I care for the Spanish gold in your pockets? Nay, do not run, Lord Berwick. You will not escape."

Kirkconnell drew his sword from the sheath at his left hip and advanced on Percy, who stood cowering and could not run.

"You will not recall," Desmond went on, walking toward Berwick slowly, "that there was a tenant farmer living on your land, named Jarrow Kirkconnell."

"Kirkconnell," Percy whispered, with dawning dismay.

"His wife's name was Jane, and they had a son, a son called Desmond."

"Mary, Mother of God!"

"Ah, I see your memory returns. D'ye mind then, one night all those years ago, when the soldiers of the Queen came and put the Kirkconnell cottage to the torch after surprising you and your fellow conspirators there? The Kirkconnells were both killed: Jane that night, by the soldiers, and Jarrow the next day, by the executioners."

Kirkconnell went on, his eyes so narrow that they were mere slits in the moonlight, "I, their son, stood in the field in front of your castle and watched my father kick and die at the end of a rope. And on that day I swore that I would avenge their death."

"Have mercy, Kirkconnell, I did not kill them, 'twas the soldiers!" Berwick went to his knees, weak with fear. The shadows of moonlight played over his twisted, ugly face.

"Soldiers who would never have come, had it not been for your conspiracy."

The long sword, unsheathed, gleamed silver in the moonlight. Desmond came slowly, steadily. Berwick could not run. There were jagged rocks at his back; and beyond, the sea.

"Have pity! I have married your wife's mother! What will she think if you kill me—how will her mother feel, how will your wife feel?"

"My wife understands and grants me my right to kill you."

"My death will not bring your parents back! They are long buried, they are at peace with God, and nothing can disturb them. Why bother to kill me! You are a Catholic—I fight for the Catholic cause! Do ye not love God?"

"Do not try to be clever by invoking God's name now. When my parents died, God must have been busy elsewhere. What are you about here—selling English secrets to Spain? Is that not Spanish gold in your hand?"

"Take it! And there is more—spare me!"

"Enough! Your money is as tainted as you are."

Kirkconnell drew his arm back, shaking. The moment had come. Berwick knelt before him.

A long moment passed.

"Jesu!" Desmond hesitated, and said angrily, "I cannot kill you in cold blood. I wonder at my own weakness. Get up, damn you!" He kicked the man before him. "Fight me!"

Berwick stood quivering there for an instant; then he turned and ran.

An arc, a flash of steel, and Desmond threw his sword in disgust. It came to rest thirty feet away, its point deep in the soft sand, nowhere near Berwick.

Berwick reached the path to the house, and bolted.

The night was quiet but for the constant lap of the waves on the sand, and far out to sea, the creak of a mast. A nightjar called plaintively. Desmond was still, and watched the last twitches of the sword before he went to retrieve it.

He stood at the ocean's edge and threw the weapon as far as he could out into the open water. Its basket hilt bobbed briefly, then was gone. There, on the horizon, was the small Spanish ship, tacking out into the channel.

He folded his arms, suddenly cold, and unconsciously turned to look toward the north, the north where Jane and Jarrow had died.

"I could not do it, Mother," he said aloud. "Forgive me. Forgive me, Father."

Ardys was awakened in the morning by a sound from below, in the great hall. Her mother, busy about the hall.

Ardys rolled onto her side and touched Desmond, who was lying on his back; his eyes open and dry as though he had not slept.

"Berwick lives still," he said quietly when he saw she was awake. "He is spying here, sending reports to Spain, probably about the English navy's strength and numbers."

She considered. "Then we must report him to someone in authority."

Kirkconnell said wanly, "Mayhap. I am tired now and care not to think more on this."

She moved so that she was in his arms, their bodies touching at chest and hip and thigh. "I like the sound of the sea," she murmured. "It changes, but it does not change: 'tis constant."

"Mayhap after we find Bleddyn we shall go back to sea . . . Ardys, I . . ."

She laid her finger on his lips. "Nay, do not speak of it. It is over now, the past is gone and we are together. We have our love; there is no more room for revenge or sorrow. We will leave, and go to Wales, and then we will go—wherever we will go. We will make new memories, and let the past stay buried. We are together, my love, that is all that matters."

He leaned over and kissed her gently, and felt his need for her.

"Aye," he said softly as he kissed her neck, her hair. "The past is gone, it has no more to do with us. We shall go on, loving each other. Always, my Ardys . . ."

"Aye," she whispered. "Always."

About the Author

Caitlin Scott-Turner holds a degree in European history and has had a passion for the Elizabethan world all her life. She has traveled extensively throughout the United Kingdom with her husband (who is, of course, British). They live in the Boston area and *The Queen's Fencer* is Caitlin's first novel.

For more information or to contact Caitlin Scott-Turner, go to www.queensfencer.com.